The Aquarius Surfboard

Read. Dream. Imagine.

Kellye Abernathy

The Aquamarine Surfboard

KELLYE ABERNATHY

atmosphere press

With love to Ian, Brendan, Mackenzie,
Melissa, Dagny and Brady

Read. Dream. Imagine.

THE HOLLOW

People say Windy Hollow is haunted. A lonely place, the tall tower of stone juts out of the sea on the far side of the cove, catching the worst of ocean gales and ragged surf. A crooked finger of shore bridges the tower to a high overlook. There the ruins of an abandoned mansion and an ancient spa hotel perch side-by-side, crumbling into the sea.

On calm days, and only at low tide, a dune of sand appears in the foaming waters below the Hollow, making it easy to wade to the tower's stone stairs. That's when Condi climbs to the top and makes her way over to sit on the orange-red rescue kayak, the one turned upside down, wedged between the two half-moon rocks.

For most of the kids in town, going to the top of Windy Hollow is forbidden.

But Grand Ella understands why she needs to go there.

Remembering is the most important thing, though it's the hardest thing of all.

Chapter One

THE BEACHLINGS

A spinning wind day, sand puffs whirl on the beach, threads of chill lace the late summer breeze; and in the outer cove, the biggest waves are crashing. From the terrace of the yellow cottage high on the cliff, Condi watches the surfer kids, straggling out to Craggy Point in slick, black wetsuits.

The surfer kids are the rich kids from the big houses around the cove, with top-of-the-line surfboards, and pro-grade wetsuits to shed the cold. But today, with a skittish breeze spinning, and whitecaps breaking higher than usual off Craggy Point, even the best surfers are fighting to get up on their boards.

Javed Holmes, a boy in Condi's class, is the first to catch a high roller. Cutting his crimson board into the curl, he skims through the cup of the wave. Condi admires the lightness of his touch, the way he slides into each fold, popping up neatly with the rise. But the ocean is unpredictable, especially today. A sneaker wave snags Javed's board, flipping him sky-high. He surfaces and paddles back out to the Point to try again.

Soon the other surfer kids stop trying. Clinging to the bellies of their boards, they slide up and down the swells, laughing into the wind. Riding waves is pure joy, on top of the water or beneath it.

How Condi wishes she was out there. Her dream is to learn to surf, but her grandmother can't afford the cost of a surfboard and wetsuit. The art shop business is slow, and Grand Ella's second job teaching yoga to the rich resort crowd is not enough. Any extra money is spent on the upkeep of the old yellow cottage overlooking the sea. "We live in paradise," Grand Ella often sighs, "but it carries quite a price."

The wind changes, throwing a veil of mist over the terrace. Sudden shifting winds signal the coming of fall in the northern Pacific—a time of strange storms and unruly tides. Wiping off her glasses, Condi sighs. Last year a wild autumn storm cost her everything.

Don't. Think. Just. Breathe.

Pressing her toes into the smooth deck of the terrace, she leans into the breeze. Eyes closed, she lifts her chin, setting her breath to the salty thrum of the sea. In her mind's eye, the wood under her feet melts into a polished surfboard. Tall and brave and strong, she rides shining curves of water, bending into each turn, gliding on the gentle waves pulsing into shore.

Never give up on your dreams.

Anything is possible, you know...

Breathe in, breathe out.

In a little while, she opens her eyes and goes to sit at the top of the zigzag stairs leading down to the beach, gazing out to sea. A black speck appears on the horizon line. A surfer kid is popping up out of the water off the shore of Windy Hollow, a place where the waves run wickedly toward a treacherous stand of rocks. Rising out of a curl, the boy slips into a lunge, then comes to standing on his molten-black board.

Squinting into the sun, Condi searches for clues as to who the new boy might be. Surfing too close to the spear-sharp rocks of the Hollow is dangerous. There the waters churn furiously, sucking unknowing surfers into the jagged teeth of the north shore.

The boy has an unusual stance. In a low crouch, he muscles the board in and out of the waves, avoiding the rocks. Then, in a move Condi's never seen before, he hops and spins in the air, backlit by sparkling wings of spray. Landing smoothly, he rides the board without a single hiccup, sliding into the shallows of the inner cove.

Jumping off the board, he shakes water from his onyx hair and glances up at the yellow cottage. She waits for him to paddle back out, or go hang with the kids on Craggy Point. But he doesn't do either of those things. Shouldering his board, he walks up the beach toward the soft curve of sand below the yellow cottage. Parking his board at the bottom of the zigzag stairs, he looks up at her.

"Hey," he says, grinning. "Coming down?"

Surprised, Condi stares at him. All summer long she's avoided the kids in the cove. Squirming, she pushes her glasses higher up on her nose. None of the other surfer kids ever talk to her. To them, she's the sad, quiet girl—the one who doesn't surf.

"I can't," she tells him.

His face splits in a grin below the fall of jet-black hair. "Aw, c'mon," he says. "I'm new in town. Come for a walk on the beach."

A strange butterfly in her chest swoops and then soars skyward. Though this bold shining boy is probably a big house kid who'll soon learn to ignore her—maybe, just maybe—she could take this chance. Why shouldn't she go join him for a walk on the beach?

"Okay," she says, standing up and kicking off her sandals. "Be right down."

When she reaches the bottom of the stairs, she decides to be brave. "What's your name?" she asks, looking into his turquoise eyes.

"Trustin," he says. "What's yours?"

"Condi," she answers quietly. She likes his name. Names are important things—they carry an identity all their own. "Short for Condoleeza."

He nods, smiling at her. "Like sea and sky."

Unexpected tears spin into her eyes. She shakes her head and starts to tell him, then she stops. This cute new boy doesn't know about Mama and Papa, and the last thing she wants is for him to feel sorry for her. He doesn't need to know that Condoleeza means sweetness in musical terms—and that Papa's favorite language was the language of music. Embarrassed, she brushes away the tears. Squaring her shoulders, she tosses back her curls and forces a smile.

"Sea and sky," she tells him firmly. "You've gotten it exactly right."

"Which way should we walk?" he asks, looking around at the wide expanse of the cove. To the south, the long, gray slab of rock called Craggy Point stretches out into the sea, a great launching pad for surfers, while the high beach road leads up through the groves of eucalyptus and beach pine, past the big houses with high decks and grand views, until it reaches the town of Dipitous Beach, sleepily resting on the folded arms of the hillside and overlooking the cove.

"There's a place we can watch the surfers," she says, pointing to the tall rock tower rising out of the sea on the rough northern shore. "People call it Windy Hollow."

"Let's go," he tells her. His wetsuit blazes with sun diamonds, lighting up the sweet blue-green of his eyes.

His answer gives her all the courage she needs. She guides him toward the far side of the cove, the side where the sea is wild, hoping desperately that Grand Ella isn't looking out the window of the yellow cottage. After all, it's been a long time since she's made a new friend her own age. She isn't going to miss this chance. This boy likes her, and he isn't asking awkward questions, at least not so far.

They fall into an easy beach rhythm, picking their way across the sharp scree of the isolated northern shore. With the waves crashing, it's hard to talk. Silently, they step across long slippery rocks scattered across the beach like dominoes, flecked with dots of spray. A circular wind whips up a froth of sand, tangling Condi's hair in the frames of her glasses.

Together they walk the remaining waterline until they reach the peninsula of the Hollow. The wind is fierce now, the sea at the base of the tower churning viciously around the jagged spears of rock. Beyond the tower, on the crest of the hill, the ruins of a decaying mansion and spa hotel shiver in the wind.

Nervously, she squints up at the sun. It is later than she thought. When they left the yellow cottage, the sun seemed so much higher in the sky. This cute boy's made her careless—it's not like her to lose track of the tides.

He follows her gaze. "Sure you want to climb?"

With the wind twirling and the waves crashing, she hesitates. Unlike the calm of the inner cove, the wind is powerful here, the tides strange, the sea impossible to predict. They'll have to wade through a nasty undertow to get to the stone stairs leading to the top of the tower. The stairs are slick and steep.

"I don't know," she murmurs.

A sunburst of light breaks over the beach, blinding her for an instant. When she opens her eyes, the churn around the jagged rocks is softening to ripples of teal. The familiar sand dune she knows so well peeks up out of the water—just as it does at low tide.

Smiling, she shyly glances over at him. "Let's do it," she says.

He smiles and they step into the water and wade through ankle-deep waves, crossing the shallows to climb up the winding stone stairs, now drying in the sun. When they reach the high ledge, she leads him over to the orange-red rescue kayak turned upside down, wedged between the two half-moon rocks.

"How'd this old thing get up here?" he asks, as they sit cross-legged on top of the sun-warmed hull to watch the surfer kids.

"No one knows for sure," she answers. "It's been here for a long time. Since the last bad hurricane, many years ago."

Thankfully, he doesn't ask uncomfortable questions, like why she comes to the lonely north shore or why she braves the crazy winds and surf of the Hollow. He's easy to be with. They laugh at the wipeouts of the surfers off the Point. Soon she relaxes, feeling like a normal girl, with a normal life, again.

"Hey, do you know those old women?" Trustin asks, shielding his eyes with his hand and pointing to the cliffs that curve around the scree beach and the domino rocks, overhanging the broken shells and crusted sand. Two old ladies are climbing down the eroding slope from a cluster of sea caves, making their way down to the beach toward the domino rocks spotted with foam, led by an old black dog.

Condi nods. "They're called the Beachlings."

The tallest of the old ladies wears a tattered green dress and tosses a stick to the dog. The dog springs high as if he's young again, bounding after the stick, splashing in the waves. Throwing back her head, the woman laughs, waist-length hair flowing down her back in a tangled net of black and silver. The second woman is frail and tiny, with a puff of white hair. She is bending over the domino rocks, prodding at the holes of foam with her fingers. Occasionally, when she finds a sea treasure to her liking, she happily stuffs it into a floppy orange sock.

"They look ancient," Trustin says. "Who are they?"

Condi pauses, not sure how to explain the small tribe of old women living in the caves of the cliffs on the desolate shore. "They're homeless. They live up there." She points to the water-worn pockets in the steep rock face. "They've lived there for as long as I can remember," she tells him.

"Homeless? I don't get it." He points to the caves. "You just said they live there."

"I know, but—" She stops, flustered. After all, she knows exactly what he means. "Of course, the caves *are* their homes, but that's not what the town believes. They say the Beachlings are smelly, homeless vagabonds—and that they should be run out of the cove."

Trustin winces, a furrow in his brow.

"My grandmother says the caves were carved by ancient waters, in times when the tide was high. The Beachlings have lived on this shore for years, and she says they have every right to be here," Condi goes on. "And the Beachlings are hardly dirty or smelly. Every day, regardless of the weather, they bathe in the sea—without any protection like wetsuits."

The old woman in the tattered green dress walks to the tip of the domino rocks and lifts her arms. The sun catches in her wind-swept hair as the old dog plays in the water, riding a wave. Gracefully, the woman bends her knees and swan dives into the water, swimming out to join the dog. After making a wide loop in the sea, stroking through azure water, she shakes back her hair and stretches out on a rock, opening her arms to the sky.

The tiny woman watches, so old and bent that she almost curls into herself like a shell. Putting down the bulging orange sock, she uncurls, darting across the rocks to plunge into a deep tide pool and splash merrily. When she rises from the pool, she picks up the sock and joins her friend to sun on the rocks.

Trustin whistles through his teeth. "Wow. These are icy cold waters." He shakes his head. "And they seem harmless enough. Why do people want to run them out of town?"

"Everything's changing in our town," Condi says bitterly. "Big resort owners are taking over. They don't like the Beachlings living in the cliff caves," she explains. "Dipitous Beach is turning into a rich tourist town. The hotel owners want to drive the Beachlings away, even though they're old, and haven't ever hurt a soul."

He looks at her. "How old are they?"

She shrugs. "Nobody knows exactly. They've been here longer than anyone in town, even my grandmother. She says they used to be known as the Beach Widows when she was young."

"People should leave them alone," Trustin says hotly. "Who are they hurting?"

The sudden set in his jaw surprises her. Looking up, she pretends to be caught up in the whirling of the seabirds. His concern makes her feel funny, even a little guilty. She doesn't often think about the plight of the odd old ladies roaming the cove.

A woman wearing a loose cotton sack-like dress

emerges from one of the high caves. Agile and strong, she scrambles down the cliff face, sidesteps over a narrow ledge and easily drops to shore, heading to the waterline. But before she reaches the women sunning on the rocks, she stops and turns, gazing up at them.

Condi throws up an arm and waves. "That's Triponica," she explains to Trustin. "She's the one all the other Beachlings listen to."

"I can see why," Trustin says. "She looks powerful."

Tall and muscular, with tough weathered skin and tight coils of steel-gray hair, Triponica waves back at Condi with a strong brown arm. Then, gathering the sack dress into her hands, she charges toward the water, high stepping through the surf before flopping face first into the foam. Her gray hair spreads out like a pewter fan as she rolls to her back and floats.

"Do you know all of them?" Trustin asks.

Condi nods. "I think so. But no one's sure how many there are. That one's Charlene," she says, pointing to the bent woman with the orange sock. "She walks the whole cove each day, picking up trash, cleaning up messes left by the tourists."

"Seems like the town would appreciate that," Trustin mutters, shaking his head. "What's in the floppy sock?"

"Sea glass and shells. All sorts of treasures," Condi answers.

"And who's that, the woman with the dog?" Trustin asks. "Graceful for an old lady. Look at her."

Dripping with silver streams of seawater, the woman in the green dress rises from the rocks, dancing across them, flowing smoothly from one to the other, and back again, like water.

"Madelaine Stinson. We call her Maddie. And the black dog is Lucky." Condi waves her arm toward the ruins of the old mansion and the pile of debris on the hill. "That's the old Stinson mansion. Maddie and her husband used to live there, back in the day. She's super old, older than the other Beachlings, they say. See the pile of junk with the tangled pipes near the house? That's all that's left of the hotel Maddie used to own with her husband. They say it was the finest spa hotel for miles around."

Trustin studies the ruins on the other side of the narrow bridge of rock connecting the tower to the peninsula. "I'd like to explore that old place sometime, but it looks like a tricky place to get to."

"It is," she answers. "Crossing that narrow ledge of rock is dangerous—especially when the winds are high." As she says it, a blast of cold air gusts off the sea, splashing the old ladies below with ragged ribbons of foam, lifting and curling so high that Condi and Trustin catch remnants of spray on their faces.

Trustin sits quietly for a while, staring at the ancient mansion and hotel. Condi thinks the mansion is looking extra lonely today, tall, blank windows staring out to sea, the sagging porch crumpled and caving in, like a witch's crooked smile.

"People say the Hollow is haunted," she tells him.

He turns and looks at her, thoughtful "And what about you? Do you believe in ghosts?" he asks.

"Maybe," she says carefully, avoiding his eyes. "People see twinkling red lights inside the old house at night." She shrugs. "My grandmother says it's only the reflections of lights from ships at sea.

"What do you think?" he presses.

Raking nervous fingers through her tangled curls, she says, "I mean, I *might* believe in ghosts, but not in the way you think." Lowering her eyes, she says softly, "I don't believe in storybook ghosts—you know, scary ghosts that stalk people."

Leaning back on his elbows, resting on the warm hull of the kayak, he says, "You mean you believe in a different kind of ghost. Not the Halloween kind."

"I guess so." She sighs. "Though some ghosts might be scary—I'm not sure. All I know is that after we die, I hope there's something more."

He sits up again beside her. "I hope the same thing."

"You do?" She peeks over her shoulder at him.

"Yep." He smiles. "What do you think the 'more' is?"

The question hits her in the heart. Without warning, as it tends to do, the pain inside her rises, threatening to choke her. Her eyes fly away from his. "You ask a lot of questions," she says stiffly, hating how she's reacting, maybe ruining the afternoon.

But he doesn't seem to care. Pointing to the shore where Madelaine is romping with Lucky, he muses, "I don't get it. If Madelaine lived in a mansion and owned a spa hotel, how'd she end up in a cave?"

Condi shakes her head. "I'm not sure anyone knows what happened. Only that the Stinsons lost the hotel. It was a long time ago—and Maddie doesn't talk."

He stares at her. "Seriously?"

"I mean, she only recites bits and pieces of poetry—old-school stuff most folks have never heard of. People think she's lost her mind. It's depressing."

"Sad," he agrees.

"Grand Ella says it's funny how memory works. Maddie remembers poems from a happier time, before bad stuff happened to her."

"Grand Ella? Is that your grandmother?" he asks.

"Yes," she answers. "I live with her in the yellow cottage."

"She sounds wise," he says.

"She is," Condi tells him, meaning it with all her heart. Without Grand Ella, she wouldn't be here.

Arms intertwined, the three old ladies walk the tideline together, braced against the wind, Lucky running circles around them. As they fade into the distance, Condi and Trustin turn their attention back to Craggy Point, where the surfer kids are catching big ones.

"Great day for whitecapping," Condi says, certain Trustin wishes he was out there with them. "Want to go back out?"

"Nope, I like being here with you," he says. "Look there—dude on the red board—going for a big one, hanging in the barrel." Without looking over, he catches her hand and holds it.

Happier than she's been in ages, she smiles. Off the Point, Javed Holmes is sliding out of the trough of a huge roller, windmilling his arms, wobbling across the wake.

"Looks like fun," she says wistfully.

Trustin squeezes her hand. "You want to learn to surf, don't you?"

"I have to wait," she replies. "Grand Ella's saving up for a surfboard and I'm helping—but it will be a while."

"I could teach you with my board," he answers. "We're close to the same height. But you'd need your own wetsuit."

"Thanks anyway," Condi shoots him a shy smile. "But I better not. Things are better when you wait."

He raises a brow. "You're kidding, right? Why wait? Life's awfully short, you know."

Instantly, her temper flares. Of course, she knows—better than anyone.

He feels her flinch. To her dismay, his eyes cloud over, blending with the turbulent blue-green of the sea. Above the neck of his wetsuit, a ridge of scars reddens like a flame.

As quickly as her irritation sparked, it fades away. A terrible thing must have happened to Trustin to cause those awful scars. He seems different from other kids, way older than his age—and maybe a whole lot sadder.

"I won't be waiting too long," she tells him. "I want to get contacts first." Playfully, she wrinkles her nose at him, adjusting her glasses. "Can't surf in these."

He laughs. "Wear goggles. You'd look cute."

Flushing, she tosses back her curls. No boy's ever told her she was cute before. For a bare second, their eyes catch and hold.

"Hey, is that your grandmother?" he says, looking over her shoulder.

She turns toward the distant shore. Grand Ella, standing on the terrace of the yellow cottage holding her silver-streaked hair off her face, is anxiously scanning the cove.

"Gotta go," Condi says, sliding off the hull of the kayak.

Reluctantly, Trustin lets go of her hand and then gently tweaks one of her long black curls. "It's been fun," he says.

"Yes," she answers, smiling.

"Come here after school tomorrow?" he says suddenly. "Climb and watch me surf?"

She nods, breathing out all the sunlight and sparkles that have been trapped deep inside her for a very long time.

"I'll be here," she answers.

Chapter Two

THE YOGA COVE

In that mysterious hour before dawn, Condi wakes up happier than usual. Coming awake in her snug bed tucked under the rafters of the loft in the yellow cottage, she can't wait to face the day. A lullaby breeze curls through the open window, ruffling the leaves of the pink bougainvillea and the winding vine of white sea lilies on the trellis outside, the flowers spilling into the room, nodding over the window frame. Stretching her arms up to the midnight blue ceiling painted with tiny silver stars, she smiles, wondering if Trustin will be at school today, and whether they'll be in any of the same classes.

Slipping into yoga clothes, Condi hurries down the ladder from the loft, landing in the living room and tiptoeing into the kitchen, awash with salty ocean air and the sweet scent of freshly baked lavender-honey muffins—the smell of love.

Nibbling on a muffin, Condi steps out onto the terrace and leans out over the railing overhung with vibrant coral beach roses, gratefully breathing in the fresh dawn air. Though she's lost an awful lot, Condi knows how much she has. She has Grand Ella—and they have the cozy yellow cottage, high on the cliff.

Grand Ella is already down on the beach, preparing for sunrise yoga, the class she teaches every morning on the small crescent of sand below the cottage. Licking her fingers, Condi finishes the last of the muffin and pulls her yoga mat out of a teak box on the terrace, then runs lightly down the zigzag stairs stretching to the beach like a zipper. Barefoot, she pads over the sand until she reaches the place everyone in town calls the yoga cove. Nestled in the crook of placid shore, Grand Ella sits in lotus pose, meditating on her mat, eyes closed, breathing in and out with the sea.

How Condi loves the sunrise, that mystical time when the air is spelled in softness. Rolling out her mat beside Grand Ella, she joins her in easy pose, relaxing her shoulders and fixing her eyes on the horizon line. Soon the peeking dawn appears, dribbling watercolor oranges and pinks into violet-blue water, the place where sea meets sky.

Smiling, Condi thinks of Trustin.

Sea and sky.

Sky and sea...

Making the words her mantra, she slows her breathing to match Grand Ella's, and tries to clear her mind. But thoughts keep popping up, making it impossible. Trustin was so nice yesterday. What if he's different today? What if he doesn't want to be friends? What if he doesn't like her at all?

What, what, what.

As so often happens, the pestering thoughts take charge, until, thankfully, a burst of giggles saves her, vibrating out through the breaking dawn. Yoga mats in arms, the rich ladies are arriving, yawning their way down the hill from the big houses, hair piled in slippery knots on the tops of their heads.

Condi folds into child's pose, face down, forehead resting on the mat. Grand Ella's taught her it's important to protect her heart. A lot of the yoga ladies are the moms of rich kids at school. Seeing the mothers of kids her own age is the worst—that other kids still have what she has lost is almost too much to bear.

At last, the ladies stop giggling and spread their mats. Sun glazes the beach, rose-peach and gold catching on the silver streak in Grand Ella's hair. Condi blinks open her eyes. Held in the hush of the tide, the sunrise yoga class begins.

Of course, the peace can't last. At the close of the practice, the ladies are resting on their backs, where Grand Ella's encouraged them to stay for a few quiet minutes. But the woman on the mat next to Condi is antsy. Refusing to stay still, she rolls to hands and knees, craning her neck toward the end of the yoga cove, where a long sliver of shore curves into the public beach.

"Not again," she mutters. Her manicured fingers

scramble in the sand, reaching for her cell phone.

The mood of the class is broken. The other ladies sit up and start rolling up their mats, resuming their usual chatter. One of them, Mrs. Jackson, asks Grand Ella to spot her for an arm balancing pose.

The woman beside Condi hurriedly places a call. "Sheriff?" she says in a low voice. "Amber Arondale, calling from the yoga cove. They're here again—you know, those awful Beachlings. Come NOW, the nasty one with the dog and her friend are digging through the trash again."

Condi stares at Mrs. Arondale, unbelieving. Then she turns and looks to the public beach, where Madelaine and Charlene are bent over an overflowing trash can, scavenging for leftover food, while Lucky runs loops around them.

Standing up in a snit, Mrs. Arondale ends the call and slides her phone into her pocket. "Those old homeless women spread filth and disease," she announces to the other ladies.

"I agree, Amber," Mrs. Walden chimes in. "The situation's out of hand. Thank goodness, Duke Holmes has hired security guards to patrol the beach front at night. The hotel guests are nervous with those horrible Beachlings roaming around at all hours."

Wishing Grand Ella wasn't out of earshot, Condi rolls up her yoga mat. It's crazy. Why isn't Duke Holmes nervous about his drunk hotel guests, the ones who party on the beach late at night, breaking bottles and littering the sand with glass and cans and other horrible stuff? Helplessly, she tries to catch Grand Ella's attention, but she's focused on steadying Mrs. Jackson, upside down in a precarious pose.

The crunch of gravel in the high parking lot off the beach road signals the sheriff's arrival. Slowly, a burly figure uncoils from the squad car and goes to stand at the top of the hill. Legs apart, he surveys the beach front.

Spotting the sheriff watching from above, Mrs. Arondale doesn't waste a minute. Flouncing across the sand, she trips over to the public trash can, glaring at Madelaine and Charlene.

Holding a crumpled coffee cup in one hand and clutching the floppy orange sock to her chest with the other, Charlene shrinks back, folding into a crouch. But Madelaine grows large. Spreading her arms, she rushes at Mrs. Arondale like an angry bird, the rags of her green dress flapping like tattered feathers around her thin shoulders.

"Sheriff Coodle!" Mrs. Arondale shrieks.

Slowly, the sheriff descends the beach stairs and ambles across the beach, clearly not in a hurry. With the sheriff dragging his feet, Condi's had enough. Jogging over to the trash can, she reaches out and touches Charlene's skinny arm.

"Wait," she says quietly, "Grand Ella will get you fresh food and something better to drink."

Charlene relaxes. She smiles, a haze of wispy-white hair floating around her gentle face, a cracked mosaic of sun and rain. She drops the coffee cup back in the trash.

The shadow of the sheriff falls across the sand. "Are these the women you called about, Amber?" he asks wearily.

Mrs. Arondale sidles up to him. Hand on a hip, she rolls her eyes. "Really Clive? Of course they are."

The sheriff's big hands hang by his sides helplessly. He shakes his head as Madelaine plants her gnarled toes in the sand and scowls at him.

"See?" Mrs. Arondale says. "She's out of her mind. Nasty and dirty and—"

The sheriff clears his throat but doesn't speak. Condi's temper spikes. "Why are you picking on them?" she blurts, glaring at Mrs. Arondale. "Because they're poor and hungry?"

Mrs. Arondale's cheeks flame. She looks flustered. "Dear, you don't understand. These women are homeless—not in their right minds."

"Dipitous Beach *is* their home," Condi answers hotly.

"Things change," Mrs. Arondale replies. "This is a respectable beach town. People want to feel safe." She shoots a warning look at the sheriff. "The Beachlings are bad for business."

"Now, Amber," the sheriff says. "I'm not sure—"

Mrs. Arondale interrupts. "Listen to me, Clive, these old women are eyesores." Crossing her arms, she jerks her head toward Madelaine. "That one tried to attack me. She's dangerous. I have a young son at home to protect—"

"What?" Condi can't believe her ears. Casey Arondale is in her class at school, the tallest boy in eighth grade. "He's almost twice her size!"

Madelaine snorts. Charlene giggles. Sheriff Coodle looks down at his boots, scratching his chin stubble, covering up a twitch.

"Clive!" Mrs. Arondale snaps, spearing Condi with a glare.

"Laughing isn't against the law, Amber," he answers.

Condi looks over at Grand Ella, pleading for support. This time Grand Ella glances up. Abandoning Mrs. Jackson, she immediately crosses the sand, breezing up to them.

"Charlene, Maddie, how nice to see you." Grand Ella nods and smiles sweetly at the sheriff. "You, too, Clive." Coming to stand beside Condi, she slips her arm around her waist.

Condi breathes out a sigh of relief.

Madelaine steps toward Grand Ella. "Man from Capri," she says softly. She holds Grand Ella's eyes.

Mrs. Arondale glowers, thrusting a long fingernail at the sheriff. "Listen to that gibberish."

Gracefully, Madelaine bends over the trash can and takes out a half-eaten hot dog, holding it out to them in her outstretched palm. "Man from Capri, don't you see?"

"Disgusting!" Mrs. Arondale exclaims. "She's crazy, Clive!"

Grand Ella shakes her head. "Crazy? Hardly, Amber. Madelaine's reciting a line from a famous poem—'Renascence' by Edna St. Vincent Millay. Perhaps you've heard of it?"

Standing dancer-straight, Madelaine fixes her emerald-green eyes on all of them and recites in a voice as clear as rain:

> *A man was starving in Capri;*
> *He moved his eyes and looked at me;*
> *I felt his gaze, I heard his moan,*
> *And knew his hunger as my own.*

Mrs. Arondale inhales sharply. The sheriff scuffs his boots nervously in the sand. Head held high; Madelaine turns her back on all of them. Taking long, proud steps, she heads toward the cliffs of the northern shore, Lucky prancing at her heels.

Mrs. Arondale chews on her lip. "Well...I still say it's a problem. Loitering *is* against the law." She narrows her eyes, looking at Charlene.

"Loitering?" Grand Ella laughs. "Don't be silly. Charlene is here for a private yoga session." Smiling at the sheriff and Mrs. Arondale, Grand Ella gently leads Charlene away from the trash can. "I'm looking forward to having you in class today, Charlene."

The sheriff, looking sheepish, says something under his breath to Mrs. Arondale, who walks off in a huff.

Tiny, trusting Charlene, hunched and curled, follows Condi and Grand Ella to a yoga mat, where she lays down the bulging floppy orange sock and smiles up at them.

Grand Ella kneels down beside her on the mat, helping her get comfortable. "We'll have a wonderful class," she murmurs. "Condi will run up to the cottage and put the kettle on. After yoga, you'll join us for breakfast."

Chapter Three

THE ORANGE-RED KAYAK

Everybody at Craggy Point Middle School is talking about the cute new boy, and what a good surfer he is.

"He's sooo hot," Jessy Pettikin moans.

"Totally," Macy Larson agrees, "but full of himself. Didn't say a word to any of us yesterday."

"Oh, I don't know," Jessy flips her hair. "Maybe he's shy."

Condi stands in front of her locker, wishing she was brave enough to interrupt the eighth-grade surfer girls and tell them that Trustin is *not* full of himself. And he's not shy, just quiet—and really, really nice.

"Where's he from?" Lindy Argyle wonders. "My mom says she hasn't seen any new parents around town."

"Who knows?" Macy sniffs. "He's a mystery. We didn't even see him paddle up to the Point yesterday. It's like he popped up out of the waves."

"Really?" Jessy's cornflower-blue eyes widen. "Amazing. He must swim like a fish."

"Ha, not *that* amazing." Lindy rolls her eyes. "You were busy making out with Finn."

"Oh, I'm so done with Finn," Jessy answers slyly. "I want to get to know the new boy." She looks at Macy and Lindy and winks.

The way Jessy curls up her mouth makes Condi flinch. Everybody knows Jessy can get any boy she wants.

First bell rings. The popular girls wander down the hall. Condi hangs by her locker, killing time. Staying away from other kids is a habit now.

"Dang! Forgot my math homework." Anda Lindgren flies around the corner, heading toward Condi, rushing toward the bank of lockers like her hair's on fire.

Condi steps aside. Anda's locker is next to hers. She and Anda used to be best friends. But that was before everything changed.

Anda opens her locker and ruffles through her backpack to find her homework. Then Anda grabs Condi's arm. "Okay, girlfriend, give me the scoop. Pretty sneaky— saw you with the cute new boy on the top of the Hollow yesterday."

Condi's heart sinks. She'd hoped none of the surfer kids saw her on the top of the Hollow with Trustin. Meeting him is her own special secret.

"C'mon. Spill it," Anda says.

"Nothing to tell," Condi answers. "We talked about surfing."

"Duh," Anda mocks, "you're so holding out." She tosses her head, narrowing her eyes. "Don't get too excited about him. You know he's a ninth grader, right?"

Condi chest tightens. She didn't know. Covering her

disappointment, she shrugs. She won't be seeing Trustin at school. Ninth graders go to Dipitous Beach High.

For a moment, she wants to tell Anda she's meeting Trustin at Windy Hollow after school to watch him surf. Anything to wipe the smug look off her old best friend's face. Their friendship is dead. After Condi lost Mama and Papa, Anda ditched her. And now, nearly a year later, Anda's changed. All she cares about is her new boyfriend, Javed Holmes—and surfing.

Anda slams her locker. "Tell you one thing, dude's incredible on a board. He's got an amazing tail slide." Running fingers through her streaky hair, she adds, "But Javed says he's a show off—way too cool for the rest of us."

Condi bites her lip. It's Javed Holmes who thinks he's way too cool for everybody else. Ever since Javed moved to Dipitous Beach and his dad built a luxury hotel called the Mirage, Javed's been the surfing king of the whole middle school.

"He's not like that," Condi says, blushing.

"Ha—now we're getting somewhere." Anda grins wickedly.

"No, I mean it. He's nice," Condi blurts.

"That so?" Anda retorts. Slinging her backpack over her shoulder, she adds, "Be careful, Condi Bloom. You're such a baby about boys."

At lunch, Condi makes her way through the bustling throngs of chattering kids and slips down a narrow hallway leading to the library. Though it's unlikely that

Trustin will be in the only shared space between middle schoolers and high school kids, she can at least hope. The library is a circular building, the sole connecting point between Craggy Point Middle and Dipitous Beach High. It's her favorite place at school. The high floor-to-ceiling glass windows command a stellar view overlooking Craggy Point, catching rays from the blue-white water of the cove.

When Condi steps into the folds of quiet, the air in the library is soft and sparkling. Mrs. Lowry, the timid, bespectacled librarian, glances up from the computer and nods at her, then goes back to cataloging books. Weaving through towering rows of shelves, Condi relaxes. Hanging out in the library at lunchtime is what's saved her this whole past school year. Being around other kids is hard. Sometimes she thinks she's the only one who knows that your whole life can turn to the worst kind of awful in the blink of an eye. But here, among the stacks of books, the world is large, way bigger than Dipitous Beach—and way more exciting than middle school. She can be a million different people, living a million different lives.

The library is deserted, except for a few nerdy high school kids doing research in carrels. She hurries past them, making her way to her favorite reading spot, a nook behind a curved bank of books. There, two chairs, one seaweed-green, one brown and saggy-bottomed, sit facing a porthole window set into a wooden beam, looking out to sea.

Settling herself in the green chair, she stares out the window. Fogged with salt spray, the circle of glass provides a smudged view of Windy Hollow. In the distance, a tall green sail wavers on the horizon line.

The sight of the proud, shimmering sail pierces her heart.

She lowers her face to her hands.

Memories crash in waves.

The valiant green sail that once belonged to her...is never coming home.

#

After school, Condi races down to the beach. Hugging the water line, she follows the curved stretch of sand across the cove to the deserted scree shore of Windy Hollow.

Preparing to step across the domino rocks, she looks at the bright haloed glow of the afternoon sun, vowing to watch the time. Grand Ella's teaching yoga at the Mirage for another hour, but then she'll expect Condi to be at the art shop, unpacking the afternoon shipments.

Reaching the rough water at the base of the tower, she hesitates. The autumn wind is sweeping, twirling itself dizzy. Not a friendly surfer's breeze.

Eyeing the high ledge of the rock tower, she fights the wind, pressing her summer-blue dress to her thighs, while she considers turning back.

No.

Of course, she won't go back.

No matter what, she'll watch Trustin surf—after all, she promised.

Gathering her nerve, she sloshes through the angry water and reaches the stone stairs. Climbing up to the top to the rock ledge will be tricky with these winds. Not much to hang onto.

Taking a deep breath, she takes the first step, cringing at the jagged spears of rocks below. One careful step at a time, she climbs to the high ledge. At the top, she shivers. Though the sun is warm today, she's never known it to blow quite so ferociously up here. Her summer-blue dress is inflating like a balloon. Holding the hem gathered in her fist, she scans the crashing ocean chop.

No sign of Trustin.

Ducking under the wind, she makes her way over to the half-moon rocks where the orange-red rescue kayak is upside down. Leaning against the hull, she sits down and hugs her knees into her chest, shutting out the howl of the wind. Through a flapping veil of hair, she stares out to the southern part of the cove, watching the curls off Craggy Point.

Suddenly, she catches a glimpse of something out of the corner of her eye. Swiveling her head, she sees a black surfboard pop up off the far north shore, where the waves are giant walls of foam. She winces at the risk. Trustin is daring to surf the blind side of the Hollow—a place surfing is prohibited.

Braving the wind, she slips out of the protection of the half-moon rocks and goes to sit on the lip of the high ledge, letting her legs dangle. Raising an arm above her head, she waves.

Lifting an arm, he waves back and carves into the tube of a huge roller, steering away from rocks as sharp as blades. Once again, the wind shifts. The ocean calms, smoothing into a pouring rush of blue and silver, curling into wheels of light, creating perfect waves known as spinners.

Surfing the spinners, he weaves in and out of the waves. Nearing the shaved cliffs beneath the ruins of the mansion, he wisely lets the last high wave enfold him, sliding off the molten-black board into the water, disappearing from view.

Patiently, Condi waits for him to pop up on the other side of the curl.

A long moment passes.

The ocean waves rock on.

The black surfboard surfaces, thrust forward by the waves, scuttled cruelly on the scree beach.

No surfer willingly abandons his board....

Condi jumps up and yanks the orange-red kayak out of the cleft between the half-moon rocks. Flipping over the heavy plastic hull, she shoves the kayak off the ledge. Bumping and scraping, it falls on the beach below. Grabbing the single paddle, she hurls it over the ledge. Flying down the stone stairs, she races to the kayak, pushes it into the shallows, and furiously paddles out to sea.

The water is icy cold.

Very cold.

What she's doing is crazy. But she's played this scene in her mind a thousand times. What if she'd seen the green sail capsize off the Hollow that fateful day? Could she have saved them?

Past the high waves rolling into shore, the water is a blank eye.

Paddling with all her might, she loops in circles, hoping to catch a glimpse of him. But there's no sign...only the tug and pull of gladiator currents, a relentless power sucking him out to sea.

Praying, she scans the water one more time.

Ruthless kicks of water slosh into the kayak, sinking it lower in the waves. Ice water washes over her feet. She looks down, staring at a widening crack in the kayak's shell.

Her mind spins out.

Crying with frustration, she digs her paddle into the crest of the next wave, turning the kayak toward shore.

Grand Ella cannot lose her, too.

But she's left it too late—

A giant wave crashes from behind.

Chapter Four

KI'S CIRCLE

A mighty vortex of water spins Condi deep into the sea, whisking her down, down, in a blinding blur of bubbles.

Thrashing and kicking, she fights, panic crushing her throat, squeezing her lungs. The water tightens its grip, making every effort futile, hopeless. She closes her eyes.

Down, down.

Mollare, Condoleeza.

Give in.

Papa's voice, speaking softly inside her head, calms her. Letting go, Condi shuts her eyes and stops fighting. With a tremendous tug, the tide yanks her back and under. Then, with shocking energy, the fist of pressure opens, the ocean's grip releases—freeing her like a gasp.

The spinning vortex slows.

Down, down.

At last, Condi dares to open her eyes. Though the waves tore off her glasses, the underwater world is clear and bright. She is floating, descending gently downward on a carousel of tiny bubbles, slowly, slowly...drifting in wide circles, toward the ocean's floor.

Shimmering light pours down from the surface waters. Above her, magnificent kelp forests of citrine and hunter green stretch up, reaching for the sun, long roots rocking in the rhythm of the tide. Below her, an endless expanse of majestic sea gardens explodes with complex patterns and vibrant color, catching the dancing light in the crystalline water.

Blinking, Condi tries to process it all. The colors and sea life are beyond anything she's ever seen. Radiant, rosy peach corals, bursting blooms in yellow and teal, clusters of spiked anemones, scarlet, electric blue, and plum. Splendid schools of fish, every shape and size, splitting the water in sudden, mesmerizing flashes.

It is beautiful here.

Peaceful.

The summer-blue dress ripples around her body. Grasping it in her hands, she sinks downward, the soft spin of the water leaving a trailing veil of bubbles. Floating like a dream, she gazes out into the distance, where a gigantic volcanic mountain puffs out slow beats of lavender mist. Soon, a curve of sand appears on the horizon, cradled by a shiny, black river of hardened lava.

With a beckoning swirl, a wave of water pushes her over to the sand. Rocked by a barely there current, she hovers for an instant, then descends, until her toes graze the dune.

Her body settles, the summer-blue dress drifting around her. As she stands on tiptoe, the wafting movements of her arms balance her as lightly as a ballerina, dark hair floating around her face, curling into the water.

Slowly, Condi looks around, marveling at spirals of lacy coral, twirling up and out of cascades of jewel-green moss, like turrets in a fairy castle. Tiny, crystal shells catch shimmering ribbons of light, glinting in the sand like diamonds. A sweep of stately white clamshells circles the sand, puffing out luminous mist—in and out, in and out, in the cadence of a breath. Silver threads of small fish weave in and out of the shells, swimming in slow, hypnotic loops.

The graceful rhythm of the fish and the rise and fall of the clamshell mist is restful; the water swirls softly, warm and silky. Her eyelids begin to droop. Oh, how she wants to stretch out...maybe go to sleep....

She closes her eyes.

"Not a good idea," a familiar voice says from behind her, snapping her awake.

Startled, she pirouettes, sending up a puff of sand sparkles. Transfixed, she looks at the figure in the wetsuit on the crest of the dune....

Impossible.

Trustin—the same—but not.

He swims over to join her, reaching out his hand. "Thought you'd never get here," he says, touching down beside her, grinning and pushing back a lock of onyx hair.

She stares at him. Though he's talking, his lips aren't moving. His voice vibrates inside her head. And, though his wet suit still shines pearly black and his turquoise eyes still sparkle like the sea, he is different.

The realization is terrifying. Frantically, she dodges his hand, pulling back, clutching her dress in fisted hands, fear beating in her ears.

His grin fades to sadness. "Please don't be scared, Condi."

"Of course, I'm scared," she cries, her own voice pouring through her head. "I don't understand! What is this place? We almost drowned."

He looks at her in concern, biting on his lower lip, brow furrowed.

His face tells her everything she doesn't want to know. This warm, underwater world, infused with color and light, is all wrong. This part of the sea is dark and icy cold.

In a hush, she whispers, "Oh, no...we *have* drowned?"

"Condi..." his voice trails off helplessly.

"We're dead," she murmurs, twisting her fingers, wringing the dress.

The furrow in his brow deepens. "No...not exactly."

"What *exactly* does that mean?" she says, turning away from him and staring hopelessly at the looping fish among the shells.

"Listen to me." Trustin grabs her elbow, turning her

to face him, his voice surprisingly fierce. "Stop. Looking. At. The. Fish."

He holds her gaze so intently she cannot look away. In desperation, she searches his turquoise eyes. "Tell me what's happening then, Trustin. Please."

He winces. "I can't, Condi. Not yet—you don't know enough."

"I know enough to know this is impossible." Wrenching her eyes away, she stares up at the distant glow of the sun, shining on the faraway surface waters. "We're under the sea...we've got to be dead...."

Cupping her chin, he draws it down to her throat. "Watch your chest, Condi. You're breathing."

Shocked, she looks down, seeing the gentle rise and fall of her breath. "Oh, I *am*," she says, looking at him in wonder.

Nodding his head at the circle of white clamshells, he explains quietly, "This place is Ki's Circle. See the bubbling mist? The clamshells are breathing for you. Ki is the ocean's breath."

Condi studies the clamshells, noticing how her breath synchronizes with the ebb and flow of mist...calm and relaxed...like the slow infinity loops of the fish....

"Condi." He grabs her shoulders and shakes her. "Stop. Looking." Urgently, he leans in and says, "You've got to listen to me. Ki's Circle is a lucky place to land—but a dangerous place to stay. If you stay here, you'll keep looking at the hypnotic fish. You'll go to sleep—and give up all your choices."

"Choices?" she says bitterly.

The jagged scar on his neck above his wetsuit flushes

bright red. "Condi, please. You have to trust me."

Halfheartedly, she shrugs. "I don't have a choice, now do I?"

Sighing, he shakes his head. "Not right now. But you will. C'mon, we're leaving Ki's Circle. We've got work to do." He reaches for her hand. "Look."

Through the clouds of clamshell mist, a majestic white sea lily floats into view. The flower's petals are open, like welcoming arms.

"Lily is a Protector," Trustin says. "She'll help us on our journey." The flower floats closer. "Hug your knees to your chest, Condi." A note of quiet urgency enters his voice, and she does as he asks.

The flower opens wider, slipping beneath her. For one sweet moment, she floats above the golden center, the petals of creamy white softly fluttering below her, like a gracious lady's fan. Gently, the petals lift, threaded with translucent veins the pale blue of a summer sky, closing around her legs and upper body, tucking under her arms.

She stares at Trustin. "Am I some kind of mermaid?"

Trustin laughs, mischief dancing in his eyes. "Mermaids aren't real, you know."

"Funny," she answers. "Like anything makes sense."

"Things make sense in time," he answers, growing serious again. "What matters is that you're safe—tucked into a lily pod—protection for our journey. We're leaving Ki's Circle now."

Alarmed, Condi asks, "How will I breathe outside the Circle?" Fresh ripples of fear wash through her. She doesn't want to leave this warm, serene place.

Trustin dives toward the sand and scoops up a small

white shell. Slipping it into her palm, he squeezes her fingers around it. "Take this. Tuck it inside the pod. Ki's shell is your breath."

With the shell tucked snugly into the pocket of her dress, Condi yearningly glances back over her shoulder at the hypnotic, looping fish. How easy it would be to just stay. Lie down on the soft sand and go to sleep....

"C'mon." Trustin quickly tugs her up off the sand. "Hold on tight to my hand. Use your other arm to steer." With a powerful frog kick, he swims them through the perimeter of the clamshell circle—out into the rough, wild water of a vast violet sea.

Condi is shocked into alertness. Outside the calm of Ki's Circle, the sharp change in temperature is stunning. No longer soft and comforting, this water is purple-blue—and cold. The dreamlike world of Ki's Circle vanishes. Her cloud of muddled thinking clears.

Am I dead?

Dreaming?

Hallucinating?

"Who are you anyway?" she asks, looking at Trustin. "How did you get here?"

"Swim, Condi," he answers, tightening his grip on her hand. "Please. Just swim."

After a while, she relaxes inside the lily pod, getting the hang of things. It's fun, shimmying alongside Trustin, moving at quicksilver speed, effortlessly as a fish. Even in the radically changing ocean currents, the lily pod slides and glides, riding the dip and flow of the tide.

Beneath them, a path of pearly sand unfolds like a storybook road. Following the ribbon of sand, they pass over miles of sea gardens, each stranger and more mysterious than the last. Exotic fish glow neon, grotesquely glorious creatures flicker electrical, opaque shadows slip into caves, then out again—plant, sea animal—or something yet unknown?

Moving rapidly over the varied terrain, Condi loses all sense of time, though it is obvious the day is waning. The light is banking, dimming in an instant, as light tends to do. The water is thick, slipping from clear to dull; the fading surface light shrinks, deepening to shadow.

In the vanquished light, the temperature falls from icy cold to frigid. Suddenly, it's hard for Condi to move her arms. She can no longer feel Trustin's fingers and her thoughts are chunked up and heavy, clogging up her mind.

In desperation, she wills herself to tug on Trustin's hand. Her arm doesn't budge. He swims on, dragging her through the gray water like a dead weight.

Help me, help me, she begs, slowly chiseling out the words in her head.

Startled, he stops swimming, looking over at her in shock.

"Oh, no," he cries, moving into action. She stares at him, frozen, unable to even blink.

"Stay with me, Condi." Urgently, he attempts to cross

her arms and fold them into the pod.

Her arms refuse to bend.

Leaning in, he looks deep into her eyes. "Remember something warm."

Somehow her brain sparks, breaking through the sludge, conjuring up an image. A crackling bonfire on the beach below the yellow cottage, under a night cast with stars, wrapped in a spun silver blanket beside Mama and Papa, nestled safely in the crook of Papa's strong arm....

Memories have power. Slowly, Condi's frozen arms thaw and Trustin bends them gently over her chest, tucking them into the pod. Once she's inside, he presses the lily petals closed around her neck.

Curled within the heart of the flower, she is warm again. The water inside is silky soft, inflating the pod with a halo of steam that wafts up through the petals around her neck, thawing out her face.

Relieved, she blinks the stiffness from her lashes and murmurs to Trustin, "Thank you."

Poking his head through the pocket of steam, Trustin tries to smile. "Sorry about that. Forgot about the temperature shift in this zone."

"Super scary," she tells him.

"This place *is* scary," Trustin admits. "It's the Dark Zone. But the only way to Koan's Place is through it. This place is called the Locker—the deepest part of the sea."

Koan? Another mystery. First Ki, now Koan. Condi sighs. And why is this part of the sea called the Locker? She wants to ask, but doesn't. Trustin told her the truth. She doesn't know enough. Besides, right now, just being warm is a relief.

Folded into the pod, she hugs her knees to her chest. This place is awful—cold and creepy. Trustin's eyes are anxiously scanning the shifting pockets of dark. She shivers. Whatever might be lurking here, they're at its mercy.

"I feel like a floating teapot," she whispers. "Sorry I'm so helpless. Are you okay?"

"Wish you had a handle," Trustin answers. As the shadows grow, it's getting harder for him to hang on to the pod. "You're slippery as a beach ball," he admits. "Currents here are tricky."

Kicking faster and harder, he holds the pod within his strong arms. The currents get meaner. Cold water slashes at Condi's face, the pod wobbling like an off-center top.

Suddenly, an underwater wave rises up beneath them, lifting the pod out of Trustin's arms, high above his head, then slamming it down. Careening like an arcade ball, the pod shoots into black.

Smack!

Bouncing off a slick, hard surface, the pod spins to a stop. Slowly, Condi's mind clears. It takes a long moment to breathe again. Squinting into the gloom, she makes out a twisted wreck of metal. A ship?

A creepy tickle grazes her cheek, tugging on her ear. Horrified, she flails within the pod; something tuberous and sticky is twining around her neck, making kissing noises in her ear.

"Heh, heh, now here's a pretty one." A nasty voice creaks through the water like an unoiled hinge.

"Get off me," she cries, bucking in the pod, trying to pull away.

"Sweet pretty one—a real little fighter." The awful voice chuckles; the kissing noises continue, nibbling on her ear.

Flipping her head from side to side, Condi struggles to free herself, but the vine only tightens.

"Leave her alone, Bernardo!"

Furious, Trustin kicks his way out of the murk. Tearing at the vine, he releases it from around her neck. Then, cradling the lily pod in his arms, he power-kicks away from the heap of metal.

"Heh, heh, well now—it's you, isn't it, Boy?" the voice rasps. "Where'd you get the pretty little thing? Is she one of the Dead Ones?"

"Shut up, Bernardo," Trustin snaps.

"Still a loser, aren't you, Boy?" The voice snarls. "Haven't figured out the answer to the riddle yet, have you?"

Trustin's arms tighten around Condi.

"I said, shut up." He stops swimming and glares at the wreck of metal.

"Figure it out, you stupid Boy!" The voice ramps up to a high shriek. "Find the answer to Koan's riddle!"

"Whether I solve the riddle or not, you're done forever, Bernardo." Trustin's voice is icy cold. "You'll never be free. You killed all those men. Your life was good for nothing."

"Good for nothing? Are you sure?" The voice vibrates with evil. "Do you know why Koan assigned you the riddle? There's a reason, you know."

Trustin goes silent. Even through the thick petals of

the pod, Condi feels him shaking with rage.

"Come closer, my pretty…" A slithery tuber slides out of a rusted hole in the twisted metal hull, snaking through the water toward her…reaching for a lock of her hair.

Without a word, Trustin rips the tuber away and fights through a growing maze of sticky, sucking plants that surround them in an instant, yanking on Condi's hair. At last, Trustin breaks them free of the tortuous wall of plants, steering the pod into open water.

Once they reach clear water, the shadows fade, and the pod comes to a stop. Exhausted, Trustin turns to look at Condi, eyes wild and angry, jaw set and tight.

Condi's heart pounds. Clutching the white shell in her hand, she slows her breath. "That voice—you called it Bernardo…" She stares at Trustin. "You said he killed people? Oh—what is this awful place?" Though the pod is safe and warm, she can't stop shivering.

Trustin's jaw softens. After a long moment, he calms down. "Condi, I'm sorry. This is the last place I wanted to bring you." Holding her close, he moves so their faces almost touch and she can see the earnestness in his eyes. "This place, the Locker—well, it is the place where evil Shadow Voices are stored."

"I don't know what you mean…" she cries, pulling away from him. "Stop confusing me."

"I know," he answers miserably. "It's hard to explain, but I'll try."

Wrapping his arms tightly around the pod, he tilts his head toward hers. "We all have a Shadow Voice, Condi. The Voice lives deep inside us, critical and negative, sometimes even evil."

Condi nods. "Grand Ella calls the awful voice in our heads our 'negative roommate.' She says the voice is the worst of us—but we don't have to listen to it."

In relief, Trustin smiles at her. "Grand Ella's got it right. What she says is true. Though we're all born with a Shadow Voice, we're also born with the power to overcome it. We don't have to listen to it. If we choose to think and do and say good things during our lives, then our Shadow Voice shrinks down to almost nothing." Trustin sighs. "But Bernardo chose the opposite. He thought and said and did evil things, living to cause suffering. When he died, his Shadow Voice had grown strong and powerful."

"Bernardo's dead?" she says slowly. "But his Shadow Voice is powerful—and still alive?"

"Yes, Bernardo is dead. But here's the part that's hard to understand..." He gazes into her eyes. "The good and evil we do in our lives continues to exist after we die," he explains softly. "It's all energy, you see—and energy never dies."

Condi shakes her head. "That's a lot to understand." She sighs. "Everything is confusing here." Fingers wrapped tightly around the shell, she takes a deep breath. "What did Bernardo mean when he asked you about solving Koan's riddle?"

Trustin winces. "Koan is the Master of the Sea, Condi— a Great Riddle himself." He turns his head away, staring off into the distance. "I can't answer your question. Koan's ways are impossible to understand."

#

The ocean pitches and rolls.

Squirt! Swish! Shhhhhh...

Clouds of black ink spray through the water, enclosing them in a darkness deep as a moonless night.

Trustin whispers. "It's okay, Condi. The creature that's coming won't hurt us."

She shudders, waiting in dread as the inked water fades into swirls of indigo. A pair of slits appear in a sea cave, blazing alien-red. A giant orange squid slips out of the rock, holding the limp body of a dead scuba diver in its long, suckered tentacles.

"Oh, how horrible." Condi gasps.

Glug, glug. Glug, glug.

A tank on the diver's back pours out a stream of useless bubbles, the cut safety line that tied him to the surface flapping behind his body like a snake.

Cradling the diver, the giant squid bows its head, covering the diver's exposed neck.

Condi recoils, shutting her eyes. "Is it eating the diver?"

"Look again," Trustin says quietly.

Reluctantly, she blinks her eyes open.

Lifting its massive orange head, the squid releases the diver. With a blast of jet-black ink, the creature squirts away, shooting toward the Dark Zone.

"That was horrible," Condi exclaims. "What was he doing to that poor diver?"

Trustin shakes his head. "Don't believe what you think you saw, Condi. The squid is one of the Great Creatures, called by Koan to comfort the dying, rocking them gently into the Last Sleep. He is known as the Distiller, and he wasn't eating the diver. He was harvesting the diver's Shadow Voice.

"Was the diver evil?" Condi asks.

"No. The diver was a good man, but he had a Shadow Voice, as we all do, " Trustin answers. "The Distiller harvests Shadow Voices, then transports them to the Locker, storing them where they can bring no more harm to the world."

Condi's heart hurts. How beautiful and horrible at the same time. She thinks of Mama and Papa, lost and drowning in the sea. Was the Distiller there to comfort and hold them close?

She is certain Mama's and Papa's Shadow Voices were very, very small. They were loving, generous people— bright, creative and kind. Remembering that last morning, before they sailed away, a great sob rises up, sticking in her throat. She misses them more than anything.

"Death is not the end, Condi," Trustin says gently. "Watch closely. Look."

She follows his eyes up to the surface water, where a burst of gold illuminates the sea. In a shimmer of diamond sea drops, a school of golden fish, tiny as hummingbirds, flutter downward and surround the diver's body, quivering like a thousand pulsing hearts.

"The diver is beautiful—covered in gold," Condi murmurs.

"Yes. The diver has a lot of goodness in him. The golden fish are Siphoners. Now that the Distiller has harvested the diver's Shadow Voice, the Siphoners are extracting his good energy. It will be infused back into the world. Good energy is called Essence, Condi. After we die,

Essence is given back to the world, where it can grow and do more good." A strange, sweet expression comes over Trustin's face. He smiles shyly. "Do you understand?"

She shakes her head. "Not exactly. But I hope it's true. How wonderful if our Essence—the good energy—lives on."

He nods. "Everything comes clear in time. There's more to learn. Come on, Koan is waiting for you."

Swimming the lily pod away from the diver's body, Trustin catches the rise of the next underwater wave and they ride the beat of the currents. The sea is light and transparent, rippling in ribbons of blue, indigo, and teal, as the water grows warmer and warmer.

When they reach a calm pool of light, Trustin lets go of the lily. The pod slows, drifting to a stop. Condi looks over at Trustin, confused.

"Time to say goodbye," Trustin tells her quietly. "The waters are warm here. You won't need Lily's protection any longer."

The creamy petals of the elegant sea lily peel away from Condi's body, exposing the golden center. As her legs unfold, she slips her hand in the pocket of the summer blue dress, finding comfort in curling her fingers around the small white shell as the gracious flower opens and slips from beneath her. Strangely, she feels stripped raw.

"Oh, how I'll miss Lily," she tells Trustin sadly. "Does she have to go?"

"Lily's never really gone," Trustin explains. "She's a

Protector, a mother flower born to love without limits. You needed her protection in the Dark Zone—but we're safe now. If you ever need her again, she'll find you. She's a true mother—always there for her children."

With a graceful dip and sway, Lily folds into a curtsy. The ethereal white-blue flower floats away on the current, fluttering with a mother's gentle kisses.

Chapter Five

SURFBOARD STORIES

Trustin and Condi swim on. Condi keeps pace, riding the waves, surrendering to the ebb and flow. The sea gardens are grander than ever, blooming with enchanting flowers. The fish are captivating and unpredictable, shivering through the water in wild, colorful bursts.

After a while, Trustin slows down, pointing to a hilltop in the distance where jewel- colored lights are bouncing off tall, oval mirrors.

As they swim closer, Condi's breath catches. Why, the tall ovals of light aren't mirrors after all! On the hilltop, fanning down into a deep ocean valley, is a dazzling forest of surfboards, standing proudly upright, casting long watery shadows. The boards are majestic, a treasure trove of color—ruby, jade, emerald, sapphire, and amethyst—hues of precious stones.

"Welcome to the Surfboard Forest," Trustin says, smiling.

"Oh! It's wonderful," Condi says in delight. "May I touch one?"

When he nods, she reaches out to touch a citrine surfboard with a blurred swirl of light in its center. The golden-green board tingles under her fingers.

Alarmed, she looks at him. "What's happening?"

"Wait and watch," he whispers. "The board will tell a story."

Leaning in, she gazes into the surface of the board, watching in wonder as a fuzzy picture comes into view. Peering through swirls of mist, she makes out the jagged silhouette of Windy Hollow.

Suddenly, air brushes past her cheek. A great whooshing fills her ears. Her eyes widen. A green sail is unfurling on the horizon beyond the Hollow. She clutches the shell in her pocket, unable to breathe.

"Don't be afraid, Condi," Trustin whispers. "Let yourself go."

She takes a breath.

Pulled into the swirls of mist, lifted from the depths of the sea, she rises, bursting out of the water. Toes dipping into the crests of the waves, she skims the sea, flying toward the boat she knows so well. At last, gently, ever so gently, the wind deposits her on the bow, the place that belonged to her.

Everything feels the same. Her long legs are propped on the rails. Papa is leaning on the cushions beside her, holding his guitar. Mama is singing, heart to sky, hair flowing from beneath the wide-brimmed white hat, scalloped like a shell.

Mama's voice is low, a lilting contralto, opening like a

rose. Papa's voice joins hers in perfect harmony, a dark night of stars, tumbling out like a river, pouring midnight blue and sure. The music, strong and sweet, holds Condi tight, wrapping her in memories of what once was, but can never be again.

Surrounded by love, her eyes well with grateful tears. They were a happy family, sailing from seaside town to seaside town, Mama and Papa doing what they loved best—making and sharing music, living the artist's life, free and flowing and pure.

The day came when Condi was ready for school, and she went to live with Grand Ella in the yellow cottage. There she learned to be content without them, breathing in the music of the sea, watching for the green sail from the top of the Hollow, waiting for them to come home.

As they always did.

Until.

The memory crashes down. A great wave arcs and falls, spilling into the boat. The breeze swirls, lifting her up, catching her in its arms, whirling her away.

Oh, no! Please let me stay! she cries.

Papa looks up and sadly shakes his head. Mama gazes at Condi with the greatest kind of love.

Audacia, Condoleeza.

Be brave.

Vivace, my Constant.

Be happy.

The music fades into soft sighing.

The ocean reaches up—pulling her down, down.

#

"No!" She cries in fury, pounding on the golden-green board with her fist and glaring at Trustin. "Why wasn't I with them that day? Why didn't I drown, too?"

Trustin shakes his head. "I don't know, Condi. There aren't answers. At least none that I know."

He takes her hand and squeezes it, guiding her away from the citrine board. She doesn't resist. The scene on the board is gone.

In silence, they swim through the forest of surfboards, making their way into the valley where Trustin lets go of her hand, pointing to a board the color of a ripe tangerine.

"No," she says, pressing her hands to her sides. "No more stories."

Trustin is thoughtful for a long moment. Then, he looks deeply into her eyes, and when he speaks his voice is firm. "I'm sorry, but it's not for you to choose, Condi. Koan wants you here. He decides what stories he wants you to hear and what things you need to learn—whether or not you want to learn them."

"Well, I don't want to," she answers stubbornly. "I can't bear any more."

"I get it." His eyes are sad. "More than you can ever know."

The catch in his voice makes her pause. The scar on his neck is a fiery slash, like something struggling within him is fighting to escape. It makes her think. He hasn't ever lied to her. Maybe she should listen.

Cautiously, she reaches out a finger to touch the tangerine surfboard. When the board tingles, the fresh scent of citrus wafts into her nose, making her sweetly lightheaded. She leans in, captivated by the scent, as a story unfolds on the board.

Again, the scene is Windy Hollow. The light is strange, an old-timey hue of wavering sepia, like streaks on an ancient photograph.

The streaks fade and the light clarifies. The landscape is not what Condi knows, except for the jagged spears of rocks in the water beneath the tower. This shoreline is lush and green, tangles of flowering vines spilling down over the rocks, clusters of orange and tangerine trees covering the hill, sea grasses softly sweeping the slope that is now only barren cliff. On the crest of the hill is a majestic mansion, sun glinting off tall, polished windows above a pristine white porch, overhung with blush-pink roses.

"The old Stinson place," Condi murmurs. "But before— a long time ago—when it was new and beautiful."

On the porch are two young women. One is a dark-haired beauty, cradling an infant with a burst of red hair. The second is a young girl, small and delicate. Nestled on the porch swing, she holds a book in her lap and presses a glass of iced tea to her cheek, under a halo of curls. Beneath the swing is a straw basket, overflowing with yarn.

"I can see the sweat beads on that glass," Condi whispers.

"You can see and hear everything in this story, Condi," Trustin whispers back. "But this scene is different. It is not your life. But there must be something here that Koan wants you to know."

The dark-haired woman with the baby kisses the infant's head. "Read me a poem, Charly. I've been up all night with this little one." She pushes back damp cobalt-black tresses. "Oh, it's so frightfully hot today, hardly even a breeze."

The young girl smiles. She uncurls and sits up straight, flipping through the pages of the book. "Alright, Miss Maddie. Here's one by Robert Frost." In a soft, shy voice, she begins to read:

> Nature's first green is gold.
> Her hardest hue to hold.
> Her early leaf's a flower,
> But only so an hour.
> Then leaf subsides to leaf,
> So Eden sank to grief,
> So dawn goes down to day.
> Nothing gold can stay.

The girl stops reading. Closing the book, she takes a sip of tea, then looks at the woman with the baby. "Do you think it's true, Miss Maddie? That good things don't last?"

The woman with the baby sighs, staring out to sea. "Oh, I don't know, Charly. The poem is sad, that's for certain." Twisting her gold wedding ring nervously on her finger, she smiles over at the girl. "I mean, it's true that 'nothing gold can stay.' But it's also true that when good things end, other good things may come. Everything changes, you know." She strokes the baby's curls. "After all, I'm so happy now. Married to the best man on earth— one of the few who survived the war." She looks up the hill where a group of men are hauling stone and bricks. "And our spa hotel will soon be finished." Her voice trails off. "Then we can help families who aren't so lucky."

The girl nods and sets down the book and tea, then leans over to pull a ball of yarn out of the basket at her feet.

The dark-haired woman closes her eyes, patting the baby and singing softly. The girl's knitting needles flash in the summer sun, spinning out a floppy orange sock.

"Madelaine and Charlene." Condi says. "I'd recognize that orange sock anywhere." She shakes her head. "They were both so young and beautiful...and Madelaine had a child." She looks questioningly at Trustin. "I wonder what happened to the baby." The thought makes her heart hurt, as it does with a certain kind of wondering.

Trustin takes her hand. They swim through the winding valley, threading through banks of surfboards in poppy reds, sunshine yellows and mountain purples. When they reach open water, the surfboard colors shift again, blending into the hues of the sea, jade to teal, indigo to ocean blue—silver-green to the color of the cove on a perfect surfing day—glittering aquamarine.

Letting go of Trustin's hand, Condi doesn't hesitate. Swimming over to the aquamarine board, she places her hand on the shining mirrored surface.

When she feels the tingle, the scene is instantly sharp and clear. Surfing the highest waves off Craggy Point is a leggy girl with dark curls, carving through the water on a shimmering aquamarine board.

"Oh, it's me—I'm doing it—surfing the cove!" Condi cries. Clapping her hands with joy, she turns to fling her arms around Trustin.

But the hug is stopped short. The second her hand leaves the board, the scene on the surfboard fades.

"I lost it," she says wistfully as the mirrored surface blurs over. "It's gone."

"Not forever," Trustin says. "If surfing is part of your story, you'll find a way to make it happen."

She nods, looking at the aquamarine board with longing, hoping she gets the chance to follow her surfing dream. To her surprise, as she gazes at the mirrored surface the blurriness recedes, though she's not touching the surfboard. She leans forward in excitement. Streaked like an old photo, another scene on Windy Hollow from years past is coming into view. The waters are frothing beneath the rock tower, crashing on the scree beach. On the peninsula, next to the stately Stinson mansion is a charming spa hotel, gleaming casement windows flung out over the sea. Beneath the windows is a broad sunny deck. Madelaine, older now, is standing on the deck of the hotel, looking anxiously out to sea.

Her gaze is on the horizon, to a hulking line of waves, where a tall, regal surfer girl is popping out of a curl, gracefully riding an aquamarine board. Throwing her head back, she laughs, red hair streaming in the wind.

"She's amazing," Condi says softly.

Sliding down a glistening wall of water, the surfer girl cuts into another wave. Bending and flowing, she follows the lead of the sea, heading toward a small inlet of water where a black puppy is stranded on the domino rocks. The puppy yips with excitement as the girl surfs closer, weaving and bobbing, skirting the ragged edges of the waves.

Condi's heart lurches. "Too close to the rocks—"

Trustin puts his hand over hers.

A swelling wave behind the girl looms large, curling over her like a tongue. Madelaine clutches her throat in a soundless scream—

The surfboard bucks, jerking beneath Condi's fingers.

Trustin yanks her hand off the board.

"No, not yet." She lunges to grab the board again. "Please. One more look," she begs.

Trustin holds on tightly to her wrist. "You won't like what you see, Condi."

"I need to know what happened." Slipping out of his grasp, she puts a finger back on the surfboard.

The scene comes into focus as the giant wave hovers over the girl and the surfboard is sucked from beneath her feet, pitching her high, tossing her head first into the domino rocks. Under Condi's finger, the shiny spot on the aquamarine board pops and goes dark—like a light bulb burning out.

"Oh, no. She died, didn't she?" Frantic, Condi turns to Trustin.

He tugs her away from the board, his limitless turquoise eyes a million miles away.

Chapter Six

THE RIDDLE

No matter how hard she tries, Condi can't stop trembling, inside and out. The sight of the red-haired girl hitting the rocks is the most awful thing she's ever seen. All she wants is to go home.

"I have to get back to Grand Ella—she still needs me," she pleads with Trustin.

Without a word, he pulls her away from the story-telling surfboards and their jeweled lights. Leaving the hill and the sparkling valley, they swim away from the Surfboard Forest.

"We're going to Koan's Place now," he tells her. "Trust me this time, Condi. Please."

She has no choice but to trust him, so that is what she does. Soon the soothing rhythm of the warm water currents calms her. She holds his hand and swims over the sea gardens, looking into the distance, where the massive underwater volcano is chugging out lavender mist. At the base of the volcano, they spiral down through the water, landing on a half-moon of silver and black sand.

"Koan's Place," Trustin says soberly, letting go of her hand. "Prepare to meet the Master of the Sea."

She nods. "I'm ready. I'll do anything. I just want to go home."

The sand dune is peaceful. Golden light pours from the surface waters, moving across the sand like spot lights. Banked high, the black and silver sand is elevated like a stage at the base of the huge volcano. In the center of the curved dune, in front of the steaming sea mountain, is a massive rock, standing alone, a hole in its center, like an eye.

"Prepare to meet Koan," Trustin whispers. "Are you ready?"

Condi nods.

Koan is coming, Koan is coming
Master of the Sea
One who knows All and is All
We are all One.

Many voices ring out around them, rich in the cadences of a vast crowd.

Puzzled, Condi looks at Trustin. "Who are the voices?"

"Sea spirits, Condi. Those who have gone before. Always with us—so we are never alone."

"Mama and Papa?" She asks, looking to him with hope, wanting for it to be so.

"We are never alone," he repeats, smiling at her sadly.

\#

In the eye of the rock, the sea undulates in unusual patterns, moving in and out, changing and catching light, casting prisms of color.

"Hello, my friends." A powerful voice pours through the sea.

Hello, great Koan
The sea is yours, Master
We are all One.

"What is happening?" Condi asks. "Where is Koan?"

"Koan is revealed in the eye of the great rock before you," he explains. "Confusing, I know. Especially since Koan *is* the sea—always present, ever changing."

"Silence, please," the mighty voice commands. "The Council of the Half Moon will come to order."

The murmuring of the sea spirits falls to a hush.

In a low whisper, Trustin says to Condi, "Koan is going to ask for an accounting from each of us. Listen—and remember."

"Who is the first to speak?" The water in the eye of the rock washes clear.

"Master, I seek permission to give my report." The Distiller swirls into view with the golden Siphoners sparkling around the giant squid's red-orange body, beating tiny fins.

"Of course, my friend," Koan answers. "The half-moon floor is yours, Distiller."

The squid humbly lowers his eyes. The creature's tentacles, slender and strong as ropes, wrap around the rocks at the base of the sea mountain.

"Thank you, Master." Lifting his head, the Distiller inflates his tubular body. "I'll come straight to the point." He pauses for full effect. "We're running out of time."

Running out of time?

What does Distiller mean?

Isn't there always time?

Oh no! Oh no!

Running out of time?

The agitated energy of the sea spirits quickens the rhythm of Condi's breath. Fumbling in her pocket, she wraps her fingers tightly around the shell.

Distiller continues, "The Locker is almost full, Koan. The loud and powerful Shadow Voices are threatening to break out and return to the Dry World. Storage is tight." The squid stretches up his tentacles in despair, long black shadows falling across the sand. Bowing his head, he cloaks himself in ink. "That is all, Master."

"Thank you, Distiller," Koan says quietly. The water in the eye of the rock thrums, a sound of deep reflection.

"What does Distiller mean?" Condi whispers to Trustin. "I'm so confused."

Trustin looks miserable. "Loud and powerful Shadow Voices take up a lot of space in the Locker, Condi. Voices like Bernardo's." He sighs. "Most Voices are small and weak, like the diver's. Small Voices shrink and fade over time. But the strongest Voices in the Locker are pure evil—and evil has a lasting and nasty energy all its own."

"Can the evil Voices really break out of the Locker?" Condi shivers.

"Only Koan knows," Trustin answers, shrugging. "And I'm not sure he wants us to know the answer. What Koan wants is for us to silence the evil Shadow Voices. The only way to do that is to solve his riddles."

Slowly, Condi nods. "So that's why Bernardo was taunting you. He was screaming at you to find the answer to a riddle." She studies his face. "But I don't understand... what happens when it gets solved?"

"Then Bernardo's Shadow Voice will be silenced forever." Unhappiness clouds Trustin's eyes and he tightens his jaw.

"Why, that's wonderful. Surely you can do it?" She smiles at him encouragingly. "Solving the riddle is a good thing," she persists. "Bernardo's evil Voice will be gone forever."

Abruptly, Trustin pulls away from her. "You don't get it, Condi. When a Voice in the Locker is silenced, their suffering is over." His voice is bitter. "Bernardo will be free—because he'll be at peace." The scar on Trustin's neck flares crimson, blazing hot. "I know it's wrong, but I want Bernardo to suffer—like he made others suffer."

Condi doesn't know what to say, so she reaches out to hold his hand. She's already said the wrong thing, and it wasn't fair. After all, she doesn't understand his pain, so she doesn't get to tell him how to fix it. All she can do is let him know she cares.

Koan comes out of deep thought. The water in the eye of the rock is soft and restful. "Though Distiller's report is troubling, there's no need for despair," he says quietly. "Let's hear what the Infusers have to say."

Pop! Shimmer! Fizz!

Above them, two tiny blue stars appear, dazzling them with brightness.

"Greetings, Koan!" The twin stars sing out in tinkling silver bell voices. After pausing for effect, they dance and twirl downward, spinning in effervescent pops of joy, until at last they come to a sparkling halt in front of the half-moon of sand.

Amused, Koan chuckles. "Greetings, Infusers. What news do you have to report?"

"Well, you know we hate to be serious, dear Koan," one of the stars ventures timidly. "We wish we had better news..."

The second star pops loudly. "Hush up, Flow. Don't drag this out. The truth is the truth."

"Yes, Ebby," Koan agrees. "Please come to the point."

"Things are looking gloomy," Ebby says bluntly. "Humans in the Dry World aren't taking care of each other like they used to. There's a lot of selfishness and anger, choking out Essence. Love, joy and hope aren't as abundant as they used to be. Good energy is harder to find. The Siphoners aren't collecting as much sparkling Essence, so we have a shortage of good energy to infuse back into the Dry World."

"It's absolutely terrible, Koan," Flow cries. "Things are getting darker."

Anxiously, the twin stars pop and twirl, dimming their sparkles.

"Hush!" Koan's voice is firm. "For heaven's sake, my dear Infusers, please calm down."

The sea spirit voices echo:
Calm down, calm down
Shadow Voices are growing.
Essence is waning.

Koan is reminding us,
Calm down, calm down.

The spirits let out a long sigh.

Abruptly, the stars stop spinning, coming to a stop on the half-moon of sand, teetering precariously on two single points.

"Dear Infusers, have you forgotten your true purpose?" Koan asks gently. "The Council of the Half Moon is about finding balance in all things. You must look past bad news and use your own gifts to infuse hope—instead of getting caught up in the Dry World's gloom and doubt."

The two tiny stars slump, bowing their heads, dropping the tips of their upper points toward the sand.

"Mend your ways," Koan tells them gently. "Don't forget who you are."

"Yes, Koan." The twin stars look up hopefully. "We'll remember." Spinning away, they twirl up toward the surface waters, shooting off sparks of light.

"What was that all about?" Condi whispers to Trustin. "They were only telling the truth—like Distiller."

Trustin sighs and hugs her close. "Each of us in Koan's world has a special purpose, something uniquely our own. The Infusers are about Truth, yes, but they are called to balance it with Love and Hope and Joy. Distiller's purpose is different."

A foaming tide swirls around and through the eye in the rock, like a mysterious cape. When the tide settles, the eye is a mirror, reflecting Trustin's astonished face.

"Well said, Trustin," Koan says. "Now it's your turn. What do you have to report about your own special purpose? As a Knower, your job is to solve riddles. How is your work on Bernardo's riddle progressing?"

Trustin releases Condi. Bereft of his arms, her heart skips a beat. As he swims toward the rock, the mirror exposes his fear. He looks very alone. *What is Trustin's purpose in this strange world?* she wonders.

Among the sea spirits, there is a nervous murmuring as Trustin hovers in front of the rock, staring at his own face, looking deeply into his own turquoise eyes.

Bravely, he answers Koan. "The Shadow Voices in the Locker are stronger than ever—maybe close to breaking out. Bernardo's is the loudest. I don't know how to quiet him. I cannot answer the riddle."

"Hmm," Koan replies thoughtfully. "Is that so? Perhaps you will recall for me what you understand your purpose as a Knower to be?"

Trustin hangs his head. "Knowers are called to discover the good which comes from every human life, even the lives of the most vile. Discovering the good that comes from an evil act is the only thing that can silence the power of a Shadow Voice." He looks directly at the mirror and says in despair. "I am failing, Koan."

The sea spirits emit a long, weary exhale.

Oh no—

Trustin cannot solve the riddle.

He is failing.

Failing.

Failing.

Oh, no—

Condi's chest is tight. No matter how firmly she grasps the shell in her pocket, she cannot seem to breathe. Poor Trustin.

"Enough," Koan says gently. "No one here is failing." The rock's eye clears, the water transparent once again. "Go toward your fear, Trustin. In your darkest hour, you'll find the answer."

The sea spirit voices lift:

Go toward fear.

All will be well.

All will be exceedingly well.

No one is failing.

The riddle will be solved.

All will be well.

"No!" Trustin bursts out, overpowering the voices. "All will not be well! The riddle cannot be solved, Koan. Some lives are pure evil. They just are. There is *nothing* good about them."

"Ah, Trustin," Koan replies, "all of my riddles have answers. I've given you a challenging one, it's true. A riddle for your own healing. A Knower's job is difficult— but in time you'll come to see my purpose."

"I can't see things the way you do," Trustin cries. "I hate being a Knower! Please, Koan, assign me a different purpose," he begs. "Make me Distiller's apprentice."

The Distiller shimmers a brilliant orange as he throws up his tentacles and groans, "Never wish to share my job of distilling evil, Trustin. It takes a terrible toll." The mighty squid cringes, cloaking himself in ink.

"Distiller is correct," Koan says quietly. "Absorbing evil is not your purpose, Trustin. Whether you like it or not, redeeming evil is your work." Koan sighs. "Besides, you ought to know me better, I'm not going to change your purpose because you're not succeeding yet. I command you to return to the Dry World and try again."

Trustin nods dejectedly. "Yes, Koan."

As Trustin swims back to Condi's side, the sea floor shudders. Beyond the half-moon of sand and the great eye in the rock, the giant sea mountain shakes and rumbles, no longer puffing out lavender mist. Instead, a thick black steam is seeping from cracks in the hardened lava river, ominously staining the water.

"Is the volcano erupting?" Condi turns to Trustin, eyes wide with fear.

He doesn't reply.

The top of the mountain cracks open. A nasty head of vapor rises out of the caldera, curling into a toxic smile. "My turn, Koan?"

The water in the eye of the rock stills. Koan says wryly, "Nice entrance Nami."

"Thanks, Koan. You know it's my turn now." The head of vapor spits out a laugh. "I've been waiting for this moment. If Trustin fails, I win this round."

"Who—or what—is that?" Condi asks Trustin, clutching his hand.

"Tsunami Volt—Nami for short," Trustin says tersely. "A terrible pain in an otherwise perfectly gentle sea mountain—if you get my meaning." He shakes his head. "Nami's out of control."

The sea spirits echo his words, a cacophony of indignant voices.

Nami is out of control.
Trustin cannot let Nami win.
Surely Koan will not allow it?
Well, he might, you know—

Times are bad.
Humans aren't connecting—-
Is it time to start fresh?
NO!
Nami is out of control.
Trustin cannot let Nami win.

The head of the steam vapor laughs manically. "If Trustin fails in his purpose, I will win! I get to wipe out the town—"

"That is quite enough!" Koan bellows. The ocean rocks violently. A huge wave of water washes up and over the sea mountain. The top of the volcano collapses inward, sucking the shouting head of vapor inside.

The water slowly settles.

"Such drama," Koan says reprovingly. "Nami is out of line. Ignore all that. Please swim forward, Condi. It's your turn now."

The water in the rock's eye twinkles. "Don't be frightened. I'm glad you're here," Koan says kindly.

"But I don't want to be here at all!" she blurts. "I want to go home."

"Of course, you don't want to be here. Few young people do."

She stares at him in horror. "Oh, no. Does that mean what I think it does? Please sir or ma'am or whoever you are—"

"Please call me Koan like everyone else, Condi. I'm your friend. I know all about you—and there's a reason you're here. You made a choice, you know."

"You mean going out in the kayak?" Condi cries. "That was stupid."

"I disagree, my dear. I believe you were very brave to try to save Trustin's life."

"I was very *stupid*," Condi repeats bitterly, "since he hardly needed saving." Summoning her courage, she asks, "Please Koan—am I dead?"

"Dead? Heavens no, my child. You're in a state of In-Between."

"In-Between?" she echoes. "Is this another riddle?"

Koan laughs. "Everything is a riddle. And really, if you think of it, everything is in a state of In-Between. Light is always shifting, tides are always turning, humans are always changing."

"Oh, I don't understand," Condi says miserably. "Please—just let me go home."

The sea spirits sigh.

She is brave to ask.

And—she did try to save him.

But that isn't the way it works—

Well, Koan does let some of them return.

While others have to stay.

Yes—you are quite right.

It is the greatest riddle of all—

She is brave to ask.

For a long moment, the only sound is the peaceful wash of waves. At last, Koan says, "Condi, I need young and brave humans like you in the world in order to save it. So you may return to your old life on one condition— you must work for me and save your hometown."

"Save my town?" Condi asks.

"Yes. You heard the Distiller and the Infusers. People in the Dry World aren't supporting one another like they used to. It's gotten very bad in Dipitous Beach. Everything's about making money there."

"But those are grown-up problems," Condi stammers. "I'm only a girl."

"Age never matters," Koan answers. "These things are about bravery and heart. I am asking you to be one of my Connectors. Find ways to bring the people of Dipitous Beach together again."

"But how? What do I have to *do*?" she presses.

"My dear Condi, I never tell humans how to *do* anything. The answers are inside you, found in everything you know *plus* everything you're willing to learn."

"That's not an answer, that's another riddle." She looks at Trustin, who only shrugs.

"It's impossible," she exclaims.

"Nothing's impossible, Condi. Trustin will be around to help you—and you must help him to solve the riddle." Koan's voice drops, as the water in the rock's eye shimmers softly. "Though there *is* one last little thing."

"Here comes the twist," Trustin murmurs in her ear.

Koan laughs. "Come, come, there's always a twist. Keeps things interesting, you know. After you return to Dipitous Beach, you won't remember what happened here, Condi. I never give humans too much of an advantage, you see. Interferes with their right to choose."

"I'll forget everything that happened here?" Condi says slowly.

"You'll forget—until it's time for you to remember. Then you might forget again. It depends. That's how memories work, after all. They're meant to serve you, not the other way around."

"More riddles," she says sadly. "It's confusing."

"You can solve this riddle, Condi," Koan says gently. "Stay open and work hard. You'll discover what you need to know. I promise you." Soft pats of water brush her cheek. "Besides, I'll be around, sending messages and clues. I always send clues, though most people are too busy to notice."

Condi nods at Koan, then gazes into Trustin's turquoise eyes. "I'll really see you again?"

Trustin smiles. "Yes, I'll be there with you."

The sea spirits murmur:

Safe travels, Condi.

Connect the town.

Watch for Koan's messages.

Work together.

"Yes—the most important thing is to work together," Koan repeats. "Now—are you ready?"

"Yes," she answers. "Please let me go home."

The vast crowd of sea spirit voices falls quiet.

A strong rich baritone booms through the waters:

Audacia, Condoleeza.

Be brave.

A soft, gentle contralto murmurs:

Vivace, my Constant.

Be happy.

Chapter Seven

WHITE SHELL

At the top of Windy Hollow, Condi struggles with the summer-blue dress, fighting to keep it from turning into an upside-down umbrella. Frantically, she scans the ocean chop.

No sign of a daring surfer boy on a molten-black board.

Of course he isn't coming.

Why did she ever think he would? In this wild wind, there are sure to be surfing warnings out.

Disappointed, she turns toward the stone stairs. With a changeable autumn wind blowing in from the north, she was a fool to climb up here in the first place. What was she thinking? Nobody in their right mind is surfing today.

The wind surges, wrapping her up and hugging her close. She pauses. A strange feeling flutters up and swirls inside her. Things are the same—but different. Holding back her hair, she takes a covert peek over her shoulder.

Yes, the orange-red kayak is wedged where it's always been—between the two half-moon rocks. Everything on the top of the Hollow is exactly the same, though she can't shake the feeling that she's gone away somewhere and has only just returned.

For good measure, she pinches herself on the arm. Thankfully, it hurts a little—exactly as it should.

Stop. Thinking. Just. Breathe.

Carefully, she makes the long descent on the precarious rock stairs.

Of course he isn't coming.

Once her toes touch down in the comforting sand of the cove, she realizes it's much later than she thought. How did she lose track of the time? As she hurries along the shoreline, troubled thoughts bob and weave, pestering her like seabirds. She feels silly. Even her sandals make sad scrunching sounds on the shell-spackled sand. He ditched her—that's all there is to it. Like a shy hermit crab, she wants to scuttle into a hidey-hole.

Volti subito, Condoleeza.

Turn the page at once.

Stop feeling sorry for yourself.

In Papa's deep baritone, the voice rumbles through her head. Lightening her steps, Condi smiles. How Papa discouraged negative thinking. Slipping her hand into her pocket, her fingers curl around a smooth white seashell.

How very strange. She doesn't recall putting a shell in her pocket. She pulls it out and studies it. The shape of the shell reminds her of Mama's scalloped-rim white hat. Stopping in the sand, she pauses, and turns around to gaze up at Windy Hollow. The sea is a brilliant dancing cerulean, the rock stairs of the Hollow shimmering with sun sparkles, winding up into the sky.

Her mood lifts. Maybe she's wrong. Maybe there's a good reason Trustin didn't show up after all.

#

When she reaches Grand Ella's art shop at the top of Upper Main, the first thing she sees is Sheriff Coodle's sand splattered black and white patrol car parked out back.

Taking a deep breath, Condi slips inside the shop, glancing at Grand Ella's yoga mat rolled up by the door. Sighing, she wonders how much trouble she's in for being late, though something else is up if the sheriff is here.

The unmistakable scent of salt, seaweed and beach smoke permeates the shop. She recognizes it instantly, the signature scent of the Beachlings. Her eyes sweep the room. Grand Ella and Sheriff Coodle are drinking cups of tea in the small alcove next to the kitchen. Madeleine, in Grand Ella's rocker, is regally watching the sheriff, Lucky on guard at her feet.

"Hello, Condi," Grand Ella says wryly, looking up. "I didn't know you were going out this afternoon."

Busted.

"I had something I needed to do," she answers meekly.

Grand Ella raises a brow, in that familiar way she has of making a point. "We'll discuss it later," she says, turning her attention back to the sheriff and Madelaine.

The sheriff studies Condi, from under thick, gunmetal-gray brows. Perched on a tall stool, leaning against the wall, he takes up way too much space.

Can he possibly know where I've been? Condi wonders. Kids aren't allowed at the top of the Hollow, and the sheriff's a stickler for rules.

But thankfully, Grand Ella and the sheriff are not focused on her. Madelaine's knobby hands are curled over the arms of the rocker, jewel-bright eyes darting back and forth between Grand Ella and the sheriff. Falling gracefully over her bony shoulders, the old woman's tattered green dress is oddly shining, faded with salt and bleached out by the sun. Lucky, even with most of his hair rubbed off, is a great black shadow of a dog, ears pinned back, on high alert.

"Condi," Grand Ella says quietly, "Sheriff Coodle stopped by because I wanted him to look at Maddie's bruises. She's injured again."

The sheriff clears his throat, squaring his bulky shoulders. Madelaine sits up straight in the rocker. Lucky growls, eyeing the sheriff.

"It's alright, Maddie," Grand Ella says, leaning over to pat the old woman's hand. "No one will hurt you here. Show the sheriff your arm."

Slowly, Madelaine extends her arm and draws back the tattered sleeve. Her inner arm is mottled with nasty purple-black bruises in the shape of fingerprints.

"I want to call a town meeting, Clive," Grand Ella says firmly. "The Beachlings are old and some of them are sick. This kind of harassment is inexcusable."

"Ella, please—you know there's nothing I can do.

There's no proof of foul play." Sheriff Coodle sags on the stool like a deflated balloon, eyes pleading.

Condi winces. The sheriff has such an obvious thing for Grand Ella. Seriously?

"Now Clive," Grand Ella says, in her best persuasive tone. "You and I have been friends for a long time." She lets her eyes hold his for a long moment. "We both know the attacks on the Beachlings are increasing."

The sheriff nods. "I don't deny it, Ella. But this town depends on tourism. The rich hotel owners want the cove cleared of the homeless."

Grand Ella's luminous brown eyes flash. "Are you suggesting the hotel owners are taking the law into their own hands?"

The sheriff opens his palms and sighs. "I don't know, Ella. Someone is—that's all I know."

Grand Ella bites down hard on her lip, a sign she's trying to control her temper. "Condi, please go put on another pot of tea," she says.

Glad to get away from the grown-ups, Condi slips away to the small kitchen in the storeroom of the shop. When the kettle sings, she pours fresh mugs of steaming brew, filling the air with the soothing scent of chamomile and strawberry.

From the kitchen, she can hear Grand Ella getting exasperated. "Clive, stop talking that way. The Beachlings aren't homeless, not really. Why, they've lived in Dipitous Beach longer than you and me!"

Trying not to slosh, Condi walks slowly, bringing fresh mugs of tea to Grand Ella and the sheriff. Then she sinks to a knee to pet Lucky. Madelaine has closed her eyes, veiny legs outstretched, black hair a mantle of snarls, woven with threads of silver.

"Good boy," she says, scratching the old dog's grizzled head, trying not to stare at Madelaine's tangled, arthritic toes. How she is able to walk, Condi can't imagine, though what Trustin said yesterday is true, the old woman moved over the domino rocks as lightly as a dancer.

In the rocker, Madelaine stirs. Opening startlingly green eyes, she fixes Condi with a lighthouse beacon stare, from under a witchy black and silver brow. Leaning forward, she jabs a bony finger close to Condi's nose, then waggles it, pointing to Condi's pocket. Then she winks, and closes her eyes once again.

Protectively, Condi wraps her fingers around the white seashell in the pocket of the summer-blue dress. Then she moves away from the rocking chair and goes to sit down on the floor beside Grand Ella. The sweet memory of Madelaine dancing across the rocks vanishes. She doesn't need some scary old woman teasing her.

Grand Ella glances down at Condi, then over at the rocker where Madelaine is dozing. "Thanks for stopping by, Clive," Grand Ella says, looking pointedly at the sheriff.

He takes the hint. Putting down his mug, he gets to his feet. "Thanks for the tea, Ella," he says gruffly. "Why don't you convince Madelaine to stay at the cottage for a few days?"

"I'll try. Maybe she'll camp on the terrace. You know how the Beachlings only feel safe in the open air," Grand Ella answers. "They can't stand having walls around them."

"True." The sheriff heads toward the door. Hand on

the knob, he turns, eyes focused on Condi. "Next time let your grandmother know where you're going, young lady. She was worried."

"Yes, sir," Condi answers, gritting her teeth.

When the door clicks behind him, Grand Ella sits quietly, stroking Condi's hair. Beside the rocking chair, Lucky raises his graying head and cocks it, looking up at his mistress. Yawning, Madelaine opens her eyes and lifts her arms, tattered sleeves fluttering like wings around the mottled bruises. Looking at Condi, she murmurs in a lilting croon, "White shell, white shell...walk by the sea."

Grand Ella smiles. "That's a lovely poem, isn't it Maddie?" She joins in, reciting, "I walked by the sea and there came to me..."

The old lady chuckles. "White shell, white shell..."

"White it glimmered, and the sea simmered," Grand Ella looks down at Condi and explains. "An old sea ballad by Tolkien. Lovely and haunting."

Madelaine catches Condi's eyes and winks again, then sinks back into the rocker. Soon the old woman is snoring, Lucky's head on her gnarled feet.

Hand grasped tightly around the shell tucked in the pocket of her dress, Condi is confused and a little scared. How did the white shell get in her pocket? And why is Madelaine acting like she knows?

But she doesn't have time to think about it. Grand Ella has stopped stroking her hair, and is now impatiently tapping her foot. "Condi, I'm waiting for an explanation. Where were you after school today?"

A made-up story pops into Condi's head, but then she sighs and lets it go. She's not in the habit of lying to Grand

Ella. They've been through too much together.

"I went to meet a boy at the beach," she answers, telling part of the truth. No need to mention waiting in wild winds at the top of the Hollow.

Grand Ella takes a long thoughtful breath. "I see."

"But he didn't show up," Condi adds sadly.

"Oh, my dear, you are growing up." Grand Ella exhales softly. "I'm sorry."

Embarrassed, Condi looks away. "I don't want to talk about it."

Grand Ella nods. "I understand—but going off alone without telling me must never happen again. When you're late, I worry. Do I have your word?"

"Yes, Grand Ella," she answers.

In the rocker, Madelaine's eyelids flutter, revealing the barest glint of green.

Chapter Eight

SURPRISE ON THE BEACH

Condi wakes up the next morning, deliciously tucked under the puffy, white covers of her bed in the loft of the cottage, smelling the tang of the sea. What a lovely dream, her mind whispers. Half asleep, she releases the sheets tangled around her legs, not wanting to let go of the dream. She was floating in a pod of petals...as if she'd been slipped into the heart of a flower.

Hello, my Constant.

The sweet voice is familiar, wafting in on the dawn breeze.

Mama?

Sitting up in bed, she slips on her glasses and looks to the open window, where dawn is barely peeking in. But there is nothing there—only an elegant white lily nodding on the shadowy leaves of the trellis outside her window. The breeze flutters the flower's petals, showing off delicate blue veins.

Her heart curls up. Oh, if only the voice on the breeze was Mama's....

Sighing, she pulls on her yoga clothes and a hoodie, slipping the white seashell into a pocket. Sitting on the side of the bed, she gazes up at the painted stars on the dark blue paint of the cottage's ceiling. "Protector stars" was what Papa called the twinkles of paint. For an instant she sees him, laughing down at her from top of the ladder. Then the memory fades. The day he painted the stars on the ceiling seems very long ago.

Slipping down the loft ladder, she creeps out to the high terrace. At Grand Ella's urging, Madelaine and Lucky spent the night, sleeping outside on lounge chairs. A beehive of blankets is spooled on the deck beside them. Madelaine is snoring, arms flung wide, embracing the ocean air.

Condi tiptoes past, going quietly down the zigzag stairs to the beach. The first rays of sun are just beginning to finger the sand, reaching for the curve of shore where Grand Ella is meditating, eyes closed, face to the open sea.

Condi pauses, caught in the hush of blushing dawn, smudged with rose-apricot and blueberry. It's true what Grand Ella says. *The hour of dawn is magical. Every sunrise is different—why do we think of them as all the same?*

Looking up, she turns to gaze at Windy Hollow, breathing in the cool sacred winds flowing from the high northern shore. The abandoned side of the cove is at its best at dawn. The rough sand glimmers with crushed shells, throwing up small shards of light. Today, though the tide is even, an occasional rogue wave rises and twists to fall across the domino rocks. A big one is rising now, swooning into the rose of dawn, tipping into a graceful tube. Crashing on the rocks, it tosses out a shimmering oval of light.

Surprised, Condi pushes her glasses high up on her nose. Skittering across the rocks in the foam of the flow is a surfboard. When the tide ebbs, the board glints on the beach, rocking on the tideline, cast upon the sand by the sea.

She doesn't waste a second. Before a wave can suck the board back out to sea, she runs across the sand to the scree beach, ignoring the ragged jabs of broken shells, and kneels beside the board. The stranded surfboard is the most beautiful one she's ever seen, a glittering aquamarine, shimmering with tiny stars. Reverently, she places her hands on the nose. Her breath catches. "How I wish you were mine," she murmurs.

Lifting the board off the waterline, she carries it on her shoulder back to the yoga cove where Grand Ella is still meditating. Without disturbing her grandmother, she makes the steep climb up the zigzag stairs to the top terrace, so excited she can hardly breathe. The board is exactly the right shape and size for her. If it's truly a lost board, maybe she can claim it as her own.

On the terrace, Madelaine is still asleep. Tiptoeing over the polished wood of the deck, Condi quietly leans the aquamarine board against the railing. She'll have to wait until after school to talk to Grand Ella about keeping the surfboard. Grand Ella will insist that Condi take the board to Mr. Marshall at the Billabong Surf Shop, where lost and stolen boards are reported. All she can do is hope that no one claims it.

A cool breeze winds out of the early autumn morning. The mirrored surface of the aquamarine surfboard blinks twice in the sun.

Facile, Condoleeza.

Take it easy, take it slow.

Condi smiles. Papa—reminding her to be patient.

"Mar, Mar!" Madelaine suddenly cries in a soft keening wail. Startled, Condi turns around. Madelaine is rocking back and forth in the lounge chair, a veined hand over her heart, staring at the surfboard.

"Mar, Mar..." Madelaine's cry fades away, breaking with a sob.

Condi cringes. She knows the sound of grief—terrible and raw. Kneeling beside the lounge chair, she pats the old lady's knee. "Can you tell me what's wrong, Maddie?"

The old woman shakes her head. "Nothing gold can stay," she says in a voice as clear as rain.

"Nothing gold can stay," Condi repeats kindly.

Madelaine pats Condi's hoodie pocket. "White shell," she whispers. "White it glimmered, the sea simmered, star mirrored...cliffs of bone..."

Voice trailing away, the old woman shudders, closes her eyes and lays back down. Lucky whines and circles the lounge chair, then flops down at Condi's feet. Condi pats his head, then covers Madelaine with a blanket. In repose, the old woman looks timeless, the creases on her face smoothed away, the tangle of hair flashing brightly in the breaking dawn.

Edging away, Condi quietly moves the aquamarine surfboard off the terrace and over to the side of the cottage, beneath the loft window. Later tonight she will talk to Grand Ella. But for now, she'll hide the board behind the high trellis, where the white lily blossoms weave up through a dark foliage of pink bougainvillea, peeking out like stars.

Running softly down the zigzag stairs, she hurries back to the beach for sunrise yoga.

At school, Condi jogs into the building, hoping to make it to homeroom before last bell. She's wearing her watermelon-red sun dress today, a happy color she hasn't wanted to wear for a long time. Sliding into her chair, she gets there just as the bell peals. Pulling off her glasses, she wipes perspiration on the hem of her dress, then pushes damp curls off her face.

"Close one." Anda looks over and rolls her eyes. "You're a hot mess—and *not* in a good way." She emphasizes the last part, saying it loud, making the popular surfer girls sitting in front of her laugh.

The comment stings. Condi wonders how she and Anda got to the place they are now. They used to tell each other everything. A twinge of guilt pokes her. After all, she's the one who's changed. Her life got very big and awful, while it stayed the same for other kids. She can't blame that on Anda.

Tempo rubato, Condoleeza.

Let things change.

Condi sighs. *Things change anyway, so go with it,* Papa was forever saying, taking care to remind her that some changes are good. And it's true. Today there was an awesome change—she got lucky and found the aquamarine board.

Slipping on her glasses, she pushes them up on her nose. Tossing back her curls, she bats her lashes at Anda in a silly way. "Better?" she asks.

The popular girls snicker, making rude faces and tossing off comments under their breath. Anda shrugs, but then her surf-blue eyes soften, and she gives Condi the tiniest crack of a smile.

Homeroom is a serious study hour. Condi quickly reviews her math, proofs her history paper and then pulls out a book about a girl lost on an island in the sea. But it's no use trying to read. Jessy Pettikin is flirting with the popular boys, looking sickeningly perfect as usual.

Dismayed, Condi watches as Jessy scribbles a note and passes it to Javed. Anda flushes, her freckles merging into ugly little splotches. Condi sighs. Now that Jessy's broken up with Finn, she's going after Javed. Jessy's into the whole mean girl thing—going after boys who already have girlfriends.

Javed reads the note and winks, then passes it on to Casey Arondale.

When Casey reads the note, he doesn't laugh. Instead, he shoots a concerned glance over at Anda, and doesn't pass the note on. Jessy flips back her ice princess hair and shoots Javed another teasing look. Anda's chest turns splotchy red.

Condi studies Casey, wondering why he isn't as awful as his mom. The way Mrs. Arondale treated Charlene and Madelaine on the beach the other morning was horrible.

Thankfully, the bell rings. The kids grab their back-packs and head to the door. Lorelei Finch, a curvy girl in a pink ruffled shirt, is at the front of the cluster.

Javed shoves his way through the crowd, muscling his way into the hall. "Move aside, Lore Bore," he snarls at Lorelei, giving her a mean shove.

Lorelei flushes, turning as bright pink as her shirt.

Following Javed, the surfer girls exit through the door like queens, Jessy in the lead. Anda lags behind with Condi and Lorelei, chewing on her lower lip.

Condi wants to tell Anda to ignore Jessy and Javed, but she and Anda aren't that kind of friends anymore. Besides, Anda wouldn't listen.

"Hurry up," Javed barks from the hall, snapping his fingers at Anda like she's his pet.

Condi looks at Anda. "You don't have to do what he says," she says loudly. "He's a bully."

Anda glares at her. "Shut up, Condi Bloom," she hisses. Bolting through the door, she grabs Javed's hand.

After school, Condi can't wait to get out outside, wondering if she'll catch sight of Trustin, though Dipitous Beach High let out a half hour earlier. In a wave of chaos, kids pour out of Dipitous Beach Middle, descending on the beach path, a wide rutted trail of grass and wild flowers, overlooking the blue of the cove. Today the ocean is sporting and playful, high ruffles of waves, peaked starch-white tips of foam.

Most of the kids are stopping on the beach path to look

longingly out to sea. Like Condi, they won't be going to the beach to hit the surf. Their parents work, and they have responsibilities at home, babysitting or other chores.

But the rich kids who live in the big houses are different. They flock to the beach to spend the afternoon on Craggy Point, sunning, swimming and surfing.

"Hey, Javed! Surf's ripe for pipe lining. Let's go!" Jessy calls to Javed, pointing to the tight row of waves curling off the Point.

Javed gives Jessy a thumbs up. "Meet you there in ten!"

Anda slumps along behind him and Condi shakes her head. Anda is only a passable surfer, while Jessy is the best of the surfer girls. With Jessy after Javed, Anda's heading for getting her heart broken.

"Javed Holmes is a total A," a quiet voice from behind her says.

Condi turns, looking into Lorelei's serious bluebell eyes.

"Totally," Condi agrees.

Lorelei sighs, gazing out at the white-tipped rollers off Craggy Point where some of the older kids are already paddling out to sea. "Don't you wish we could be out there, too?" she murmurs.

"More than anything in the world," Condi answers.

Chapter Nine

THE BILLABONG

Perched high on the hilltop of Upper Main, the Wafting Rafters Art Shop has a grand view of Lower Main, the primary street in the town. The day is sunny and warm, but only a few people are out on the street, hunkered over cell phones.

Condi sighs. Working after school in the shop is lonely. The art shop doesn't get many live customers during the week. People mostly order online these days. Today time is hanging heavy, dawdling along.

The chimes over the door jingle. To Condi's surprise, Grand Ella breezes into the shop in a swirl of cotton and gardenia, her favorite scent.

"Toddlers and Moms yoga was cancelled," Grand Ella explains. "I'm going to miss doing animal poses." Laughing, she stashes her yoga mat in the antique umbrella stand by the door and puts the kettle on. "How are sales today?" She flops down in her rocker and stretches, pointing and flexing her toes.

"Better than usual," Condi answers, scrolling through the computer, reading the online sales out loud. "The new scarves are the best sellers. I hung up a few of my favorites after Maisie dropped them off." She waves an arm toward the hand-painted scarves hanging from the ceiling beams, wafting from the rafters, affirming the shop's name.

"Excellent." Grand Ella says. "Maisie Hollister needs the money. Working in the kitchen at the Mirage doesn't pay much, and five children is a lot of mouths to feed." The shop thrives on supporting local artists; nothing pleases Grand Ella more than helping them along.

Going over to a stack of boxes in the corner, Condi lifts out a beeswax candle in a small milk-can jar. "Gloria Johnson's candles came in today. She's naming the scents after beach plants and flowers. Listen to these fun names—Musings of Lily of the Nile, Cantankerous Cranberry Rose, Sea Thistles Among Eucalyptus."

Grand Ella smiles. "Gloria's always been creative. After Ben died, she said she wanted to find a way to remember their morning beach walks. I'm sure those candles are infused with joy." When the teakettle sings, she pours a cup of honey vanilla tea and leans against the kitchen counter, taking slow, meditative sips. Offhand, she remarks, "When I was out trimming the bougainvillea this morning, I found a surfboard stashed under the side trellis. Would you happen to know how it got there?"

The unexpected question catches Condi off guard. "Oh, Grand Ella, I'm sorry," she says quickly. "I found it on the beach before sunrise yoga. The night tide brought it in. I was going to tell you about it tonight at dinner."

Grand Ella nods. "It's a lovely board, my dear. But no matter how tempting it is to pretend it is yours, you must take it to the Billabong and report it to Mr. Marshall this afternoon." She leans over and brushes a curl off Condi's cheek. "Then we'll just have to wait and see. Run along now and take the surfboard down to the Billabong before dinner. You've been a big help today, as usual. I can handle things here. Besides—it's a great day to watch the surfers off Craggy Point."

Condi jumps up and hugs her grandmother. "Thank you." Slipping on her sandals at the door, she takes off for the high beach road, heading to the yellow cottage to retrieve the aquamarine board.

Hot and sweaty by the time she gets back to the inner cove with the aquamarine board on her shoulder, Condi pauses at the long beach stairs leading down to the Billabong and stops to catch her breath, scanning the waves off Craggy Point. No sign of a boy on a molten-black board.

Disappointed, she heads down to the shop and slides the aquamarine surfboard into the rack on the porch. Swinging open the broad screen door, she steps inside. The delicious smell of salt, suntan lotion, and buffing polish greets her.

Behind a long counter, a proud old man with a regal mane of bleach-white hair looks up and grins, letting his eyes twinkle at her. Hunched over a surfboard, he is vigorously waxing the board with a soft rag.

"Hey there, my girl." Slowly, he straightens up,

keeping a careful hand on his back. "What's up?"

"Hi, Mr. Marshall," Condi says, smiling. "I came to check the Lost and Found postings." She tilts her head, directing his gaze to the aquamarine board on the rack outside the front window. "Anybody looking for a lost board like that one?"

Mr. Marshall glances out the window at the board. A look of astonishment crosses his leathery face. Throwing down the waxing rag, he hurries out of the shop.

"Whew! She's sure a beauty, Condi," he tells her, running his calloused fingers eagerly over the length of the surfboard's graceful rails.

Surprised to see the laid-back surf master lit with excitement, Condi's speechless. No one in Dipitous Beach is sure how old Mr. Marshall is—he's been around so long the locals say he's old as God. But now he's fired up with the zeal of youth. "This is a valuable vintage board," he tells her. "Haven't seen anything like her for a long, long time."

"What do you mean?" Condi asks uneasily. He's scaring her. It's never crossed her mind that the board might be valuable.

Mr. Marshall doesn't answer right away. Carefully, he turns the board over and examines the bottom, where a deep cut exposes raw wood, a wound in the board's surface. "Lanced by a rock," he mutters, poking a thick finger into the groove. Squinting at Condi, he asks, "Where'd you find her?"

"On the north beach below the yellow cottage—beyond the yoga cove—on the domino rocks beneath the Hollow," Condi answers, hoping that finding the board in such an isolated location bodes well for her hopes of keeping it.

"Beneath the Hollow...well, well, well..." The old man's hand goes to his grizzled chin. "Who knows where she comes from or where she's been?" He looks at Condi. "The sea around the Hollow is a keeper of secrets. The waves are funny about giving up bits of treasure whenever they're good and ready. This board was probably holed up in a coastal cave, out of wind and rain for years. She's in prime condition except for the gouge. Amazing—she's at least fifty years old, maybe more."

"How can you tell?" Condi asks.

"The old school design, and she's made of balsa redwood," Mr. Marshall replies, "light and strong as they come." He touches the board again. "This color was popular back in the day. Glittering blue-green, same as the sea. Yep—old girl's a real vintage beauty."

"Can the gash be fixed?" Condi asks.

"I believe so." He grins. "Leave her to me." Thoughtfully, he strokes a small symbol on the nose of the board, partially obscured by the gash. "Strange. Never seen a shaper's mark like this one before."

Condi leans closer, peering at the symbol on the board. "Shaper's mark?" she asks, confused. The mark is hard to make out, but it looks like a half-moon, part silver, part black.

Mr. Marshall explains, "A shaper's a dude who makes surfboards. And a symbol like this one is called a mark. It's the shaper's brand." The old surf master sighs. "Shaping is almost a lost skill. Except for Pacific Islanders, who still take pride in shaping their own boards, most surfboards are mass produced nowadays." His eyes crinkle at the corners. "A shaper's mark is good luck, Condi. This board is unique. We'll post a photo without revealing the mark. Doubt if anyone can present a legitimate claim."

"How long do we have to wait?" she asks.

"Three days," the surf master replies.

"You mean I get to keep her if no one claims her by Friday?" Condi squeals.

He chuckles, then grows serious. "Whoa...slow down, my girl. Your grandmother will have my head if I say you can keep this board without her permission."

"Grand Ella knows I'm here. She told me to come," Condi tells him. "She'll give me permission." Fingering the shell in her pocket, she rubs it for good luck.

"Sure?" he asks.

"Positive," she answers.

The sun disappears behind a cluster of clouds, casting the old man in shadow. For an instant, Condi sees Mr. Marshall as he must have been when he was young—a hunky surfer dude with wind-whipped hair, living to ride the big ones.

The sun blazes bright again. Light catches on the surf master's sagging shoulders. Cracking a weary smile, he shuffles back into the shop. Reaching under the counter, he brings out a wobbling pile of shiny old wet suits. "While we wait to see if anyone claims the board, I'll fix the gouge. She'll be waiting for you. If the board is yours, I'll make you a promise. If one of these fits, you can have it. No market for used wetsuits anymore. Seems like everyone who surfs in Dipitous these days is rich—they can afford to buy a new one made of the best materials." He shakes his head. "Place has changed. We used to be a town where money didn't matter. Nobody cared if you were rich or poor—it was all good, as long as you loved to ride the waves." He sighs and stares out to sea, looking back into the good old days.

"I'm sure one of these will fit," Condi answers gratefully. Longingly, she fingers a newer style, black with lilac-colored sleeves that looks like her size.

Grinning, Mr. Marshall pulls out a basket filled with miscellaneous surfing gear. Rummaging through the basket, he comes up with a pair of bright pink goggles. "You'll need these, too—unless you plan to surf blind."

She laughs, remembering how she told Trustin she was waiting to get contacts. But that was before she knew she might have a board of her own.

"Tell your grandmother to stop by the shop on Friday, so she can give me the okay." His wise old eyes smile. "Bring the board inside for safekeeping."

"You're the best, Mr. Marshall!" she exclaims, dashing out the screen door to the porch.

"Hey. Where'd you get that sweet surfboard?"

Condi turns toward the voice, blinking into the sun. In the blaze of late afternoon, a long-legged girl is sitting on the bottom step of the beach stairs. Amber hair slides over her shoulders, smooth and shiny as sea glass.

Condi grips the aquamarine surfboard.

The girl stands up, brushing sand off her shorts. "Looks like a board I used to have," she says, reaching out to touch the surfboard.

Without a word, Condi backs away, opening the screen door and tipping the board under the doorframe.

"Hey, I'm not trying to claim it," the girl says, stepping back.

Condi flushes. Guiding the board inside the shop she leans it against the inside wall, feeling silly. Nodding at Mr. Marshall, she goes back out to the porch where the girl is sprawled on the wide deck of the Billabong, face to the sun. When the screen door slams, she jumps up.

"Sorry I acted weird," Condi mumbles.

Tossing back her spill of hair, the girl sticks out her hand. "How 'bout we start again?" she says. "I'm Marissa Davis."

"Condi Bloom," Condi answers. The girl is gorgeous—and she has serious muscles. Everything about her is sleek and strong and shining.

Marissa grins. "I'm new in town. My father just bought the old Stinson mansion."

Surprised, Condi blurts out, "That old place? It's falling down."

"A real mess, right?" Marissa shrugs. "We're staying at the Mirage while the house is rebuilt. My father's going to reopen the spa hotel."

Condi doesn't reply. She was starting to like this girl, but now she's not so sure. The town doesn't need another hotel bringing in pampered strangers.

"The hotel will have a whole new name and look," Marissa goes on. "The old spa hotel was called the Double Palm. Sounds dated, exactly like the forties, when the old place was built." Her eyes dance. "I want my dad to call the new spa The Last Resort."

Condi laughs. "Ha. Sounds desperate."

Marissa laughs, too. "That's my point. You know how desperate rich ladies are—terrified of losing their looks."

A gust of wind swirls, lifting and twisting their hair,

Condi's thick and curly, Marissa's fine and straight. A cloud passes over the sun. The light in the girl's eyes dims. She looks up at the tall silhouette of Windy Hollow in the distance. "Not sure about living up there though. It's a lonely place, don't you think?"

Condi is silent, contemplating the stone tower and the old remains of the Stinson place. In the waning light, the wind-swept peninsula is a shadow, towering over a crashing sea. The bones of the mansion look stark and empty. Lonely, for sure. But then a thought comes to her fiercely—the Hollow may be a lonely place, but it's *her* place, and she doesn't want it to be the site of a busy spa hotel. Shrugging off the thought, she holds her tongue. If Marissa's father has purchased the Hollow, there's nothing that can be done.

"Oh, how I love dogs," Marissa murmurs wistfully. She is looking at the far shore where Lucky is chasing gulls, playing in the surf. In a blast of spray, he bounds out of the water and streaks up the beach to greet them.

Falling to a knee, Marissa hugs the chaos of wet fur to her chest. The old dog licks her face, wagging his black and gray tail, as if he's known her forever.

"Where's Maddie?" Condi says softly, reaching down to scratch the old dog behind the ears. Her eyes roam the beach, searching for Madelaine, thinking she must be close by. But the long stretch of shore stretching to the cliffs of the Hollow is empty.

After a long whimper, the old dog nuzzles Condi's hand and gives Marissa a last long lick. Then he takes off running, a smear of black, heading back to the cliffs.

For a moment, Condi considers telling Marissa that

Lucky belongs to Madelaine Stinson, the original owner of her new home. But she thinks better of it. She's not sure Marissa would care right now. Lost in her own head, the red-haired girl is idly letting sand sift through her fingers.

"Well, I guess I'll get going," Condi says, turning toward the yellow cottage.

Marissa looks up. "Sorry. Didn't mean to zone out." Sweeping a long arm toward the ocean, she tries to smile. "Dipitous Beach is short for Serendipitous Beach, right?"

Condi nods, surprised. Most people don't ever catch onto the meaning of the town's name.

Marissa cocks her head toward Craggy Point where Jessy and Javed are carving lines across foaming pipeline curls. "Know those kids?"

"Yeah. They're from school," Condi answers, wanting to sound offhand. "Best surfer kids in town."

"No, they're not," Marissa tells her. "Those two aren't the best."

Annoyed, Condi shoots her a look. "Yeah—I'm pretty sure they are. I've lived here a long time."

"Don't take this wrong, but look—" Marissa points to a distant line of waves where an onyx-haired surfer boy is rising out of the sea, slipping into a surfer's crouch. "That's Trustin Davis, my twin brother. Have you met him yet?"

On her walk back home from the Billabong, Condi's tries to process that Marissa Davis is Trustin's twin. She never would have guessed. Why, they don't even look alike, except maybe for their blue-green eyes (Trustin's a little more green, Marissa's a little more blue).

At the yellow cottage, she finds Grand Ella relaxing on the terrace, patting a place on the lounge beside her. Burrowing into a beach blanket, Condi snuggles into the pillows. "Where's Madelaine?" she asks, as the sun melts to honey, slipping into the sea.

Grand Ella sighs. "At the caves in the cliffs, I suppose. She and Lucky were gone when I got home from the shop." Sadly, she looks down at Lucky's empty water bowl.

"I saw Lucky at the Billabong," Condi says. "Maddie wasn't around."

"How odd," Grand Ella says. "Those two are rarely apart." A furrow appears in her brow. "How did things go with Mr. Marshall?"

Condi's eyes sparkle. "He says the aquamarine board is super old. I get to keep it if no one claims it by Friday. He's even giving me a used wetsuit and goggles." She can't keep the excitement out of her voice. "Can you believe it? I'm going to get to surf!"

"Oh, Condi, I don't know—"

"But you promised—" Condi stares at Grand Ella.

"I know—but I said *someday*. I was hoping you could wait a little longer. It's a dangerous sport. Your mother and father..."

"They were sailing, not surfing!" Condi interrupts. "And Papa was a master sailor. You've always said that accident was one in a million."

Taking a deep breath, Grand Ella nods, shaking away the faraway look in her eyes. "You're right, my dear. I'm not thinking straight tonight."

"What is it?" Condi asks. Her grandmother's usually

serene face is grave.

"I heard some distressing news in town today. Surfers have been seen surfing the Hollow recently. Kids—taking risks." She winces. "Those aren't surfing waters, Condi. You know that, don't you? The rocks of Windy Hollow are treacherous—sharp as shark's teeth."

"I know," Condi says earnestly. "I promise I'll never surf there."

Grand Ella sighs. "I'll hold you to that, my dear."

Chapter Ten

A TALK IN THE LIBRARY

On Friday morning, Condi jumps out of bed before dawn and leans out of the loft window, eager to start the day. The sea lily on the trellis brushes her cheek, a clean ocean breeze sweeps back her hair. The day is kissed with promise, a cinnamon tea sunrise blinking the world awake, early morning tide sipping at the shore.

Running lightly down the zigzag stairs to the beach for yoga, all she can think about is surfing, claiming the aquamarine board, and Trustin. Maybe if she learns to surf, they can be friends.

Rolling out her mat on the damp sand, she folds into a lotus pose. Closing her eyes, she imagines herself balanced on the aquamarine board, looking over her shoulder, laughing with Trustin, riding shimmering banks of curls.

In a little while, the rich ladies arrive for the sunrise class, hardly awake and barely moving. But today there's a surprise waiting for them. Three Beachlings are making their way to the yoga cove from the caves in the cliffs. Tiny, bent Charlene, and a pair of ancient sisters.

Grand Ella nods and smiles at the visitors, calmly rolling out extra mats. She introduces Charlene and the sisters, Pippa and Glinda. The Beachlings nod and smile shyly, shaking water from their hair, the last droplets from their pre-dawn swim.

The rich ladies glance warily at the old women. But since outspoken Amber Arondale no longer attends class, the ladies make room. It's only yoga, after all. Condi and Grand Ella guide the Beachlings to their mats.

When class begins, things are tense. Pippa and Glinda struggle, grunting and groaning. The rich ladies grit their teeth and glare at them. Thankfully, Charlene, though bowed and bent, proves to be amazingly flexible and spry. Her sweet trusting smile helps the rich ladies relax. Soon Pippa and Glinda grow quiet, and the class moves along in a stately rhythm, ebbing and flowing. The sun rises in a crimson and apricot arc, breaking over the beach.

After class, Charlene is the only Beachling awake. Pippa and Glinda are fast asleep. To Condi's surprise, the rich ladies smile at the two sleeping Beachlings. Mrs. Wainright, on the mat next to Charlene, stretches and asks the tiny woman if she enjoyed class. When Charlene claps her hands with joy and answers "yes," the two sleeping sisters wake up. Startled, they look around, remembering where they are. In the bright light of day, Pippa grows suddenly fearful. Eyes wide, she cringes and scrambles to her feet, whimpering.

Her sister snorts in annoyance, yanking on Pippa's

arm. "C'mon, Pippa. No whining." Without saying goodbye, the sisters pick up the yoga mats and scuttle across the sand, hurrying back toward the cliffs.

Charlene shakes her head. "Pippa is often afraid," she explains to the rich ladies in a soft voice. Looking at Grand Ella, she asks, "Thank you for the wonderful class, Ella? May I keep my mat, too?"

"Of course," Grand Ella answers kindly.

Feeling brave, Condi steps forward, smiling at Charlene. "Please tell Pippa and Glinda to come back to our class again."

Mrs. Wainright nods. "Yes, please come again. I can't wait to see you all tomorrow morning."

At school, Condi keeps her eye on the clock, anxious for the bell in homeroom to ring. Javed is being super obnoxious, flirting with Jessy, upsetting Anda, passing nasty notes—one of them an especially mean drawing of Lorelei in a ruffled pink swimsuit. Thankfully, Casey Arondale intercepts the note and puts it in his pocket before Lorelei sees it.

When the bell rings, Condi hangs back, waiting for Lorelei. Casey also hangs back, sticking close to Condi and Lorelei as Javed shoves past them.

"Move it, Arondale." Javed snarls at Casey.

Casey shrugs, shielding the girls with his tall, lanky body. Lorelei smiles up at him, while Condi fumes.

"Dude's the *worst*," Condi mutters under her breath, hating how Javed keeps a tight grip on Anda, putting a finger through the belt loop of her jeans and yanking her through the door out into the hall. Oddly, today Javed's forearm is wrapped in a tight white bandage. For an instant, Condi wonders whether he got hurt surfing yesterday, scratching his arm on coral or getting tossed into the rocks. When she thinks about how he treats Anda and bullies Lorelei...she hopes it hurts really bad.

Heading down the hall toward Science, Condi sticks close to Lorelei and Casey. Though the hall is crowded, Casey protects them from the pushing and shoving.

"Ready for lab?" Lorelei asks.

Casey's ears turn red. "Today's the ocean disturbances experiment, right?"

"Yep, the one with the water tank," Lorelei answers excitedly, launching into a lively conversation about seismic fault lines and unstable rims.

When they get to Science, the three of them grab stools at the lab table in the front of the room, near a huge aquarium. Inside the tank is a small underwater volcano set in a strange underwater moonscape. Air bubbles pop and fizzle from the volcano, giving an illusion of steam.

Mr. Poirot, the science teacher, enters the room, wearing an old-school jacket with shiny black patent leather shoes, hair sprouting around his ears like sea grass.

"Come to order, class." Banging on a test tube with a ruler, the teacher raises his voice to a dramatic pitch. "Today we are simulating the movement of oceanic water." He stands at attention next to the giant aquarium. "Can anyone tell me the difference between a tidal wave and a tsunami?"

Lorelei's arm shoots up in the air.

Mr. Poirot smiles at her. "Yes, Miss Finch?"

"A tidal wave is caused by the gravitational influences of the moon, sun, and planets. A tsunami is caused by a sudden movement of the ocean floor—like an underwater earthquake or explosion," she explains.

From the back of the room, Javed groans and whispers loudly, "Lore Bore's a raving Wikipedia."

The students in the back of the class titter.

"Silence, Mr. Holmes," Mr. Poirot glares, then turns his attention back to Lorelei. "Correct, Miss Finch," he says. "Tidal waves are predictable. However, tsunamis are not. They are extraordinary events, occurring with little or no warning." He pauses for effect. "Dipitous Beach is in a high-risk tsunami zone."

Condi shivers. Tsunami warning signs are posted all over Dipitous Beach. Most of the time she forgets about them, but, like everyone who lives in a beach town, she knows the signs give a false sense of security. The truth is, by the time tsunami warnings sound, it's probably too late to make it to higher ground.

"What's the first sign of a tsunami?" Mr. Poirot asks.

Casey shyly raises his hand.

"Mr. Arondale?"

"An earthquake?" Casey's voice wobbles awkwardly, then cracks.

The back of the class snickers.

"What should you do if there's an earthquake, Mr. Holmes?" Mr. Poirot stares at Javed.

"Run like hell for the inland!" Javed calls out.

The kids in the back of the room lose it.

"Language, Mr. Holmes," the teacher says dryly. He waves the ruler with a flourish. "Pay heed—this is no laughing matter. An earthquake in our area is a serious event. Dipitous Beach is close to an unstable part of the ocean's floor. Miss Bloom, can you tell me what I mean by that?"

Condi nods. "Dipitous Beach is not far from the Ring of Fire, the big underwater volcanoes of the Pacific."

"Excellent," Mr. Poirot nods approvingly. He steps to the aquarium and flips some switches. "Let's see what happens when the ocean floor disturbs one of those volcanoes."

The tank buzzes, and the volcano inside begins to shake, spouting bubbles. Puffs of sand in the tank whirl, churning the water. The spewing changes into violent spurting, waves rock the tank, and soon a curve of water is sloshing from side to side.

"Here comes the big one!" Mr. Poirot exclaims as he flips another switch. The next wave crests over the side of the tank, splashing his shiny shoes.

The kids cheer.

Mr. Poirot smiles with satisfaction. Not for the first time Condi wonders about the eccentric science teacher and his strange inventions. He certainly goes to great lengths to make a point.

"Alright, class," the teacher says as he mops up the water on the floor. "Take out your textbooks and answer the questions at the back of chapter three. Divide in groups and work with the partners at your table."

Relieved to be at a table with Lorelei and Casey, she pulls her stool closer to theirs. Lorelei spins her open book around on the lab table. "Hey guys, take a look at this." Condi and Casey lean in, studying a small orange submarine with bubble hatch windows. "Isn't it just the cutest oceanographer's sub?" Lorelei exclaims, looking at Casey. "I want to major in oceanography when I go to college. I'm interested in underwater weather. Sea storms are going to be my specialty."

"Weather?" Condi asks. "I never thought about there being weather in the ocean."

"There are all sorts of weather conditions in the deep sea," Lorelei answers. "Earthquakes, volcanic eruptions, sea floor fissures—even blizzards of sand that stir up weird, buried sea creatures."

"I'm all about sea creatures—and the weirder the better." Casey says, grinning at Lorelei. He flips through the pages of her book. "Like this one." He points to a picture of a blobby thing on the ocean floor that looks like an old rug. "Called a wobbegong. Looks harmless—but it's a carpet shark."

Condi examines the thing in the photo. "A shark? It looks like a nice little floating plant."

"Trust me—it's a shark." Casey says. "Glides over the bottom of the ocean floor like a piece of carpet. When a tasty prey floats by..." He pauses and looks at Lorelei, then scrunches up his face, and makes a lot of goofy gobbling noises.

Lorelei giggles.

Condi winces.

Some boys...

#

After lunch, Condi hurries to the library, passing Javed and Anda in the hall. Pressed up against a bank of lockers, they're making out, Anda's hand cupped around Javed's neck.

Yuk.

How Anda can be such a fool, Condi will never understand.

Entering the calm of the library, she returns a few books to Mrs. Lowry, trying not to get her hopes up. The library is the only possible place she can run into Trustin at school. But it's been ages since the walk on the beach, and it's not likely that she'll find him here. He's probably way too cool to read. And why would he hang out in the library at lunch? Everyone at school is talking about the Davis twins. They're super popular, and definitely the best surfers, like Marissa said. Every day after school they surf Craggy Point, while Condi's stuck working in the art shop.

"I found a new book on ghosts for you, Condi," Mrs. Lowry says with a smile. "Take a look." The librarian hands her a cellophane-covered book, shimmering a vaporous silver.

"Thanks," Condi says, glancing over the back of the book jacket. "Looks good. I'll try it." At least if she does run into Trustin again, she'll have something new to talk about.

After Mrs. Lowry scans the book out to her, she takes it and slips away from the check-out desk, vowing not to think about Trustin anymore. After all, she needs to remember that he didn't show up at the Hollow. She's still a little bit mad about that—though, of course, there *were* surfing warnings out that day.

Soundlessly, she weaves through the stacks heading for the nook with the two chairs next to the porthole window. Rounding the corner, she stops short.

"Wha—" Startled, she steps back.

"Hey," Trustin says, looking up from the open book on his lap and smiling. "Isn't this a great reading spot?" He's sitting in the seaweed-green chair, salt etchings on the window casting a sprinkle of fairy dust behind his head.

She nods. "It's where I always come," she tells him.

"Want to sit?" He asks, waving an arm toward the saggy-bottomed brown chair.

Hesitating, she remains standing, not sure if he really means it. "What are you reading?" she asks politely.

"Research," he says, shrugging. He holds up a large book with black-and-white photos on the cover. Leaning in, she studies it.

In bold letters the title reads, *Pacific Sea Catastrophes. Oh, no.*

Her heart twists into the horrible, familiar knot. The photos are of helpless people drowning—sucked into the sea.

"I'll find another place to read," she says quickly, trying to sound offhand. She has to get away before he sees her cry.

"Don't go," Trustin says. Closing the book with a snap, he tosses it on the floor, face down. "Sit here, in the green chair. It's way nicer."

He stands like a gentleman. Taking a deep breath, she calms down. Then, smiling shyly, she slips into the seaweed-green chair. He grins and flops into the saggy-bottomed brown one.

"Hard to get comfortable in this old thing," he says. Flailing, he flops and twists, until at last, he throws both legs over the arm of the brown chair, making the springs collapse with a ridiculous groan.

She stops feeling bad and laughs. He looks so crazy and his silly antics give her the chance she needs to wipe a tear away and settle her glasses primly on her nose. Grief lifts, drying like the tear. For an instant, she wishes she could tell him everything, why she got so sad, but that's stupid—after all, he'd never understand. Instead, she nudges the book he tossed on the floor with her foot. "What kind of research are you doing?"

"Something for a dude I know." Leaning over, he picks up the book and puts it back on his lap, tapping his finger on the cover. "An old wreck off Windy Hollow. A long time ago. Back in the forties—World War II."

"A shipwreck?" Condi asks. "I've never heard of one off the Hollow." She sighs. "Though there've been plenty of surfing and sailing accidents."

"Not a ship—a submarine." He hesitates. "In 1945. The end of World War II."

She makes herself study the photos on the cover of the book again. Suddenly, she feels stupid. If she hadn't freaked out, she would've noticed that the photo is grainy and blurred, an iron-gray submarine with an old-timey periscope in the background.

"It's a diesel sub," he explains, his face grave. "They were a lot like boats, floating mainly on the top of the ocean, instead of staying submerged. Diesels collect oxygen from the surface." Biting on his bottom lip, Trustin stares out the porthole window, shoulders tensed.

Condi stays silent. Whatever the research is, it's upsetting him. She wonders a lot about Trustin's friend. An old submarine accident from World War II doesn't seem like something a kid would care about.

Putting a smile into her voice, she changes the subject. "How'd you learn to surf like a pro?"

Shaking off his gloom, he turns back to face her, grinning. "Well—let's just say I was born in the waves."

"Sure—let's just say that," she says, rolling her eyes, shooting a grin back.

They laugh together again. It makes things better, as laughing tends to do. Condi relaxes; the tension in the air unwinds. Easy with one another now, Trustin goes back to his book, and Condi does the same. Her new book is enthralling. She had no clue there were so many different legends about ghosts, crazy what some people believe.

The rest of the lunch period flies by. When the bell rings, they close their books at the exact same time, chuckling at the snap. When Trustin stands up, Condi stays seated, not sure what to do, wondering if he wants to walk out with her. After all, he's a high school kid. He might not want to be seen with an eighth grader.

But he waits patiently, standing in front of the seaweed-green chair, nodding his head toward the porthole window. Through the etchings of salt spray, they look out at the waves, high and tumbling, rocking a sea of crystal blue.

"I'm surfing the Point after school, Condi. Come and watch?"

She shakes her head. While she's relieved that things are good between them, she doesn't want to get hurt again. Maybe there's a good reason he didn't show the other day, maybe it was the weather—but still, she can't forget. He's a popular surfer kid—way too cool for her.

Maybe if she gets the aquamarine board and learns to surf, one day she'll be out there, too. Right now, she can only hope.

"Sure?" He studies her face, a question firing in his eyes.

"Yes," she answers.

Flipping an errant lock of onyx hair off his forehead, he slips his backpack over one shoulder and stretches out a hand, helping her out of the seaweed-green chair.

They walk side by side to the front of the library. At the door, he turns to the left and heads off down the hall to the high school. For one yearning moment, she follows him with her eyes. Mrs. Lowry glances after him, then gives Condi a sympathetic smile.

Embarrassed, Condi turns and hurriedly heads down the hall to the right.

Breathe. Reset. Focus.

Today after school she's going to the Billabong—to claim the aquamarine board

Chapter Eleven

SHAPER'S MARK

After last bell, Condi runs down the high road overlooking the cove and dashes down the beach stairs to the Billabong. Flying through the screen door, she plops her backpack on the floor and leans against the wall, trying to catch her breath.

Mr. Marshall looks up from the counter where he's buffing a lime-green board. "In some kind of a hurry?" Chuckling, he winks at her.

Grand Ella is at the surf shop, too, waiting, just as she promised. Smiling at Condi, she asks, "How was school?"

"Too long," Condi mumbles. "I couldn't wait to get here." Anxiously, she monitors Mr. Marshall's face. *Please, please, let the board be mine...*

He grins, giving her the thumbs up sign. "She's yours, young lady. Not a single inquiry all week."

"Yay!" Condi hugs Grand Ella.

"The board is yours," Grand Ella repeats, hugging her back. Nervously, she twists her infinity necklace. "I'm happy for you, but you know I have safety concerns. I've arranged for you to take surfing lessons with Mr. Marshall."

The old surf master nods. "That's right, my girl. You'll be joining my junior surfing class."

"There's a session bright and early tomorrow morning," Grand Ella goes on.

Condi stares at them. The joy of claiming the aquamarine board takes a nosedive. They can't be doing this to her. Junior surfing classes are for little kids, held on the beach, not in the water. Kids practice surfing moves—but with boards firmly planted on sand.

"Great," she says dismally. *I'll feel like such a baby.*

"You'll like the class, Condi." Mr. Marshall reassures her. "A couple of junior surfer champions are helping out. I think maybe you met Marissa Davis the other day?"

Condi moans inside. Grown-ups are clueless. Stuck in a class with little kids—taught by a super-surfer ninth grader—totally humiliating.

"Marissa has a twin brother," Mr. Marshall adds. "His name is Trustin. He won Surfing Pacifica last year; Marissa placed second."

Grand Ella beams at her. "Isn't it exciting? You'll be learning from kids your own age." She hugs Condi again. "Mr. Marshall and I made a trade. On Sundays, I'm teaching a yoga flow class for surfers, in exchange for your lessons."

Condi sighs, trying to look happy. Grand Ella's done all this for her, taking on another yoga class on her only day off.

The screen door of the surf shop swings wide. "Hi, everyone. How's it going?" Marissa Davis steps into the Billabong, swinging her shining hair over one shoulder, shooting them a confident smile.

"I asked Marissa to stop by so she can meet you, Ella," Mr. Marshall explains. "Marissa, this is Condi's grandmother."

"Please call me Grand Ella. Everyone in town does." Grand Ella steps forward and smiles. "Welcome to Dipitous Beach."

"Nice to meet you, Grand Ella," Marissa answers, with light and airy charm. "I love it here already." Turning to Condi she adds, "What's up, Condi?"

"Hi," Condi says flatly. After the news she just got, it's hard not to resent everything about the older girl. She's glowing today, sculpted arms burnished with sunscreen, setting off the gold in her amber hair.

"You alright, Ella?" Mr. Marshall asks.

Brows knitted together, Grand Ella is studying Marissa. "Of course," she shakes her head. "Sorry. It's just that you look very familiar."

"Pippi Longstocking or Ginny Weasley or that girl in *La La Land*?" Marissa jokes. "I look like all the crazy redheads."

Grand Ella laughs. "Certainly not Pippi Longstocking," she answers.

Mr. Marshall looks confused.

"May I go get my surfboard?" Condi asks.

"Polished her up good." Mr. Marshall jerks his head toward the storeroom. "Ready and waiting for you."

"I'll come, too," Marissa says quickly.

Making an eager exit, the girls pick their way through Mr. Marshall's workshop, dodging an assortment of surfing equipment and clutter. Odd-shaped tools, every kind of polish and wax, racks filled with expensive surfboards, in varying stages of maintenance and repair.

"Wow, Mr. Marshall's some kind of surfboard savant," Marissa comments.

"Yeah, he does it all," Condi agrees, flinging open the door to the storage room and stepping inside.

Streaming through a giant window, the afternoon sun bathes the surfboards in a golden glow. Unlike the surfboards in the workshop, these boards are in prime condition, neatly hung in racks or mounted in sturdy wooden floor mounts. Dappled sunshine dances on the polished surfaces of the boards, tossing out tiny rainbow prisms of light.

"Magical," Marissa whispers.

Crossing to the far side of the room, Condi goes to where the boards in ocean colors are hung—cobalt blue, emerald teal, shimmering silver and aquamarine.

Gently, she touches the aquamarine surfboard. Mr. Marshall's worked a miracle—the board is like new. The deep gash on the nose is gone. The shaper's mark is clear and bright. Leaning in, she studies the mysterious brand, made by an unknown artist many years ago. Two tiny blue stars, hovering above a black and silver half-moon.

A tingle flows up into her fingers as she traces the shaper's mark.

"Magical," she agrees.

Chapter Twelve

TIDE POOL LESSONS

The next morning dawns bright and clear. After breakfast, Condi puts on a cute yellow polka-dot two-piece, hoping she looks okay. It's her favorite swimsuit—though it's more than a little faded—and it inspires Grand Ella to sing a crazy beach song from back in the day.

Today's no exception.

"She wore an itsy bitsy, teeny weeny, yellow polka-dot bikini," Grand Ella sings out. Grabbing Condi's hands, she tries to dance her around the kitchen.

"It's not itsy bitsy, Grand Ella!"

Grand Ella drops Condi's hands and stops dancing. "Oh, Condi. I'm sorry. Of course it's not."

"Does it really look okay?" Condi asks anxiously. "Or should I wear the purple one?"

"The yellow's perfect," Grand Ella assures her. "How fast you're growing up." She strokes Condi's hair. "What a dark-haired beauty you are!"

Condi looks at Grand Ella, wanting more than anything to believe her. Slipping into her yellow hoodie, she makes sure the white shell is in her pocket.

"Enjoy your first surfing lesson," Grand Ella says, gently pushing her out the door of the cottage. "No matter what, choose joy, my dear. You've waited a long time for this day."

Condi hugs Grand Ella, then swings her way into the blue and pink and yellow of a perfect beach morning, with the aquamarine board on her shoulder.

In the cove on the shore below the Billabong, Condi parks the surfboard in a mound of sand, loving how the aquamarine of the board matches the shining blue-green of the sea beyond. The ocean is whisper-soft today, though the day promises to be hot and sultry. Already the sand is warm between her toes, the sun urging her to slip out of her hoodie. But she leaves it on, not wanting to get too comfortable until Marissa and Trustin arrive. She wonders what the older girl is wearing. Probably not an old yellow suit with a hoodie, that's for sure.

The first group to arrive at the beach for the junior surfing class is a gaggle of three little boys.

"I told you to go to the bathroom before we left the house, Nicky," their harried mom sighs. "Jake, take your brother up to Mr. Marshall's please—ask to use the bathroom."

Jake moans and yanks Nicky by the arm, dragging him up to the Billabong.

Condi sighs.

The smallest boy cries, "Mom, look!" On the top of the

hill, Anda's parents, Mr. and Mrs. Lindgren, are pulling in with their pastry food truck, Sweets and Sippers.

"No, Danny," his mother says firmly, "you just ate breakfast."

The boy scrunches up his face and lets out a pitiful whine.

Any hope that the junior surfer class isn't going be too horrible ebbs out of Condi. Wanting to get as far away as possible, she goes over to sit on the rocks and stare into a tide pool. What were Mr. Marshall and Grand Ella thinking, putting her in a baby class?

Soon another cluster of little kids arrives, as obsessed with the pastry food truck as Danny. In desperation, one of the moms volunteers to buy a round of mini-donuts for the kids, just to shut them up.

Today's going to be a nightmare. As she gazes into the pool, her hair falls around her face; her reflection wavers, while her thoughts spin in circles, dark as her mood.

"Hey, is that a baby sea pig?"

Condi looks up. Marissa, tall and lithe in a navy swim suit, kneels beside her, leaning forward to study a pale pink wriggle in the tide pool.

"Sea cucumber, I think," Condi says.

"Nope, sea pig," Marissa answers. "Sea pigs and cucumbers are from the same family—but sea pigs have tiny little legs. They're the vacuum cleaners of the ocean—always sucking up tons of bad microbes."

"Hmm," Condi murmurs politely, adjusting her glasses.

"Yep, I can tell you most anything about sea creatures," Marissa says. "Spectacular and amazing—

dangerous and creepy. Life under the sea is a whole other world—totally bizarre and beautiful—the kind of stuff you can't make up." She smiles at Condi.

Condi smiles back, feeling better. Who knew? Marissa Davis may be gorgeous but she's also a sea nerd, like Lorelei and Casey.

"Hey, Marissa," Jessy Pettikin's voice floats over to the tide pool. A loud wolf whistle follows.

Grinning, Marissa stands up and sends a big wave to the surfer kids on their way out to Craggy Point. Jessy and Javed Holmes lead the pack, while Anda is struggling through the sand, trying to keep up.

Condi slips into a low crouch by the tide pool, hoping the kids don't notice her, wishing she could be swallowed up by the sand. The last thing she wants is kids at school seeing her in a little kid class.

Javed yells, "Come surf!" Jessy puts a hand on a hip and pouts. Anda holds up a bag of goodies from her parents' food truck, shaking it enticingly.

Marissa points to the little kids gathered on the beach. "Can't," she yells back. "Later."

The surfer kids shrug. Turning their backs, they continue to the top of the Point.

"Sorry you can't surf with them," Condi says stiffly, getting to her feet and brushing sand off her suit.

"No biggie," Marissa says. "We can hang out with them later."

Condi doesn't answer. She's working at Wafting Rafters after the lesson. No hanging out for her.

Mr. Marshall and Trustin emerge from the Billabong, arms loaded with surfboards and boogie boards, and clank their way down the beach stairs.

Condi's heart lurches.

Cute as ever...

Trustin lays out boogie boards on a stretch of sand. Blowing the whistle around his neck, Mr. Marshall calls out each kid's name, points to a board, and instructs them to sit beside it. To Condi's relief, he doesn't call her name, so she sits as far away from the little kids as she can get, next to the aquamarine board.

Trustin catches her eye and winks. Shyly, she smiles at him. Maybe the class won't be so bad after all.

Mr. Marshall sticks the tail of a surfboard in the sand and blows his whistle. When the kids quiet down, he asks, "What's this part of a surfboard called?" He points to the thin strip of wood running vertically through the center of the board.

"The stringer!" Nicky calls out.

"What's it do?" Mr. Marshall counters.

"Makes the board stronger!" the kids chant.

"What do we say about the stringer?" Mr. Marshall prompts.

"The board lasts longer—because the stringer makes it stronger!"

The kids collapse in a fit of giggles. Trustin shoots Condi a sympathetic glance. Marissa rolls her eyes.

For a while, Mr. Marshall drills the kids on the various components of a surfboard, stuff Condi already knows. Then he launches into a boring lecture about safety and surfing etiquette. "Thousands of surfing accidents occur each year," he declares. "Most due to a lack of respect for the ocean."

While he drones on and on about deadly undertows, raging rip currents, and sly sneaker waves, Condi sneaks a peek at Trustin. To her amazement, he's looking at her, too. He grins, holding her eyes in the cutest way.

#

"Time to practice on the boogie boards," Mr. Marshall says. "Trustin, you can work with the younger boys while I work with the little girls. Then we'll switch off."

Marissa jumps to her feet. "Great plan, Mr. Marshall. I'll work with Condi." Under her breath she mutters, "Hurry. Come with me." Grabbing the aquamarine board, she strides to the far side of the sand by the tide pool, and lays the surfboard down.

"Grommets get on my nerves. I know they can't help it—but baby surfers are annoying." Marissa confides. "I'm not like Trustin. He's the patient twin. Me? I like to get things moving." All business, she taps the center of the board. "Like now. Hop on."

The instant Condi steps onto the aquamarine board, joy ripples up through her feet. She may not be on the waves yet, but she's on her way to becoming a surfer. Taking off her yellow hoodie, she tosses it on the sand.

"Ready?" Marissa asks.

"Ready," Condi answers, spreading out her toes.

"Left foot forward, toes straight, right foot back, at forty-five degrees," Marissa instructs. "Keep your hips forward, then bend into your left knee."

A smile twitches at the side of Condi's mouth.

Marissa laughs. "See where we're going with this?"

"Warrior one pose in yoga," Condi says in delight.

Marissa crosses her arms and nods. "Yep. Surfing is yoga on a board. Now—set your intention, and keep your eye gaze on the horizon line."

Slipping deeper into the yoga pose, Condi focuses on the silver sliver of the horizon. Leaning into the breeze, she sets the rhythm of her breath and lifts her arms, opening and expanding, reaching for sky.

Breathe in, breathe out.

"Crescent lunge," Marissa orders.

Condi slides into a crescent lunge, arms like jet wings.

"Fingertips on the board," the older girl adds.

Sliding into a classic surfer's crouch, Condi lets her imagination take over. Instantly, she feels a rush of water under the board, energy flowing up into her feet.

Breathe in, breathe out.

The lesson flies by, with Marissa calling out yoga poses, making slight adjustments to Condi's body on the board.

"Reverse warrior."

Condi slides into the pose, left arm skyward, right arm reaching for her calf.

Marissa smiles proudly. "Like most things, surfing is about confidence. You're a natural, Condi. Once you learn how to get on and off a board, you'll be ready for real waves."

Condi does a silly little happy dance on the board, grinning at Marissa. *I can do this,* she marvels. *I really, truly can.*

"Let's call it quits for today," Marissa says. "I want to watch the surfing skill games. If I have to teach the groms next week, I need ideas."

Leaving the aquamarine board by the tide pool, the girls grab water bottles and wander over to the shoreline to watch Mr. Marshall's class. The kids are divided into two teams for the games. So far, it's pure chaos. Danny and Nicky are doing handstands and flips, accidentally-on-purpose kicking sand on the girls.

"Alright, you two monkeys," Trustin says, picking up a boy under each arm and carrying them to the head of the line. "You two are team captains. You get to go first, how about that?"

"Yay!" Nicky and Danny cry, giving each other fist bumps.

Mr. Marshall blows his whistle for order.

"Time for the paddling contest," Trustin says when the kids settle down. "First up, Nicky and Danny. Step right up, gentleman." Trustin points to two boards prone on the sand. "On your tummies!"

The boys flop down on the boards and plant their toes in the sand.

"Go!" Trustin yells.

Lifting their chests, the boys pump out a few furious breast strokes.

"Paddle harder!" Trustin kneels down beside Danny, holding his ankles. "Imagine the current is sucking you back. Fight harder to get out to the waves!"

Danny grunts and paddles harder, stroking through

nothing but air while Trustin cheers on Nicky. Both boys are turning scarlet, battling imaginary waves, slick with sweat.

"Ha, that's my bro," Marissa says. "Pure genius. He's teaching *and* wearing them out." She shakes her head. "Grommets love him. I don't think I can handle it. When it's my turn, I'll be screaming and beating them over the head with boogie boards."

Condi laughs. "You two are really different."

"My dad can't believe we're twins," Marissa says serenely. "Yin and yang, you know. Together we make a perfect whole." She grins at Condi. "The thing is, Trustin is patient, but he gets stuck in his head sometimes. I have the opposite problem. I'm always moving, rushing in without thinking." She gazes out to sea. "Trustin likes to *know* things, while I like to take action, even if it's not a good idea." She sighs. "My brother drives me crazy sometimes. Like right now he's trying to solve this one particular problem. The answer is right in front of him, but he can't get out of his head to see it."

"If you know the answer, why don't you help him?" Condi asks.

Marissa shrugs. "He wouldn't listen to me. Sibling rivalry and all that. Trustin thinks I move too fast through the world—take way too many risks." She flips her hair back and winces a little. "He's probably right. Besides, you can't solve other people's problems—only your own."

"True," Condi agrees. "But I think there's one thing you have in common—both of you are kind."

"Kind?" Marissa rolls her eyes. "Most people don't think I'm kind. They think I'm bossy."

"Well, maybe a little." Condi laughs. "Kind is about caring," she goes on. "When you're kind, you give people confidence, like you did for me today. I never would have figured out the yoga/surfing connection on my own."

Marissa shakes her head. "Don't give me too much credit, Condi. You're brave—and brave people figure stuff out, because they're not afraid to fail. That's all surfing is— getting up, wiping out, then doing it all again."

Marissa takes a last sip of water and stands up, gazing toward the tide pool where Lorelei, in a pink swimsuit with ruffles, is poking at the pool with a stick. "Hey, do you know that girl over there?"

Condi nods. "She's a friend."

"Let's go over and say hi," Marissa suggests. "She's been watching us, though she's totally acting like she's not."

They trudge back to the tide pool. Lorelei, butterscotch hair twisted into a knot on her head, leans close to the water, studying it intently.

"Hey, Lorelei," Condi says, as her shadow falls across the pool.

"Uh, hi." Lorelei looks up and blushes, gaping at Marissa. Stammering, she says in a rush, "I saw you all practicing. Hope it's okay I'm here." She points to the aquamarine surfboard, glittering on the sand. "Condi, is that yours?"

"Yep." Condi grins. "Can you believe it? I found it the other morning on the north shore."

"You're so lucky." Lorelei sighs.

"Hey, I'm Marissa Davis," Marissa says matter-of-factly, stepping forward and swinging a long athletic leg over the rocks so she can perch on the edge of the tide pool. "What's in there?" She nods her head toward Lorelei's stick, peering into the contents of the pool.

Lorelei's eyes light up. "It's a By-the-Wind Sailor," she says eagerly. "Isn't it beautiful?" Gently, she nudges a triangle of what looks like blue gauze floating in the pool.

"Nice. Don't see many of those." Marissa studies the tiny, translucent blue creature unfurling in the pool like a small sailboat.

"Is it some kind of jellyfish?" Condi asks.

"Absolutely not," Marissa and Lorelei burst out, looking at each other and laughing.

"Okay, okay." Condi holds her hands up in mock surrender.

"Sorry, Condi," Lorelei says. "Not everyone's into sea creatures."

"By-the-Wind Sailors aren't jellyfish," Marissa explains. "Jellyfish are underwater creatures, like submarines—sailors are like boats, floating on top of the water."

"That's right." Lorelei looks at Marissa with awe.

Mr. Marshall blows his whistle three times, signaling it's almost the end of class. Condi goes over to the aquamarine surfboard, lifts it easily onto her shoulder and glances at Marissa. "Coming?"

Marissa doesn't answer. She is studying Lorelei. "Saw you watching Condi's surfing lesson," she says. "You want to learn to surf, don't you?"

Lorelei flushes. "My family can't afford it," she mumbles. "Besides, I don't have much free time." She forces a smile.

"What about now? Seems like you're free Saturday

mornings," Marissa points out.

Lorelei nods. "My mom is off until noon on Saturdays. This is the only time in the week I don't have to watch my little brother and sister."

"Well, maybe we can include you in the surfing class next week," Marissa tells her confidently. "I'll talk to Mr. Marshall."

Lorelei's face flashes with hope, then she shakes her head. "I can't pay—and I don't have a surfboard."

"Don't worry about paying. My brother and I have a special deal with Mr. Marshall." Marissa winks. "It's worth a lot to be junior surfing champions, you know. And I have a spare board you can borrow."

"But I don't have—" Lorelei starts to object.

"Mr. Marshall will loan you a used wetsuit," Condi interjects. "He's got a ton of used ones at the Billabong."

Marissa laughs. "Any other excuses?"

"Just one," Lorelei hesitates. "I'll probably be terrible at surfing. Look at this body, short and well, you know—I'm shaped sort of like a beach ball."

Marissa frowns. "Don't talk like that. You've got good muscles and a low center of gravity—you'll do just fine."

Condi slips her arm through Lorelei's. "It'll be great. We'll learn to surf together." She points up to the top of Craggy Point where Casey Arondale is standing, gawking at the three of them. "Look at that—Casey Arondale is so crushing on you."

"No way," Lorelei says, flushing as bright pink as her suit.

"There you go again," Marissa says in a big sister tone. "Tearing yourself down. First rule of surfing—you have to believe. Can you do that?"

Lorelei takes a big breath and nods, eyes filled with hope.

#

While the little kids help Trustin stack boogie boards, Condi shows Mr. Marshall her yoga surfing moves.

"Good work," Mr. Marshall says in approval. "Won't be long before you can go in the water."

"How long do you think?" Condi asks breathlessly.

The surf master shakes his head. "Ah, the impatience of the young. No need to rush." He looks at Marissa. "You've done a good job, too. Next week Condi can work with Trustin, while you work with the groms." When Marissa groans, he shrugs. "All part of junior surfer instructor training."

"Okay, okay," Marissa agrees, letting her eyes sparkle at him. "But can we include Lorelei Finch in surfing lessons next week? I need her to help with my class. Please? She babysits all the time, and I'm no good with kids, I could really use some help." Taking a deep breath, she adds, "I'll loan her one of my old surfboards. You can put my earnings toward the cost of her lessons."

Mr. Marshall throws back his head and guffaws. "Marissa Davis, you're a clever one." He nods. "Lorelei can join the class. No need to cover the expense, I'm happy to offer her a scholarship. I know her situation at home. Her dad's worked to the bone at the Mirage. And her mother is constantly on call, because of that snooty old Mary Hardy." He snorts, glaring up at the top of the hill above the

Billabong, where the steep pitched eaves of the rambling Hardy mansion look down their noses at the town.

Condi smiles over at Marissa. *Kind.* She has it right. The Davis twins are kind, but in different ways. Trustin, patient and steady, Marissa bold and bossy, insisting that good things happen for kids who deserve a break.

With a last long shriek of the whistle, Mr. Marshall adjourns the surfing class. The little kids squeal, falling over each other, charging the Lindgren's food truck.

"Look over there," Marissa whispers, nudging Condi in the ribs. "Love is in the air." She tilts her head, a tiny smile playing around the corners of her mouth. Casey Arondale is jogging over the sand, hunter-green surfboard under one long arm. Headed for the tide pool, he makes a beeline for Lorelei, lying on her tummy, straining her neck to squint into the crevices of the pool.

"Those two are perfect for one another," Condi declares.

Then, because she can't help it, she sneaks a peek at Trustin, racing up the beach stairs to return the boogie boards to the Billabong. Her breath catches. He's beautiful, held in a blaze of sun, moving like water, easy and strong. At the top of the beach stairs, he stops, puts down the boards, and gazes down at her, shaking back a lock of onyx hair. Raising an arm, he waves.

Her heart sings.

Beside her, Marissa groans. "C'mon, Condi. Not you, too?"

Chapter Thirteen

THE ART SHOP

On Monday morning, Condi rushes to the library at lunch to wait in the seaweed-green chair by the porthole window, hoping Trustin will show up. But the reading nook is empty.

The next two days are the same, and she starts to lose confidence. Maybe he doesn't like her after all.

Dejected, on Wednesday afternoon, she drags her feet to Science. Today Mr. Poirot's hair is slicked back, his too-tiny glasses pinching his bulbous nose. Huffing and puffing, he heaves a metal box up onto the front lab table and raps for order with his ruler, causing his billowing gray lab smock to swirl like smoke.

"He's got a whole Snape thing going on today," Lorelei whispers to Condi and Casey.

Casey wiggles his eyebrows crazily and drops his voice. "Welcome to the Dark Arts, my dear."

Lorelei goes into a fit of giggles and Condi groans inside. Everybody in eighth grade seems to have a crush. Javed and Anda cruise by the front lab table. Anda ignores Condi, lifting her chin. Javed smirks at her. The wound on his arm is professionally taped today, the white bandage wrapped in plastic, so he can still go out to surf. Nothing stops Javed Holmes from getting what he wants, Condi thinks bitterly.

"Class, come to order," Mr. Poirot says. Dramatically, he taps on the metal box with the ruler. "Observe my latest invention, a portable magno meter, designed to predict earthquakes." Mr. Poirot taps the box softly, and the needle of the meter quivers. He raps more firmly, and the needle fluctuates wildly.

Raising a brow, Casey looks at Lorelei. "I don't believe this," he whispers. "Guy's lost it."

"Mr. Arondale," Mr. Poirot says sternly. "Kindly pay attention." He slides the magno meter to the center of the lab table, so the needle bobs directly in front of Casey's nose. "A magno meter records 'the intensity of tremors coming from the sea floor, on a scale of one to ten." He looks out at the class. "Last month's magno meter readings ranged from three to five. However, this month's readings are staying at a fairly constant eight. What do you think this might mean?"

Lorelei's hand shoots up in the air.

"Yes, Miss Finch," Mr. Poirot nods, acknowledging Lorelei.

"Well...it *might* mean there's increasing seismic activity in our area but..." She hesitates. "No offense, Mr. Poirot, but earthquake prediction is unreliable. There are lots of factors we don't understand."

The teacher frowns, fixing his gold-rimmed eyes on her. "True, Miss Finch. That is why I was careful to use the word *might*." He sniffs.

"So can that thing tell us if there's going to be an earthquake or not?" Finn calls out from the back of the room.

"Of course it can't," Javed scoffs. "Scientists have been threatening us with The Big One for decades."

The kids laugh.

Mr. Poirot pounds the ruler like a gavel. "Mark my words," he says ominously. "One of these days a volcanic eruption in the Ring of Fire will cause a massive earthquake and tsunami along the coast. Dipitous Beach sits on the edge of the Ring. Our cove could be destroyed." Stepping quickly over to the door, the science teacher flips off the overhead lights. "Let me show you what I mean." He projects a computer screen onto the broad white wall. "Behold! The mysterious depths of the sea."

"That's the ocean?" Macy murmurs.

"Looks more like a planetarium," Finn says loudly.

The screen is a deep blue. A cluster of luminous sea stars float into view. Silently, the class watches the hypnotic spinning of the stars.

"What you are seeing is a live underwater camera feed from an oceanographer's sub," Mr. Poirot says, his nose glowing red in the reflected light from the screen. "The camera is recording the activity of an active underwater volcano not too many miles off the coast of Dipitous Beach."

The camera zooms in on an underwater mountain,

more indigo than black.

"I read about this discovery," Casey exclaims. "It's a rare asphalt volcano, about sixty-five feet tall and super old."

"Exactly," Mr. Poirot says approvingly as the screen flickers eerily and the volcano shudders.

"An eruption," Lorelei says breathlessly.

The mountain belches a small spurt of black magma.

"Lava doesn't flow underwater. It binds with seawater and floats," Mr. Poirot explains.

The spurt of magma separates and clots, slowly drifting down to settle around the volcano's base, soft and fluffy, like small sofa pillows.

Mr. Poirot switches off the projector. After he flips on the lights, he points to the magno meter, where the needles are twitching from four to five on the dial. "We experienced a small earthquake a few moments ago when the volcano erupted."

"I didn't feel it," Javed says with disdain. "Not much of an earthquake. You're just trying to scare us."

The teacher raises his bushy brows. "Indeed?" He shakes his head. "The ocean is a cruel deceiver, Mr. Holmes. That volcano off the coast is alive and well—don't ever doubt its power."

At last, it is Friday afternoon. When the last bell rings, Condi dashes out of school, not allowing herself even a backward glance toward Craggy Point. There are storm warnings out for the weekend, and though the day is clear and bright, the waves are pitching and rolling higher than usual. The surfer kids will soon be racing toward the beach stairs, rushing down to the cove to catch the sweetest of the high rollers, Marissa and Trustin among them. And Condi doesn't want to think about it. Not seeing Trustin in the library this week has made her anxious about seeing him tomorrow.

Forte, Condoleeza.

Be strong.

Condi sighs. Of course, Papa's right. She has to stay strong. It's not the worst thing in the world if Trustin doesn't like her. Besides, right now, she has work to do.

Hurrying up the hill to Upper Main, she follows the steep winding road up to Wafting Rafters. Maisie Hollister is delivering a new assortment of painted scarves this afternoon. Grand Ella will want them unpacked and displayed in time for Saturday's shopping rush, the best day for in-person sales by far.

When Condi reaches the shop, a carton is already waiting by the back door. Maisie, with her five young children, must not have had time to wait. Punching in the key code, Condi opens the door and drags the carton into the shop. After making a mug of her favorite cinnamon honeycomb tea, she starts unpacking. Soon the tart sweetness of the tea relaxes her. The scarves shimmer and slide through her fingers, falling into soft folds, in rich and luminous colors.

Going to the small alcove by the back door, Condi pulls out a wooden ladder. Hanging the new scarves from the ceiling beams will be fun. She plans to do a beach theme. The colors are perfect. Maisie's painted this batch of scarves with the changing colors of the sea, foaming ivory, slate blue, sand-washed green, deep horizon indigo.

Before she can pick out a scarf and climb the ladder, the front door chimes ring. The door opens, letting in an unusually brisk autumn breeze.

Condi looks up. Anda is slumping into the art shop, wild with dismay, face blotchy from crying. Twisting her long yellow hair around one wrist, she flings herself into Grand Ella's rocker.

Condi stops unpacking the scarves and stares at her old friend, not sure what to say. Anda hasn't stopped by the shop in forever.

"What are you doing here?" Condi asks, trying not to sound annoyed.

"My parents found out about Javed," Anda wails. "They put a locator on my phone. You're the only friend of mine they trust. They're going to be checking to see if I'm here at the art shop with you."

Wow.

It's all Condi can do to bite back the first hot words that come to mind. Bending over the box, she lifts out a scarf, letting the gossamer folds shiver through her fingers. How she wants to tell Anda that, as far as she's concerned, they're no longer friends.

Anda's phone pings. Instantly, she scrambles around in the rocker, fishes it out of her jeans pocket and dives into the screen.

"Jav—heading out to surf," she moans, jerking a shoulder toward the beach front. "All the kids are there."

"Not *all* the kids," Condi says evenly, holding up a translucent blue and silver scarf and shaking the wrinkles loose, more vigorously than necessary.

Anda ignores her. Bowing her head over the phone, her streaky hair shields her face as she frantically taps out a reply.

That does it. Condi glares at Anda. She's tired of being invisible. "Just so you know—we haven't been friends for a while," she says darkly. "You have a lot of nerve showing up here."

Shocked, Anda looks up. "What?"

"You heard me," Condi answers.

Slowly, Anda puts down the phone. Her blue eyes widen, her lower lip quivers, and she starts to cry. "Oh, Condi, I'm sorry."

Anda's tears fluster Condi. While she's used to her old friend's flair for drama, maybe this time the apology is real.

As she opens her mouth to reply, Anda's phone pings again. Forgetting Condi, Anda grabs her phone and focuses on the screen.

Nothing's changed.

Turning her back, Condi slowly climbs up the ladder to hang the blue and silver scarf in a prime spot from the iron rod below the rafters.

"My dad caught me sneaking back in the house last night," Anda says, not even glancing up at Condi. "Parents are so awful!" Still transfixed by her phone, Anda launches into a long story about how she's been meeting Javed Holmes on the beach at night. "My parents are driving me crazy. They won't let me grow up!"

Condi's heart curls into a tight knot and hardens. Oh, if only Mama and Papa were here to drive her crazy...

"You shouldn't be sneaking out," Condi says flatly. She descends the ladder and reaches into the box for an ivory-pink scarf the color of the inside of a shell, vowing to tuck her hurt away. Anda can't be trusted.

"Oh, Condi, you don't get it," Anda blurts out. "Wait till you get a boyfriend."

Climbing back up the ladder, Condi pushes away her grief and stays silent. Anda is so into herself these days, the jab isn't worth a reply. She hangs up the pink scarf and goes back down the ladder to choose the next one, a pale lavender with blue-gray squiggles—the color of coastal rain.

"Javed's into me and I'm into him," Anda prattles on. "When you're really into a boy, you want to be with him, no matter what. You'll do anything...absolutely anything..."

Condi shakes her head. From the top of the ladder, she looks down at Anda, wishing she'd be quiet. A strange light is falling through the front window, shining on Anda's tear stained face. Squirming in the rocker, she's yanking on her yellow hair—hard—as if to stop a hidden pain. It occurs to Condi that Anda is lost and alone.

Concerned, she hurries down the ladder. "Oh, Anda, you really like him that much?"

Anda nods, choking up. Flushing, she turns her head and looks into the light streaming from the window. Her shoulders crumple and shake, the sobs coming from deep within. At last, she stops crying and turns back around, her voice urgent and low, "No judgment, Condi. Promise?"

Condi sits down on the floor beside the rocker, holding her hands open on her lap, as Grand Ella's taught her.

When the shoulders are open, so is the heart.

"Promise," Condi answers.

"You can't ever tell anyone." In a quicksilver change of mood, Anda's eyes go faraway and she smiles dreamily.

Nervousness creeps up Condi's spine. She regrets the promise.

"You know how they say the Stinson mansion is haunted?" Anda leans over and whispers. "Well...it's nice and private up there."

"You and Javed go to the top of the Hollow?" Condi can't believe it. "What about the security teams patrolling the beach?"

Anda looks smug. "The security teams work for Mr. Holmes. They let Javed do whatever he wants," she replies airily.

"Oh, Anda..." Condi is speechless. She's horrified—in more ways than one. Javed is an awful bully and the narrow rock ledge connecting the tower of Windy Hollow to the mansion is unsafe, treacherously looming over the jagged stand of spear-tipped rocks.

"The Stinson mansion is the very best make out spot in the world," Anda announces proudly.

"It's dangerous," Condi says helplessly, thinking of the slippery stone stairs winding up to the top of the Hollow. She's never dared to cross the narrow ledge connecting to the mansion and spa hotel. The ruins are practically sliding into the sea.

"Not really. There's nothing scary about it. Those flickering red-gold lights that people always say are ghosts are campfires, Condi." Anda's voice is bold. "One of those crazy old Beachlings was squatting in the mansion, until

Javed ran her off. You know, that one with the terrible hair and the creepy old dog."

Condi feels sick, thinking of Madelaine and Lucky. She imagines Maddie building a fire in the ruins of her old home, sweet Lucky by her side. Then a horrible thought rises.

"How did he run her off?" she asks carefully.

Anda tosses back her hair. "Oh, Condi, why do you care? I don't know exactly what he did. All I know is that he ran her off because his dad wants to clear the beach—you know that."

Anda's phone pings again. When she reaches for it, Condi stops her. She touches Anda's wrist, and looks into her eyes. "I'm asking you—did Javed hurt her?"

"Hurt her?" Anda's face crumples and she looks uncertain. "Why, I don't think so..." She hesitates. "Why would he?"

"Because Javed Holmes likes to hurt people, that's why," Condi answers fiercely.

Anda sits back in the rocker. For an instant, nothing in her face argues with what Condi's just said. But then, her face closes back down. Jumping up out of the chair, she heads for the door. Hand on the knob, she turns around.

"Well, you listen to me, Condi Bloom. If Javed hurt that awful old woman, she deserved it. Her vicious dog attacked him. Bit him on the arm."

Condi is stunned. It all makes sense. Poor Madelaine, covered with nasty bruises—and Javed wearing that huge honking bandage on his arm all week.

Pausa, Condoleeza.

Wait...listen to what's not said.

Condi takes a deep breath. Putting her hand in her pocket, her fingers close around the shell. Her eyes drop to Anda's outstretched arm. A bubble of memory floats up. Javed's hand, closing tightly around Anda's wrist, Javed and Anda making out by the lockers, him holding her hips, hands like a vise.

She slowly studies Anda, frozen by the door. Getting up from the floor, Condi walks toward her. Anda's long sleeved T shirt has ridden up, exposing an ugly band of purple bruises. Going pale, Anda tugs at her shirt, pulling it over her wrist.

"Please don't tell." Anda's eyes well with tears. "He doesn't mean to hurt me. Javed really loves me."

"Loves you?" Condi repeats. How do you tell someone love never looks like this?

"And I love him, Condi. I really do. He doesn't mean to hurt me...he's just stronger than he knows." Wiping her cheeks with her hair, Anda sniffs.

"We need to tell someone," Condi says softly.

Anda's head jerks around. "Oh, no, you don't, Condi Bloom! You promised. Say one word, and I'll tell on you for meeting Trustin Davis at the top of the Hollow the other day."

She storms out the door, slamming it hard behind her, letting in a vicious kick of wind. The painted scarves ripple across the rafters like an angry tide.

#

Later that night in the yellow cottage, Grand Ella notices Condi's strange mood. "Is something wrong?" she asks quietly, pouring them each a mug of bedtime hot chocolate. Outside the evening is cold and the wind blustery, spinning off a wild and ragged surf. Condi curls up on the rose-splotched sofa, holding a warm mug in her hands.

"I'm okay," Condi mumbles. "Really."

"I won't press—but it's clear you're distracted, my dear," Grand Ella says. Then she smiles. "I saw Andy Marshall today. He says you'll be ready to take to the waves soon—surfing for real. Tomorrow's your next lesson."

"I hope so," Condi answers. Taking a sip of hot chocolate, she forces a smile. But even the thought of a surfing lesson with Trustin can't dispel the sick feeling in her stomach. What Anda told her today is awful—and scary.

This isn't the kind of secret you should keep, Mama's voice whispers in her head.

I don't have a choice, she thinks miserably. *Lots of kids sneak out. And Anda will deny it. No one can prove what Javed did to Madelaine—or to Anda. The news will upset Grand Ella and it might make things worse. Mr. Holmes has it out for the Beachlings. If Javed gets in trouble, who knows what his father might decide to do to them next?*

Thoughtfully, Grand Ella smooths a stray curl off Condi's forehead. "Isn't it wonderful that more Beachlings are coming to yoga?" Grand Ella says brightly. "The resort ladies are really warming up to them."

Condi nods. Today the rich ladies showed up at the sunrise class with new yoga mats and gave them away to the Beachlings. Even the most timid of the old women ventured down out of the cliffs to collect a mat.

"Yes," Condi says, trying to match Grand Ella's positive mood. "And some of the Beachlings actually *do* yoga—"

"—if they don't go to sleep first," Grand Ella says as they burst into giggles. Sunrise yoga is looking a little like nap time in kindergarten.

Grand Ella takes another sip of hot chocolate. "Amazing what happens when we take the time to know people who are different from us. I've lived long enough to learn that we only change the world one relationship at a time." She sets down the mug, concern clouding her eyes. "I only wish Duke Holmes wasn't stirring up a pack of trouble among the other hotel owners. Pushing for a program to provide incentives for the Beachlings to get out of town."

"Not the one-way bus ticket idea again?" Condi exclaims.

Grand Ella sighs. "Yes. If the Beachlings have family somewhere, then Duke Holmes plans to send them on a one-way bus ride. They won't be able to afford to come back if their families won't take them in."

Condi hates what she's hearing—and she hates Javed Holmes for hurting Anda and Madelaine. And she hates his stupid father, Duke, for being rich and mean and powerful. And she hates herself for not telling Grand Ella what Javed did to Maddie. But she's sure her grandmother will speak out, and then Duke Holmes will do something even more awful—and probably get away with it.

"Why are some of the people in this town so stupid?" she says miserably.

"Oh, Condi, it's complicated. The hotel owners believe that if we continue to tolerate the Beachlings, then tourism in Dipitous Beach will fall off." Grand Ella shakes her head. "I'm a business owner myself. I certainly want to protect the safety of our beaches—but the Beachlings aren't the problem."

Grand Ella rubs her forehead with two fingers, massaging her temples. The two of them sit quietly. Stretching out her legs, Grand Ella murmurs softly, "Who knows what the answer may be?"

An unexpected draft swirls through the room, raising goose bumps on Condi's arms. The lamplight flickers, casting them in shadow. Setting down the mug, Condi jumps up, suddenly needing air. Throwing open the door to the upper terrace, she steps out into the star-crossed night and goes to the railing, squinting into the darkness. If only Madelaine and Lucky would show up. There's a storm coming in the next few days, and she needs to know they're okay. Leaning into the wind, she says a prayer for them, held in the mysterious black folds of night.

If only...

Grand Ella comes outside, throwing a blanket around Condi's shoulders and slipping an arm around her waist, offering the kind of comfort that doesn't need words.

The night deepens. One by one, the stars twinkle out and moonlight blazes a trail across the water. "Come back inside," Grand Ella says after a while. "Time for bed. You've got a surfing lesson tomorrow if the weather holds. Going without sleep never helps a thing."

Climbing the ladder up to the loft bedroom, Condi slips under the covers, wondering if she can handle any more surprises or secrets. Everything is changing, catching her off guard. A few weeks ago, she never kept secrets from Grand Ella—now she's keeping far too many.

Chapter Fourteen

SAPPHIRE KELP

In the mercurial way of the northern Pacific coast, Saturday morning dawns more like winter than autumn. An ominous hood of clouds is covering the cove, sun glaring through gray like a stark eye.

"Be careful on the beach today, my dear," Grand Ella says anxiously to Condi as she finishes breakfast. "There are tropical storm warnings in the south. Watch for lightning."

Condi gives Grand Ella a reassuring hug. They both know the horrible consequences of ignoring bad weather. But right now, Condi's not worried about storms. She's wishing she didn't have to wear her thick yellow hoodie over her swimsuit just to stay warm. She wanted to look extra cute for Trustin today.

Grand Ella bites her lip. "Don't you want something more on your legs? There's a mean wind out there."

"I'm fine," Condi tells her. No way is she going to appear at the beach in too many layers. She'd rather freeze to death.

On the long walk to the inner cove, she starts to regret her choice. Looking cute for Trustin is one thing, but being covered in goose bumps is another. A ruthless wind is whipping flecks of chilled foam off the waves. Not a good beach day. Not a good beach day at all.

When she reaches the shoreline below the Billabong, Mr. Marshall is hurrying to bring the display surfboards propped against the front porch of the surf shop inside. He waves at her, then ducks through the screen door, the rising wind sending it clanging behind him.

Condi spies Marissa perched on a rock next to the tide pool, lost in thought and staring out at the Hollow, a small purple surfboard lying flat in the sand beside her. An indigo board with orange rails leans against a twisted jacaranda tree, next to Trustin's molten-black board and a tangled pile of wetsuits.

"Hey, Marissa," Condi calls out as she goes over to the rocks, dropping the aquamarine board in the sand. Dressed in an oversize camo sweatshirt, Marissa looks wickedly cool today.

Marissa turns and smiles. "Hi, Condi. Good news. Junior surfing class is cancelled. Mothers don't want their precious grommet-babies out in the cold."

Condi grins. Sliding onto a rock beside Marissa, she scans the beach, wondering where Trustin might be, especially since his board is underneath the tree.

One by one, noses of brightly colored surfboards pop up in the distance. Some of the best surfer kids are cresting the top of the dune, heading out to the Point.

Condi frowns. "That's crazy. There are bad weather warnings out today."

Marissa shrugs. "Storm's stalled down south. Be a while before it gets here. Those gnarly ones off the Point are incredible today, Condi. Wild weather makes great surfing, you know."

Condi bites her lower lip, embarrassed. Marissa's a junior surfing champion. Of course she loves rough tides. "Are you and Trustin going out after class?" she asks, looking at the wetsuits under the tree.

"Maybe. We'll see. If we decide to surf, we can change later."

At the mention of Trustin, Condi's eyes sweep the beach.

Marissa notices and laughs. "Don't worry. He'll be here soon. He's on the north shore helping Triponica." When Condi looks puzzled, she goes on, "We've been getting up super early each day, sneaking out of the hotel, going to the Hollow when the stars are still out." She shakes her head. "Living at the Mirage isn't our style. Stuck up rich people everywhere." She sighs. "Our dad's busy. Besides, the Hollow's going to be our home. The past few mornings, we've gone to the cliffs to hang out with the Beachlings." She studies Condi. "Trustin says you know them pretty well."

"Not exactly," Condi answers, suddenly wishing she knew the old ladies better. "Grand Ella's the one who knows them best. Sometimes Madelaine and Charlene stop by the shop or the cottage for tea. A few of the others come to sunrise yoga."

Marissa grins. "Sunrise yoga sounds fun."

"It is," Condi answers. "If you and Trustin are out before dawn, you should join us. In fact, I'm surprised I haven't seen you. The yoga cove has a clear view out to the Hollow."

"Thanks for the invite. Maybe one morning we'll stop by."

"I hope you will," Condi says, thinking it's odd that the twins' dad would let them sneak out to the Hollow before dawn. "What do you think of the Beachlings?"

"I haven't met them all, only Charlene, Triponica, Pippa, and Glinda," Marissa replies. "I want to meet Madelaine, but she hasn't been around. Hear she's a whiz at reciting poetry."

Condi nods. "That's right."

"Trustin and I plan to get to know them all. After all, they live right next to the Hollow. They're our neighbors." She smiles. "They're all kind of amazing, don't you think? I mean, they swim in the coldest part of the cove, live off what they catch in the sea, whatever they can scavenge on the beach." She shakes her head. "It's a hard life. I hate it that sometimes they go hungry." She leans over and whispers, "Don't tell—but Trustin and I sneak leftovers from the buffet at the Mirage and bring them to the cliffs. Criminal how much food at that hotel goes to waste."

Condi looks at Marissa with admiration.

"There's another thing I hate about the Mirage," Marissa goes on, glancing up at the high parking lot, where the Sweets and Sippers food truck is parked. "That awful Javed Holmes is always around." Huddled at the awning window of the food truck, Javed and Anda are getting hot chocolate in steaming to-go cups. "Can't stand that dude. He orders everyone around because his rich daddy owns the place." Her sweatshirt slides down over one shoulder. Irritated, she yanks it back up. "And he's so jealous of Trustin. Yesterday when we were pipelining, I caught him trying to ram Trustin's board. Stupid move. Nobody can catch my bro—but I swear Javed wanted to send Trustin straight into the rocks."

Condi clenches her teeth.

No doubt Javed wanted to do just that...

At the bottom of the beach stairs. Casey carefully leans his hunter-green board against the rail, then helps Lorelei pull a shocking pink sweatshirt over her head. When her head pops through, she turns a blooming rose, smiling up at him.

"They're pretty cute together," Marissa says.

Condi smiles. "Yeah."

Standing up, Marissa grabs the purple board and demonstrates how it barely comes up to her chin. "Outgrew this board ages ago. Think Lorelei will like it?"

"She'll love it," Condi answers.

Suddenly, Marissa's smile dims. A line in her forehead appears. Javed Holmes is jogging down the beach toward them, leaving Anda standing by the food truck looking lost, holding two cups of hot chocolate.

"Teaching today, Rissa?" Javed says, strolling up to Marissa, ignoring Condi.

"Don't call me Rissa," Marissa snaps.

In a short-sleeved wetsuit, the thick bandage around Javed's bare forearm looks like a wrestler's cuff. Flipping back his hair, he says, "You look hot today, *Marissa*. Hope you're coming out to the Point." He holds onto her eyes, letting them slide slowly over her bare shoulder, where the camo sweatshirt has slipped again. "Don't tell me you're teaching Lore Bore and Grief Girl how to surf." He jerks his head toward Casey and Lorelei, trudging toward them through the sand. "Why waste your time?"

Marissa smiles sweetly back at him for a long moment. Then, tossing back her hair, she steps forward. "Get out of here, Holmes," she says coldly. "Go back to your spineless girlfriend."

Javed's eyes harden. "I'll get you, Marissa Davis," he says under his breath. Squaring his shoulders, he walks off toward the food truck.

"Dude needs a serious lesson," Marissa tells Condi. "And what's the deal with that chick, Anda Lindgren? Follows him like a sick puppy."

"She's messed up," Condi mutters. "And Javed Holmes is awful."

"Hey, guys." Lorelei and Casey join them at the tide pool. A gust of wind blows up a puff of sand. "Getting nasty." Lorelei glances nervously toward the Point where the breakers are foaming. "Can't believe kids are actually out surfing."

Casey looks startled. "I'm going out, too, Lore. Those waves are rad." He hesitates. "Unless you want me to stay here?"

Lorelei's cheeks flush. "Guess I've got a lot to learn about what makes good surfing weather." She waves Casey off. "No way. Go on out. I'm nervous enough already."

When Casey jogs off to the Point, Marissa picks up the

small purple surfboard. "All yours. Sorry I don't have a pink one."

"Purple's my second favorite color." Lorelei gazes at Marissa with adoration. "Thanks for loaning me your board," she adds shyly.

"I call her Amethyst," Marissa answers. "She was my very first board—the one I learned on." She grins. "Just the right size for you."

Condi winks at Lorelei. "Should I call my board Aquamarine?"

Marissa and Lorelei laugh.

"I like it," Marissa says. "Ocean colors. Amethyst and Aquamarine. The color of the shallows." She puts a hand on the surfboard leaning against the tree. "And this sweet baby is Indigo—the color of the deep."

A rogue streak of sunlight breaks through the clouds over the Hollow. In the distance, coming from the north shore following the tideline, Condi's relieved to catch a glimpse of Trustin, Triponica, and Charlene. The three have their heads together in deep conversation. Triponica grips a tattered net slung over one shoulder, glittering a brilliant blue-purple in the sun.

As they approach the beach below the Billabong, Triponica leans in to say something to Trustin, then turns on her heel, striding back toward the caves in the cliffs. Condi is not surprised. It's unusual to see Triponica close to town. As far as Condi knows, she never leaves the Hollow to venture into the inner cove.

Gentle Charlene is different. Small and fragile, she lives as she always has, despite the risk of harassment from security patrols. Every morning she faithfully walks the beach, bent and curled, picking up trash left by tourists and gathering her precious shells. Today, as she and Trustin reach the waterline below the surf shop, she sits back on her heels and shakes out the floppy orange sock. After sweeping the sand with the hem of her bleached white skirt, she lays out her shells, showing Trustin each of her treasures. Patiently, he kneels beside her and studies each one, asking quiet questions. Her face is animated as she answers, looking up at him, mouth wreathed into a smile.

All Condi's fears about Trustin not liking her leave her.

Charlene never shows anyone her shells.

Eyeing the low cloud cover slinking in from the south, Mr. Marshall signals to Trustin to hurry. "Nasty storm on the way," the old surf master tells them. "Just a quick lesson, then you kids need to head home. Stay focused."

Battling the wind, Mr. Marshall and Trustin set up two saw horses and balance Condi's aquamarine board between them. At the end of each saw horse is a curved groove. Placing the nose of the board in the groove of one sawhorse, Trustin swings the tail into the groove of the other, docking the surfboard in place.

The old surf master double-checks the stability of the elevated surfboard, then looks at Condi. "She's locked in good. Stay grounded through your feet—that wind's capricious."

His eyes twinkle. "Mind if I leave you with this young man so I can help Marissa with Lorelei?"

"I'll take care of her," Trustin rushes to say.

"Oh, I know, son." Mr. Marshall winks at them.

Condi blushes.

"You'll do great," Marissa whispers to Condi. Jogging over to the tide pool, she goes to help Lorelei practice on the sand.

Shyly, Condi and Trustin look at one another.

"Marissa says you were with Trippy at the Hollow this morning," Condi says, hoping to break the awkwardness.

His eyes light up. "Yeah. When Marissa and I got to the cliffs this morning, Triponica was braving an awful tide, swimming around the spear-tipped rocks. That churn around the Hollow was a washing machine."

"What in the world was she up to?" Condi asks. "I know she's a strong swimmer, but that sounds crazy."

Trustin looks at her with surprise. "It's the autumn equinox, you know. During the equinox, Trippy harvests the rarest kind of seaweed in the world—sapphire kelp. Right now, because there's a big weather change on the way, the kelp is floating close to shore. Tidal currents are pulling it up out of the depths, tangling the kelp in the rocks." He smiles. "It's so darn beautiful, Condi, clusters of sea kelp grapes sparkling on the rocks like blue and purple jewels."

Condi is quiet. Of course she knows all about the autumn equinox, the shift of tides and seasons—but she's never heard of sapphire kelp.

"Trippy makes a medicine from the kelp, an elixir that helps relieve pain," Trustin explains. "The kelp collects on the sea side of the rocks, where the rip tides are strong. I gave her a hand hauling in the net."

"Triponica makes medicine?" Condi asks slowly. "That's amazing."

Trustin laughs. "She's a nurse, Condi. Didn't you know? When she was a girl, she drove ambulances the last year of the war."

"The war?" Condi stammers, not sure she heard him right.

He hesitates. "World War II."

"That can't be..." She stares at him. "How old was she back then?"

"Who knows? She lied about her age, I'm sure. Lots of kids did back then." The turquoise in his eyes deepens. "Some people are ageless, you know. Especially those with the gift of healing."

Thoughtfully, Condi rubs the white shell in her hoodie pocket. How could she not have known all this before? It explains so much that's mysterious about the Beachlings. Why the people in the town call them witches...why Triponica never comes to town...why none of the old ladies seem to get sick.

"Thank you for telling me," she says. "I had no idea."

He grins. "I like to know things about people. It's fun to hear their stories." The wind whips a lock of hair over his eyes. "Ready to practice?"

"Ready," she says, pulling her hoodie closer.

A blast of wind sweeps up and over the dune, peppering them with sand. The puckered ridge of scars on Trustin's neck glares purple in the chilly air.

"Are you cold?" she asks, shivering.

"Naw," he shakes his head. "I never feel the cold." Smiling, he holds out his hand and says, "C'mon."

Strong fingers close around hers. A shaft of light breaks through the clouds. Sitting on the elevated surfboard, she uses his hand as support and gracefully swings her feet onto the board. Rocking forward on her toes, she comes to standing, centering her weight.

"Good," he says approvingly. "Settle into feeling balanced."

"Got it," she murmurs.

"Move through some yoga poses," he instructs.

She slides through a few warrior poses, ending in a low lunge.

"Good. Pretend there's a golden ball in your core, tucked beneath your ribs. When you're out in the water, everything moves around that ball."

Nodding, Condi visualizes a golden ball under her ribs. Holding the ball steady, she smoothly slides out of the lunge, into a surfer's crouch, then up to standing.

The next hour flows by, in the rhythm of the tide. Her dark curls tumble and lift, swirling around her face like strands of rain.

Never has she felt so right—or so free.

"Focus on the horizon," he tells her, a crack in his voice. "The place where sea meets sky..."

Lifting her chin toward the horizon, she smiles. That small crack in his voice is so sweet. She glances to the north side of the cove. The ragged shore is bathed in light, the tower of Windy Hollow shining...like the turret of a castle set in a sparkling sea.

#

The sky continues to darken, the winds tightening into short strong bursts. A flash of lightning cuts across the sky. Some of the surfer kids out on the Point are leaving the water and starting for home. Mr. Marshall blows his whistle, signaling the end of class.

Lorelei, Marissa, and Mr. Marshall hurry over to join Trustin and Condi. "You did well, my girl," the surf master tells Condi. "You're bonding with the board." He pats her on the arm. "If the weather's good next Saturday, we'll put you in a wetsuit and get you out in the surf. You're ready."

"Not me," Lorelei wails, wrinkling her nose up in disgust. "I'm a lost cause. I can barely stand up, even when the board is on the sand. My toes keep sliding off."

"You're fine," Marissa tells her. "Hang loose—and for goodness' sake, stop whining." Spreading her own toes wide, she goes up on tiptoe. "Practice the ten-toe grip. Walk on your toes a lot. Surfers need strong feet."

Lorelei sighs. "Ha. Easy for you to say. You're super graceful. I have hobbit feet."

As Trustin lifts Condi's surfboard up off the sawhorses, he looks at Lorelei. "Don't give up. Only giving up does you in."

Lorelei takes a deep breath. "You're right." Going up on tiptoe, she prances around, high stepping through the sand. "I've waited a long time for this—I won't give up."

A rumble of thunder shudders in the far distance. Wind gusts shovel a wave of sand off the dune. Brushing sand out of his hair, Mr. Marshall winces, glancing up at the sky. "See you kids later," he says. "Got to get back to the shop. These winds are a warning—the next few days will be bad."

When Mr. Marshall is out of earshot, Marissa winks at Trustin. "C'mon, bro. Let's take a few surfing runs."

"You're kidding. You're really going to surf?" Nervously, Lorelei eyes the breakers frothing off the Point.

"Yep." Marissa grins at her mischievously. "And you should totally come watch." She points to Casey, gazing at them from the top of Craggy Point.

Lorelei gazes longingly at Casey. "I'm supposed to be home to baby sit soon," she says slowly.

Trustin gazes at Condi. "Can you come?"

"Well..." Condi looks at Lorelei. "I'm supposed to be home soon, too...but maybe we can go to watch just one run?"

Lorelei grins. "Okay."

"We'll grab our boards and wetsuits. Meet you at the Point." The twins head to the tide pool. Lorelei and Condi lift their boards, bowing into the wind, trudging toward the Point.

A high shrill scream breaks above the wind—

Startled, the girls look up.

On the high ledge of Craggy Point, Anda is shrieking. Next to her, Casey is crossing his arms back and forth over his head. Finn bounds down over the rocks, dashing across the sand toward the parking lot where the Lindgren's food truck is parked.

"Call 911!"

Trustin and Marissa drop their wetsuits by the tide pool, charging toward Craggy Point, surfboards on shoulders, legs and arms bare.

"Surfer down," Marissa yells.

Dropping their boards, Condi and Lorelei take off running for the Point.

Chapter Fifteen

RESCUE

When the girls reach Craggy Point, a fine mist is falling. The long rock ledge is slippery and cold. The surfer kids are huddled together, towels clutched to chests, watching for a sign of the lost surfer.

Anda rushes up to Condi and grabs her. "It's Jav! He's gone under. Oh, Condi, I'm so scared."

"Finn's gone for help," Condi says quietly. putting her arm around Anda's waist.

Casey, talking fast, tells Trustin and Marissa what happened. "Jav went out too far. Showing off. His board washed in." He points to a ragged shoal—Javed's crimson surfboard is marooned, impaled among the rocks.

A bolt of lightning slashes in the distance, lighting up the sea. The surfer kids on the rock ledge gasp.

"We shouldn't be out here!" Jessy cries. Scurrying down off the rocks to the beach, the kids run for cover.

The mist is falling thicker now. Casey pulls Lorelei

under an overhanging rock. Trustin and Marissa stand out on the seaside tip of the Point, scanning the waves, boards by their sides. Anda, dazed, sinks to her knees, rocking back and forth. Condi kneels beside her.

"Javed wanted to show everyone he's still the best," Anda sobs. "He hates that Trustin is a better surfer." She turns her anguished face to Condi. "I told him it was stupid to go out that far."

Condi squeezes Anda's hand. It was stupid. She tugs Anda under the low ledge next to Lorelei. Silently, they watch the waves pitch and roll, looking for a sign of Javed.

"There! To the south. I see him!" Marissa jumps up and down.

On the distant horizon, Javed's head bobs above the waves. He throws up an arm, then disappears.

Without hesitating, Trustin steps to the edge of the Point. Holding his black board like a knife, he dives, slicing into the curl of a breaker. Marissa stands unmoving, the indigo board nestled in the crook of one arm, held like a staff in her hand.

Anda loses it. Dashing out from under the ledge, she screams and screams. Condi rushes to her, shaking her. Nothing works. Helplessly, Condi scans the waves. Trustin and Javed are nowhere to be seen.

The sea is furious, the sky a flat slate gray. Suddenly, without a trace of thunder, a mighty slice of lightning flickers in the sky, cutting a gash in the sea. The light shifts—the water blooms orange—a giant red creature rises from the waves.

"A Humboldt squid!" Lorelei cries.

"Look at the size of that thing!" Casey gasps. He turns

to the girls, eyes wide. "Humboldts can attack."

Anda stops screaming and stares at him, horrified.

"Sorry," Casey mumbles. "They're known to eat divers."

The great red eyes of the giant squid turn toward the Point, shining out of the mist. Then the creature slowly folds up and disappears, sinking back into the sea.

Anda buries her face in Condi's shoulder. Wrapping her fingers around the white shell in her pocket, Condi fights to breathe.

Decrescendo, Condoleeza.

Calm yourself.

Holding on to Anda, she prays, watching the waves—and waiting.

The surf groans. A flash of orange-red cuts the waves like fire. The giant squid surfaces, tentacles wound around a molten-black surfboard, Javed's limp body splayed on top of it. A head pops up beside the board—Trustin, gasping for air. With a mighty tentacle the squid pulls Trustin to the board, where he hangs on tightly. Head bowed, the squid gathers the board with the two boys up into its arms.

"It's eating them!" Anda shrieks.

"No," Condi murmurs.

The giant squid spreads like a magnificent fan, gently releasing the surfboard with the two boys into the waves. The molten-black board catches the next big roller. Riding the crest, the two boys and the board are raised up high, then flung downward as the wave breaks, sending the board skimming toward the Point.

Lifting its great red tentacles skyward, the squid retreats back into the sea.

#

"Hurry," Marissa snaps into command. "Grab towels. I'm going down to meet them." Swinging down over the edge of the rock ledge, she drops to a small sliver of sand among the rocks below.

"I'm going, too," Condi says.

"Oh, Condi, be careful!" Lorelei begs.

"I will," she promises. Swinging out over the ledge, she drops beside Marissa on the rough sand.

Marissa looks over at her and grins. Through the foaming chop, Trustin is making his way toward them, holding Javed's limp body secured to the molten-black surfboard, slowly kicking to shore. When the board touches the rocks, Marissa rolls Javed's unconscious body off the board, onto the sand.

Trustin heaves himself out of the water. "Wrap him," he gasps.

From the high ledge, Casey and Lorelei pass down towels. Condi and Marissa quickly wrap Javed's body. His eyes are closed, lips bruise-blue—but he's breathing.

"EMTs!" Lorelei yells.

A team of rescue workers appears on the lip of the ridge. One jumps down to join them on the sand, quickly securing Javed's body to the surfboard with ropes.

"You kids okay?" he asks them.

Condi and the twins nod.

The EMTs hoist Javed to safety. Trustin helps Condi climb back up to the top of the rock ledge while Marissa scampers up behind.

"That was amazing!" Lorelei exclaims, "A real Humboldt squid. They're known to attack humans—but never close to shore."

"Storms alter ocean currents," Casey says. "Changes in currents affect the behavior of sea creatures. That's why the squid attacked."

"The squid wasn't attacking," Marissa tells him.

"What? That Humboldt attacked Javed," Casey stammers.

"It wasn't a Humboldt," Marissa tells him.

Lorelei opens her mouth to say something, then closes it, looking from Marissa to Casey. Putting a hand on Casey's forearm, she whispers, "Let it go."

Marissa's eyes soften. "We don't know what we don't know—about sea creatures—or the ocean."

"You were super brave...under a long time." Condi looks at Trustin.

Lorelei nods, studying him. "Yeah, you *were* awfully brave—but you should have hypothermia. That deep water off the Point is icy. You aren't wearing a wetsuit."

"Yeah," Casey jumps in. "Javed had a wetsuit on, but you—"

Marissa glares, sighing a pointed sigh.

Lorelei elbows Casey. "Never mind. I want hot chocolate. C'mon, let's go up to Sweets and Sippers."

They retrieve their surfboards and head up to the food truck where a small crowd is gathering, discussing the impending storm. The talk at the food truck is that the tropical storm may be upgraded to a hurricane, something this part of the coast hasn't seen for over fifty years. A slow mover, the storm is stalled on the southern coast, gathering power from warmer waters.

Lorelei and Casey cuddle up together. Trustin sits next to Condi. As Marissa blows steam off her hot chocolate, her eyes flicker over to her twin. The two burst out laughing.

Condi smiles, not quite getting the joke. Sipping her cocoa thoughtfully, she ponders the happenings of the day.

Strange and beautiful...

A mystery....

"I better get home," she says at last, turning to Trustin. "Thanks for the lesson. I'm glad you and Javed are okay. I was scared to death."

He smiles, catching her eyes and holding them. "See you tomorrow, Condi."

Chapter Sixteen

AN EMPTY COVE

That evening the weather channel announces that winds in the south are escalating, moving in unusual circular bands. The wide front window of the yellow cottage is a show of jagged spurts of lightning, breaking through mist, illuminating the sea.

After dinner, Anda calls to tell Condi that Javed is staying overnight in the hospital. He's got a concussion from being hit on the head with his surfboard.

"And Mr. Holmes wants to thank Trustin for saving Javed's life," Anda explains. "Isn't that sweet? He wanted me to ask you—where does Trustin live, Condi?"

"Funny Javed's dad doesn't keep track of his own hotel guests," Condi answers curtly. "The Davis family is staying at the Mirage."

"Mr. Holmes is a busy man, Condi." Anda laughs. "He doesn't have time to notice all his guests, I'm sure. Thanks for the info, though. Gotta go. My dad's yelling at me to come to help unload the food truck. The storm's looking bad."

"Later," Condi answers. Annoyed, she puts the cell phone back on the charger in the kitchen and wanders into the living room where Grand Ella is monitoring the weather. The storm's been upgraded to a hurricane.

"We haven't seen a hurricane in these parts for fifty years," Grand Ella says. "But it may miss us yet. Stalled storms often spin out to sea."

"Let's hope that's what happens," Condi says, throwing herself down on the rose-splotched sofa beside her grandmother. "This weather is scary." She explains the strange events of the afternoon, how somehow—no one knows quite how—Trustin and Javed are safe, though they encountered a giant squid.

"Oh, my goodness," Grand Ella exclaims, putting her hand over her heart. "It's the weather. Mysterious things happen when there are circular winds. Unlikely creatures come close to shore. Javed and Trustin are lucky to have survived a giant squid attack."

Condi doesn't bother to correct Grand Ella. Sighing, she slips her hand into her pocket and folds her fingers around the white shell, nervously watching the weather radar on TV. The celestial swirls of the hurricane bands are hypnotic...spinning, spinning...lighting up the screen.

"White it glimmered, the sea simmered..." she says under her breath.

Joining in, Grand Ella softly recites:

I walked by the sea, and there came to me,
as a star-beam on the wet sand,
a white shell like a sea-bell...

Lamplight shivers across the polished wood of the cottage floor, catching on the silver streak in Grand Ella's hair. Abruptly, her voice fades away and she reaches for Condi's hand. "Oh, Condi, I'm worried about Maddie. No one's seen her for a week." Her eyes fly to the big front window of the cottage. Rain is spitting on the glass, night falling fast.

"I know," Condi tells her. "I'm worried, too."

Standing, Grand Ella moves quickly to the mahogany bookcase in the corner. The bookcase is tall, with a moon and stars design carved above two slender, shining glass doors. It holds Grand Ella's most cherished books, family favorites and all the old classics Condi's grown to love. Opening the bookcase with the silver key kept in the latch, Grand Ella draws out a well-worn blue volume.

"Tolkien," Grand Ella says, tracing her finger over the embossed book cover. "Maddie read this over and over the last time she was here." She flips through the pages. "The poem is called 'The Sea-Bell' by J.R.R. Tolkien." She looks at Condi. "Do you want to hear more? It's quite long."

"Read the part about how 'the sea simmered,'" Condi tells her. "That feels exactly like what's happening now."

Sitting beside Condi on the rose-splotched sofa, Grand Ella reads:

...on the hidden teeth of a perilous reef;
at last I came to a long shore.

White it glimmered, and the sea simmered
with star-mirrors in a silver net;
cliffs of stone pale as ruel-bone

A sharp chilling beep from the TV interrupts. A meteorologist's voice crackles into the room. "Coastal areas...prepare to evacuate by midday tomorrow. Storm surge is expected. Secure all ocean vessels...extreme flooding up and down the coast..."

Grand Ella groans. "The last hurricane to hit Dipitous was when I was a little girl. I hoped to never see another. The damage was extensive." She sets the book aside. "Tomorrow we'll take what we can up to the art shop and prepare to spend the night there. It won't be safe to stay here in the cottage."

A sudden draft chills the room. Wind whistles through the eaves, pitching and falling, a mournful human whine.

Condi and Grand Ella jump up, speaking the same thought at the same time, "Madelaine."

Wordlessly, they hurry to the terrace and step outside.

The terrace is empty. Wrapped in a heavy hanging veil of beaded mist, the zigzag steps to the beach appear to lead to nowhere.

"How soft the tidal sounds are," Grand Ella whispers sadly. "The storm is sucking up water from the sea, pulling the tide back from shore."

"Creepy." Condi shivers. "Do you think Maddie's okay? That wind sounded just like her."

Grand Ella hugs Condi close. "I don't know. If the storm stays on course, we'll have to evacuate the Beachlings from the cliffs in the morning, and make room for them up at the art shop. Perhaps we'll find that Maddie is perfectly fine."

"We'll need lots of help. You know they won't want to go," Condi exclaims. "People in town can be so mean—most of them don't care about the Beachlings."

"People change during a crisis," Grand Ella answers. "Sometimes for the worse...but often for the better. I'm sure others will help."

Condi hopes so. Getting the Beachlings off the north shore and cramming all of them into the art shop is going to be a nightmare.

"If the storm is as bad as they say, it could strip the whole beach." Grand Ella shakes her head. "Andy Marshall might lose the Billabong."

"Do you think the beach hotels will evacuate?" Condi asks. The Mirage, with its walls of glass and chrome, sits close to the water. She can't help thinking of Trustin and Marissa. Where will they go?

"Yes," Grand Ella says. "The beach hotels, the Billabong...any building in the inner cove. Nothing there is safe."

"What will happen to the yellow cottage?" Condi asks anxiously.

"Who knows?" Grand Ella answers, stroking Condi's hair. "The cottage survived the last hurricane, but one never knows with storms. The important thing is to keep people safe—we can't worry about the rest. Come on, let's go in. Tomorrow will be a long day. Time for bed." Kissing the top of Condi's head, she leads her back inside.

After saying good night, Condi climbs the ladder up to the loft. Crawling into bed, she snuggles up under the covers, and thinks about Trustin for a long time. The day was beautiful and scary. She wonders if tomorrow will be the same. He told her he'd see her, and she hopes that's true. If they evacuate the Mirage, who knows? She stares up at the twinkling protector stars on the ceiling. At last, she hears the television go off. Grand Ella's bedroom door clicks closed, and Condi falls into a heavy sleep.

A few hours later, she wakes with a start. Something is different. The cottage is quiet, way too quiet. The crooning tidal sounds are gone. Creeping down the loft ladder, she slips out to the terrace. The mist is thick and dripping now, the clouds dense. She can't see a bit of the cove. The silence is eerie. The ocean has disappeared.

A half orb of moon floats out from behind a cloud. A patch in the mist thins, creating a clear eye. Through the eye, she can make out the tower of Windy Hollow and beyond, seeing the high hill of the Stinson property and the crumbling white cliffs where the Beachlings live. The small eye in the mist blinks. A sparkling red-orange light appears on the peaked crest of the hill, dancing among the splintering bones of the old mansion.

Condi stares at the strange flickering lights. Grand Ella says that when lights are seen on the Hollow, they're reflections from the lights of ships at sea. But tonight, with the ocean receding, ships are pulled back from shore.

Those lights cannot be ships....

Quickly, she tiptoes back into the kitchen. A plan is forming in her mind, a reckless plan, but a necessary one.

Stealthily, she takes the cell phone off the charger in the kitchen. She can't go without a light. Putting on her thick yellow hoodie, she slides the phone into the pocket with the shell, and sneaks out the door to the terrace.

The air is a peppery black mist. Hugging herself for courage, she summons her nerve. This is the darkest kind of dark—the kind that dares you to go out in it.

Barefoot, using the terrace railing as a guide, she sidesteps down the zigzag stairs to the beach. When her toes touch sand, she makes her way toward the lip of shore she knows so well. Without moon and stars to guide her, walking the ocean's curving waterline is the only sure way to get to the Hollow.

Pulling the phone from her pocket, she slowly moves the flashlight over the beach.

The cove is empty. No water anywhere—only wet clots of sand. The ocean's pulled back, far from the original tideline.

Turning away from the barren seabed, she sweeps the phone light over the shore. A ripple of sand marks the old watermark. The light glares angrily off the mist, blinding her. Reluctantly, she turns it off and slides the phone into her pocket.

Marsiale, Condoleeza.

March...

One foot on dry sand, one in the wetness of the old seabed, she tracks the boundary of the old shoreline, finding her way through the dark—until at last she reaches the familiar rough scree of the Hollow.

Suddenly, like a cloak flung aside, the black dark lifts. A sleepy shrouded moon breaks through the mist, hanging above the tall tower of the Hollow, spilling pinpricks of light over the splayed domino rocks and the rough scree beach.

Amazed, Condi stands by the desolate ocean floor, gazing at the sparkling strands of sapphire kelp strung over the rocks, winking blue and purple in the starlight, the steep stone stairs up to the top of the tower slippery slabs of silver.

The Hollow is silent. Without the usual foaming sea, the seabed is a mucky mess. But there's no time to lose. Wading through piles of prickly algae, she marches on, over to the winding stairs of the tower where she climbs, placing each foot carefully, heart pounding, refusing to think of the spiked rocks below.

At the top of the stairs, she staggers over to the orange-red kayak between the half-moon rocks, and stops to catch her breath. In the starry sky, the moon breaks into a wide smile.

Untangling the hair from the frames of her glasses, she looks to the peninsula where the orange-red lights in the old Stinson mansion flicker, giving her the will to go on. On hands and knees, she crawls across the treacherously narrow rock bridge, only to find that the steep slope to the top of the hill is a slide of mud.

In desperation, she looks up at the moon.

Cadenza, Condoleeza.

Improvise—find a way.

A lone tree clings to the muddy slope. Grabbing a branch, she tests it. It holds firm. Scrambling for toe holds, she uses the branches of the tree to claw her way up the slope.

On solid ground, she bends over, gasping for breath, hoping she has the strength to do what she's come to do.

She has no choice...

She owes Madelaine.

This is the terrible price of keeping Anda's awful secret.

Taking out the phone, she gathers her courage and shines the light.

As the light sweeps over the wind-swept peninsula, her heart sinks. Blocking the path up to the mansion is a roped off area spiked with red construction flags. The open jaws of a bulldozer yawn ominously over a huge excavation pit filled with black water. Mr. Davis isn't wasting any time building his fancy spa hotel....

Sickened, Condi surveys her options. Wading through the pit of spooky water is the only way to get to the mansion. Beyond the pit, the moon shines on the ruins of the Stinson mansion. The old house spills out its guts, scattering broken wood and stone across the hillside. Inside the mansion, a solitary figure hunkers by a campfire, swaddled in swirls of smoke.

Condi breathes a sigh of relief.

As she steps bravely into the murk, an icy cold grabs her, surging past her knees. With shaking hands, she sweeps the light across the black water. Twists of ancient copper pipes catch the light; old spa equipment snakes up and out of the pit—the last remains of the elegant facilities that once made the Double Palm Hotel the finest spa around.

Drip, drip, drip.

Her head jerks toward the sound—water plinking off an old shower head, impaled in the exposed white tile walls of an old steam room. Eerie dark shadows dip and spin across the cracked tile of the rain-washed walls.

Clutching the light and holding it high, she steps forward. The slippery mud craters, sending her sliding into a drop-off, water rushing around her waist. Holding the phone still higher, she moves forward, testing the mud underfoot, searching for shallow water.

A voice vibrates from behind her, chilling her to the bone. "Oh, no, you don't."

Frantic, she high-steps through black water, fighting her way over to the old steam room.

"Heh, heh, heh," the nasty voice rasps as something long and winding wraps around her neck, yanking her backward. Ensnared, she tosses the phone into the steam room. It skitters across the floor. In a blinding white flash, everything goes black.

The water closes over her body like a lid. Flailing, she grabs at the surface, clutching for air. The thing around her neck tightens, sucking her down, winding around her arms and legs, encasing her in slime. She cannot move, cannot breathe.

"Prepare to join the Dead Ones," the awful voice says.

The slime grows thicker and heavier—tighter and tighter—

Furiouso, Condoleeza.

Con brio!

Fury—and vigor!

Rocking and bucking, Condi summons all her strength, struggling to break out of the slime cocoon.

Doppio movimento!

Twice as fast.

Rocking, she manages to slosh water from side to side. Each wide curved wave allows her head to surface, long enough for a breath.

Strong arms enfold her, lifting her up out of the water, gently placing her on the tile of the steam room floor. A familiar hand tenderly slides her lost glasses over her ears, pushing them up on her nose.

"No!' the evil voice roars. "You are not allowed to help her, Boy!"

"Shut up, Bernardo."

"No!"

"She helped herself first, Bernardo," Trustin says quietly. "So I am allowed to help her now."

"It isn't fair, you haven't answered Koan's riddle yet. She must die."

"Nothing's fair," Trustin answers wearily. "Face it, Bernardo. This time you lose."

"Solve the riddle!"

The voice fades away. The slimy binding thing unwinds from Condi's body. Cheek on cold tile, she falls asleep.

Why am I so cold?

She blinks awake.

Cold, wet dark...the slow drip, drip of a shower head. Drawing her knees up to her chest, she sits up and looks around. Fuzzily, she remembers—slipping in the pit, throwing her phone clear, everything blank after that. Retrieving the phone, she slips it back into her pocket, letting her fingers brush over the comforting contours of the shell.

Continua, Condoleeza.

Keep going.

Getting to her feet, she climbs out of the pit and makes her way up the hill to the mansion. On the sagging front porch, a muscular bundle of fur bounds out of the dark, jumping up to lick her face.

"Lucky," Condi breathes, burying her face in the comfort of the old black dog's neck.

With a plaintive whine, he impatiently tugs at her sleeve, pulling her into the house. She follows him across the chipped marble floor of a once-grand hall. The room retains a wistful glory, wallpaper peeling off the moldy walls like tendrils of dying leaves. In the heart of the room is a broken chimney, a sputtering fire crackling, smoking to stay alive, mist sizzling into the grate. Hunkered in a blanket, bent and broken and still, is Madelaine.

"Oh, Maddie," Condi cries, rushing to kneel beside her. "Hurry—you must come with me. We've got to get back to the cottage. A bad storm is coming. It's not safe to stay here."

Slowly, Madelaine turns her face up to Condi's, her mouth laced with pain. Condi inhales sharply. The old woman is hurt, face badly bruised, red scratches clawing across one cheek, one arm twisted awkwardly, like a mangled bird's wing.

Madelaine shakes her head, falling back on the blankets. Lucky moans, licking the old lady's drooping cheek.

"We've got to go," Condi says urgently. "I'll help you." She helps Madelaine sit up. Draping the old woman's good arm across her shoulders, she gets her to her feet. Fine rain bleeds from the rafters, dredging the air with smoke. Maddie coughs fitfully, collapsing once again. "Be strong," Condi whispers.

Madelaine staggers to her feet. Condi half drags, half carries her into the brisk night.

When they reach the narrow ledge that stretches over to the tower, Madelaine stops, turning her battered face toward the mansion. "Heart," she cries, thumping her good fist on her chest, "Stay. Hollow." She digs her gnarled feet into the mud.

"No. We cannot stay. The ocean is being sucked up by a hurricane," Condi explains quietly. "There will be a huge storm surge tomorrow when the water returns. Waves will reach high into the cove, over the cliffs. Come on, Maddie, we've got to go."

"Heart," Madelaine repeats, sinking down to her knees, almost dragging Condi with her into the mud. "Stay. Hollow."

"Maddie, please." Condi struggles to haul the old woman to her feet. "We've got to get to Grand Ella. She'll make you well again."

Maddie shakes her head, eyes faraway and lost, her body a weight of despair. Moonlight falls across her face, shimmering across her cheeks, in an awful and terrible beauty.

"Hollow," Madelaine says, touching her breast. "Heart." A lone tear drips off the tip of her nose.

"Yes. The Hollow is your heart, Maddie—" Condi nods. "But tonight, you must leave it and come to the yellow cottage with me. Grand Ella and I love you, you see."

Affrettando, Condoleeza.

Hurry.

Lucky nuzzles his mistress. The wind lifts. Wrapping her good hand around Condi's wrist, Madelaine slowly rises to her feet. Together, arm in arm, Condi and Madelaine let Lucky guide them down the slippery slope. Condi prays, hoping for a way to avoid the excavation pit. Maddie cannot safely wade through that harsh black water.

The moon brightens and blinks. Lucky charges ahead, diving through the brush, forging a path through the overgrowth, around the gaping jaws of the pit. Condi leads Maddie through a tangle of branches and vines, skirting the edges of the pit, until at last they reach the narrow rock bridge.

"Almost there," Condi whispers.

Without hesitating, she steps out onto the bridge, holding tight to Maddie's hand. Carefully, they cross the narrow bridge of rock, Lucky a wedge of protection between Madelaine and a fatal fall to the rocks below. When they reach the top of the rock tower, Condi guides Maddie past the orange-red rescue kayak between the two half-moon rocks, leading her over to the stone stairs, where they safely descend down to the beach.

When her toes touch the familiar sand of the cove, Condi hugs Madelaine's weary body, and bends to stroke

Lucky's matted head.

What a relief. The mist spins silver beneath the partial moon, the sea beats in the distance, thrumming on a distant shore. A sprinkle of stars bursts out above them, moonbeams catching on tide pools like diamonds, illuminating the curve of sand leading to the yellow cottage. Condi points Madelaine toward the welcoming curve of shore.

The moon blinks again.

With a wild jerk, Maddie spins out of Condi's grasp and darts toward the pockets of glittering water in the empty seabed. "Home!" the old woman cries.

"Maddie! Come back!" Condi lunges for Maddie's cloak, swirling in the wind.

Lucky blocks the way. Hurling his body in front of Condi's, he seizes Madelaine's cloak in his powerful teeth. Running at full speed, he pulls his mistress through the waves of silt in the seabed, toward what was once the open sea.

Condi runs as fast as she can, chasing the pair through the empty mouth of the waterless cove. But no matter how fast she goes, she falls farther and farther behind. Around her, the wind is ragged, the tide invisible and loud, thundering and crashing on an unseen shore. In the distance, silhouetted by the light of the moon, Madelaine is dancing over the sand, light and wild and free, Lucky by her side.

"White it glimmered and the sea simmered," Madelaine cries.

Bent though I be, I must find the sea!
It is later than late! Why do we wait?
I leapt in and cried: Bear me away!

A wind gust lifts Madelaine's tattered cloak and peels it away.

The moon bursts through a cloud, scattering starlight.

Condi stops, dazzled by the brilliant scene before her.

On the shining expanse of shore is young Maddie, cradling a strong black dog in her arms. Turning, she blows Condi a kiss and plunges into the water. Laughing, they ride the crest of a wave. The wave peaks and falls. Maddie's arms arc to the sky. In a gliding streak of light, the ocean draws them under a blanket of shimmering water, sweetly tucking them in.

Home.

The moon smiles down.

Two stars tremble, twirling and spinning—and dive into the sea.

Chapter Seventeen

CAVES IN THE CLIFFS

"Condi, darling, wake up," Grand Ella says, shaking her awake at dawn. "Sheriff Coodle's downstairs. We're going to the cliffs to round up the Beachlings. The hurricane's heading straight for Dipitous—it will reach the cove by nightfall."

"What?" Condi murmurs. She rubs her forehead, wanting to remember the strange dream she was lost in. Scary, but wonderful...Maddie and Lucky were in it, and Trustin, too. He was saving her from something horrible....

Scrunching up her eyes, she tries to remember the dream, but the dream fragment fades and slips away, like dream fragments do, just when you want them to stay.

Sitting up, she glances outside at the thick gray clouds, and complains to Grand Ella, "Why is this pokey old storm so slow? I want it to be over. I hate the waiting."

"Me, too," Grand Ella answers quietly. "Storms that move slowly—well, they are often the worst of all." She steps to the loft window. "The ocean's pulled away from shore. Come and see."

Condi puts on her glasses, slides out of bed, and joins her grandmother. "Oh, it's terrible," she bursts out, turning to Grand Ella in dismay. "The ocean's gone."

Where yesterday there was a pounding tide, today there is only a blank seabed of wet sand, with sickening pockets of left-behind sea life drying out and dying.

The view of the lost sea is incredibly sad.

"Hurricane winds are brutal, but the storm surge will be worse," Grand Ella says somberly. "Record breaking, they say. The huge incoming waves may wipe out everything in the cove."

"How high will the water get?" Condi cries.

"Forecasters are predicting thirty-foot waves," Grand Ella answers. "Get dressed. Pack what you can in a backpack. We need to be up at the Art Shop with the Beachlings by afternoon."

Frantically, Condi pulls on her clothes and stuffs her favorite books into a backpack. She and Grand Ella hurry downstairs and scurry around the yellow cottage, gathering up food, clothes and essential belongings. Sheriff Coodle helps, loading boxes of Papa and Mama's music and all the photos of them into Grand Ella's old gray van.

"Here, Clive," Grand Ella says to the sheriff, handing him an overflowing box of first aid supplies. "Put these in the patrol car. We may need them."

Condi stares at the first aid box and shivers. If the

storm is bad, a lot of people might get hurt. And who knows what shape the Beachlings will be in. Getting them down from the cliffs will be hard. She gazes over at the Hollow. Beyond the rock tower, the bones of the mansion suddenly break through the clouds. A fragment of her dream returns...red flickering lights...oh, could it be?

"Grand Ella," she blurts out, "I need to tell you something. I'm worried Maddie might be up at the Stinson mansion."

Sheriff Coodle snorts. "Impossible."

Grand Ella puts a hand on the sheriff's arm. "Condi?"

"I had a dream," she says awkwardly, avoiding the sheriff's eyes. "That Maddie and Lucky were at the mansion...there were flickering red lights..."

Sheriff Coodle guffaws. "Not that old ghost story!"

Condi glares at him. "I'm not talking about ghosts," she says coldly. "The lights could be a campfire."

"That narrow rock bridge is slippery and wet," the sheriff replies, looking irritated. "She could never climb up there."

"Hush, Clive." Thoughtfully, Grand Ella studies Condi's face. "Dreams are important things," she says softly. "Clive, can we send someone up to the Hollow to check?"

Sheriff Coodle crosses his arms across his burly chest. "Absolutely not, Ella. I'm sure we'll find Madelaine at the cliffs with the other Beachlings."

"Please?" Condi begs. Suddenly, getting to the top of the Hollow seems urgent.

The sheriff glowers at her. "Don't borrow trouble, young lady. Scaling the Hollow in these winds means risking a rescue worker's life."

Grand Ella nods. "Of course. You're right, Clive," she says. "I didn't think of that."

Condi turns away. In silence, they finish packing up the van.

"Time to head to the cliffs," the sheriff says, glancing nervously at his phone.

"One more thing," Grand Ella says, shooting him an apologetic smile. "Condi, come back inside with me. Hurry."

Condi follows her grandmother back into the cottage. Swiftly, Grand Ella goes over to the mahogany bookcase and opens the glass door with the silver key.

"We must take these," she says quietly.

Carefully, Condi helps Grand Ella lift the well-worn volumes off the shelves and place them in a duffel bag. Soon the bookcase is bare.

"My surfboard," Condi says anxiously. Right now, the board is safely stored on the terrace, but if the storm destroys the cottage, she'll lose Aquamarine for sure. "I know it will take up the last of the space in the van."

Grand Ella smiles. "We'll make room."

Condi retrieves Aquamarine and carries the board through the stripped cottage and out to the van, trying not to think that it may be the last time she sees her home.

The sheriff groans when he loads the bulging duffel bag into the van

"Books, Ella?" He sighs.

Grand Ella smiles her calm and patient smile. "Where would we be without our poems and stories, Clive?"

"I guess you're right, Ella," he smiles back at her,

holding onto her eyes a moment too long.

The exchange annoys Condi. Ignoring the sheriff's offer of help, she loads the surfboard herself, maneuvering it into the space between the tops of boxes and the roof of the van.

Grand Ella firmly shuts the front door of the yellow cottage. "I'll come pick up the van after the Beachlings are safely up at the shop," she tells them. "At least we're packed and ready to go."

"Let's get moving. We've only got a few hours. Rescue buggies are on the way, coming across the dunes to transport the Beachlings up to town," the sheriff says. "Down to the beach. Hurry."

"Everything is dead or dying," Condi exclaims in horror when they reach the empty seabed below the zigzag stairs.

Whirling white seabirds are crying mournfully, swooping into the wind, picking off parades of helpless crabs. Stranded starfish in faded colors splay out over the bare ocean floor—arms spread like legs running—losing the race to the sea.

"Not everything is dying," Grand Ella says softly. "The sea is the great life source. When the storm passes, there will be a renewal of life, you'll see." She slips a comforting arm around Condi. "Look." She points to the inner cove, where three of the ladies from the sunrise yoga class are emerging from the mist. "There's good news."

Sheriff Coodle moans. "Ella, really? Those three lightweights are more trouble than they're worth.

Climbing the cliffs is strenuous."

"Be nice, Clive," Grand Ella whispers. "They're stronger than they look."

When the yoga ladies arrive at the old shoreline, dressed in tennis shoes and work clothes, the sheriff runs his big hand over his unshaven chin and tries to smile. "I'd say good morning, ladies—but it's clearly not."

Mrs. Wainwright frowns. "No. It's creepy." She studies the clouds. "They say it will get dark as night soon."

"Eerie," Mrs. Hsu agrees. Her eyes dart nervously to the jaw of the waterless cove. "I don't know...maybe we shouldn't do this after all."

"Stop it," Mrs. Ragsdale snaps. "You promised, Jasmin. We have plenty of time to get the Beachlings to safety."

Mrs. Wainwright eyes the sheriff. "Where are the security teams from the resort hotels? They should be here to help by now."

Sheriff Coodle winces. "Duke Holmes ordered them to stay at the Mirage and try to secure the property—the guests evacuated last night."

Condi's heart sinks. She wonders where the Davis twins are. Evacuated is a serious word.

"Trained rescue workers will be here soon, I'm sure," Grand Ella declares. "Let's get on our way." Confidently, she strides off across the sand, heading toward the cliffs.

"Onward, ladies," the sheriff commands, matching his stride to Grand Ella's.

A few paces behind, Mrs. Ragsdale slips her hand into Condi's. "I've grown to love the old ladies who come to our yoga class," she confides. "I wanted to be here to help."

Condi squeezes Mrs. Ragsdale's hand and smiles.

High in the caves in the cliffs, the Beachlings stare down at the sheriff, refusing to cooperate. They are not afraid of storms, and they don't listen to news or weather. They are not coming down out of their caves, especially when ordered to do so for no good reason by Sheriff Coodle.

"Come down, I say," he bellows up at them.

Charlene pokes her head out of the lowest cave, her tiny body curled over the floppy orange sock. Sadly, she shakes her head at the sheriff. "We're not leaving our homes," she calls down to him.

"Okay, then. I'm coming up," the sheriff yells. Going to the least steep side of the rock face, he sweats and swears, looking ridiculous as he searches for footholds for his huge heavy boots. But the mist has dampened the rocks to a glassy sheen, and he keeps slipping back down to the sand.

Finally, standing below the caves, he gives up, mopping his brow with his handkerchief. "Ladies, you must come down. A bad storm is coming!"

"Charlene, please come out!" Grand Ella calls. "A hurricane is headed straight this way."

Charlene's face grows worried as she listens to Grand Ella. More frightened eyes peek out of the crevices in the rocks.

"Monster-sized surf," the sheriff shouts, drowning out Grand Ella's voice with his booming one. "Waves as big as houses!"

Charlene makes a face, waving the sock and pooh-poohing him, then retreating back into her cave.

A twisting gust of wind throws up a blast of sand. The

air turns an unsettling blend of warm and cold.

"This is crazy," Mrs. Hsu declares. "We need to get out of here. Do something, Sheriff."

Sheriff Coodle takes off his lawman's star and flings it toward the beach. The star catches in the swirling wind and sails off.

"Ladies, I am not here as the Sheriff of Dipitous Beach," he declares dramatically. "I'm here as your friend. Please come out of your caves. We'll get you to safety."

The Beachlings don't budge, and Condi isn't surprised. Friendship has a track record. When a uniform treats you badly, you don't trust it—star or no star.

"Clive," Grand Ella tells him. "Let me handle this. You're annoying them."

More thunder rumbles over the beach, setting off a steady rain of gravel, sifting down from the cliff ledges.

"It's getting bad," Mrs. Hsu shrieks. "Someone do something!"

"We can't wait," Condi tells Grand Ella. "I'm going up."

Grand Ella bites down hard on her lower lip, then slowly nods her agreement. "Be careful."

Swinging herself up onto a low ledge, Condi adjusts her weight. After finding small finger holds and toe grips in the cliff face, she stretches out and hugs the stone, inching up the rock until she reaches the lip of Charlene's cave. Pulling herself up and over, she crouches low and slips inside the crevice.

"It's me, Condi," she calls, squinting into the darkness. "Please come out, Charlene."

"Not even for you." Charlene sighs, a long sad wheeze of a sound. "Go home, child. We'll be safe here. The

Beachlings have weathered many a storm in these old caves."

"Not like this one," Condi tells her, as her eyes adjust to the dark. She crawls on hands and knees toward the back of the cave where Charlene is pressed into the wall, shaking her head, holding the orange sock tight to her chest. Her yoga mat is rolled out like a mattress, covered neatly with layers of worn blankets. Next to the mat, on the smooth stone floor, is a mosaic of shells.

"My art..." Charlene's eyes mist with tears. "I can't leave it, Condi."

"You must," Condi says quietly, taking the frightened old woman's hand. "The sea is far away right now, but when the tide returns, it will be high and terrible."

For long moment, she studies Charlene's mosaic—rippling green and blue sea glass, knobs and swirls of white shells—unmistakably the magnificent tipping waves of Windy Hollow. What a shame to leave something so beautiful behind.

Semplicemente, Condoleeza.

Simplify.

The idea comes to her like a flash. "We'll bring your shells, Charlene. Every single one," Condi says excitedly. "You're an artist—you'll make new art again—but you must be alive to do it. Hurry."

Charlene nods. Together they disassemble the mosaic and fill up the floppy orange sock, wrapping the rest of the shells and sea glass in blankets. Charlene rolls up her yoga mat. Arms loaded with treasures, they creep outside.

At the lip of the cave, Condi passes down the yoga mat, the sock and the blanket with shells to Grand Ella. Then she helps Sheriff Coodle lift Charlene down to the sand.

When Charlene is safe, Grand Ella looks into the tiny woman's eyes. "Charlene, you must tell the other Beachlings to come with us. They'll listen to you."

Turning to face the cliffs, Charlene claps her hands three times. In a clear, strong voice she calls up to her friends. "Come out, come out."

Slowly, weary old women poke their heads out of the caves and watch as Charlene gestures to the vacant seabed.

From a cave opening off a middle ledge, several stories off the sand, Glinda appears, supporting Pippa, dragging her yoga mat. "We're coming down, Charly," Glinda yells.

Other Beachlings emerge from an assortment of caves in the middle and low ledges, tossing yoga mats and other assorted belongings down to the sand. Slowly, old women make the precarious descent downward, dropping from one ledge to the other, landing on remarkably strong knees. Glinda helps Pippa swing down to meet Condi on the lowest ledge. Sheriff Coodle gallantly sticks out his hand to help her safely to the sand. When Pippa sees the sheriff's stern face, she refuses his help. Slapping his hand away, she starts to wail.

"Hush up, Pippa!" Glinda snaps. "I don't like the old hypocrite either, but we don't have time for whining. Get going."

"Stop bossing her, Glinda," a powerful voice commands. Triponica, formidable arms crossed, tight gray curls springing up into the wind, is standing in front of a wide cave on a thick ledge thirty feet above the sand.

Abruptly, Pippa looks up at Triponica and stops crying.

She glares at Glinda. Primly, she takes the sheriff's hand and allows him to help her down.

One by one, the rest of the old ladies follow Pippa's lead, making their way down from the caves, Condi and Sheriff Coodle helping each of them to safety.

At last, Condi swings down to the sand. Only Triponica remains outside her cave, braced against the wind.

"Tell her to come down, Charlene," Grand Ella implores.

Sadly, Charlene looks at Grand Ella. "It's Francie, you see. Trippy will never leave her."

"Francie?" Grand Ella repeats, puzzled.

"I don't believe you know her, Ella. She's one of the oldest of us. She hasn't walked for years," Charlene explains. "She lives in the highest cave. Up there."

"With Triponica?" Grand Ella squints up at the place where Charlene is pointing.

"No. The small cave above Trippy's." Charlene guides Grand Ella's hand. "There—do you see it? The slit in the rock above Triponica's cave."

"That's a cave?" mutters the sheriff.

"For years, Francie has lived up there alone," Charlene goes on. "Trippy sends food, water and medicine up in a basket. Francie used to sun herself on that narrow rim of rock outside her cave, but now it's crumbling away." She wrings her hands. "There's no way to get up there. The rim won't hold Triponica's great weight, but she'll never leave Francie.'

"Clive, we need the rescue crew," Grand Ella turns briskly to the sheriff. "To help Triponica and Francie." She takes a long deep breath. "And to see what's happened to

Maddie. I don't see her anywhere."

Alarmed, Condi searches the exhausted cluster of bedraggled Beachlings.

Maddie and Lucky are not among them.

\#

The sheriff checks his phone. "The crews are tied up in town, Ella." He studies the small rim of rock outside Francie's cave, hardly a ledge. "None of us can climb up there without safety equipment and ropes."

The Beachlings whisper anxiously among themselves. The yoga ladies fidget nervously. The blackening eye of clouds is smudging a long line of shadows over the sea.

"We've got to go," Mrs. Wainright declares.

"I agree," the sheriff says. "Go. Get the rest of the Beachlings up the hill, head to the low parking lot. Emergency crews are on their way. They'll meet you there."

"I'm not going," Charlene says to Grand Ella.

"Nor I," says Glinda. "We don't abandon one another."

"Please," Mrs. Ragsdale begs.

"This way," Mrs. Hsu cries, tugging on Glinda's arm, who fiercely shrugs her off.

"No," Glinda says. "I'm staying." She looks at Pippa. "You go on with the others, Sister. We can't all stay. If things get bad, you'll have trouble keeping up."

For an instant, Pippa raises her chin defiantly—then her shoulders sag. "I hate being weak—but I know you're right. It won't help if you're worrying about me, too."

Glinda hugs Pippa tight and sends her toward the yoga

ladies setting off down the beach, leading the band of straggling Beachlings across the sand.

Stricken, Grand Ella stands with her hands over her heart, looking up at the caves, searching for a sign. "Maddie?" she repeats over and over, saying it softly, like a prayer.

"Ella, my dear," Charlene gently places a small, wrinkled hand on Grand Ella's arm, slowly straightening her bent back. "All is well. Maddie and Lucky have gone home."

Sheriff Coodle barks into his cell phone, demanding assistance from the emergency crew. "I need ropes and safety harnesses. Experienced climbers."

Charlene and Grand Ella huddle with Glinda and the sheriff, looking up at the caves while Condi paces back and forth along the old shoreline. Another fragment from last night's dream is nudging at her, pricking her memory. Oh, if only she could remember....

"Hey!" A shout sings out over the wind.

Through the spitting rain, four kids break through the gray mist, racing toward her, Trustin and Marissa in the lead, Lorelei and Casey not far behind.

"What's up?" Marissa asks when they reach the cliffs.

"There's a sick Beachling in the top cave," Condi explains, pointing to the slit above Triponica's head. "Her name's Francie. She can't walk."

Trustin and Marissa's eyes meet. "We've heard about her," they say.

Jogging over to the sheriff, Marissa tells him, "We're going to climb and help Triponica. The rim outside of Francie's cave won't hold Trippy's weight—but it might hold ours if we work fast."

Sheriff Coodle puffs out his chest. "No one but emergency personnel are climbing that cliff face, young lady."

Marissa holds the sheriff's gaze, smiling sweetly.

"No time to lose." Trustin adds apologetically.

Dashing around the sheriff and grinning, the twins run to the cliffs and scale them like spiders, easily pulling up to the high ledge where Triponica is waiting. Without a word, Triponica and Marissa give Trustin a boost to the fragile rim outside Francie's cave. Moving fast, Trustin pulls himself up and over the narrow rim, then vanishes into the cave. The rim of rock shudders—but the rim holds.

"He's over the edge and inside," Casey says incredulously. "Wow, that takes some kind of strength."

"And stupidity," Lorelei says darkly. "That rim could give way at any moment."

In the next seconds, Trustin pokes his head out of the cave, a frail old woman draped over his shoulders. The lip of the rim carves off, raining loose stones.

"Won't hold much longer," Triponica shouts up to Trustin. "Anchor your feet in the cave, hand Francie down to Marissa and me. Be as gentle as you can."

Trustin rolls Francie over the edge of the fragile rim into Trippy and Marissa's waiting arms. When Trippy has Francie secured on the high ledge, Marissa jumps down to the middle ledge where Casey is waiting to help. Cradling Francie like a baby, Trippy passes her down to them, and

Casey carries her down to the sheriff. Once Francie is safe, Triponica goes back into her cave. When she reappears, she has a small leather nurse's pouch in one hand and a net of sapphire kelp slung over her broad shoulders. Dropping from the high ledge, she moves from ledge to ledge downward, with the silent grace of a queen. On the lowest ledge, she dodges the sheriff's hand, regally jumping down to the sand.

Waiting on the middle ledge, Marissa lets out a whoop. "We did it!" Tucking into a crouch, she somersaults through the air, landing on her feet next to Sheriff Coodle. Rock rains off the cliff face, sending up spirals of dust.

"Going to break your neck someday." the sheriff mutters, brushing sand off out of his hair. "Crazy kid."

"Coming down!" Trustin shouts from Francie's cave.

Condi waves up at him.

"Clear the way!"

But a single step onto the rim is too much. It shaves off, swallowing him in an avalanche of rubble.

"Trustin!" Condi cries.

"Relax," Marissa says.

Out of a cloud of dust, Trustin appears, barefoot and smiling, surfing a landslide of loose rock, down to the sand.

"Sorry I scared you," Trustin tells Condi, dusting himself off.

"Way to be her hero," Marissa says, teasing him.

"Way to be a show off," Trustin flips back.

"That was amazing," Lorelei says, shaking her head.

"Hey, what's this?" Casey is scuffing something glittering out of the sand. Triumphantly, he bends over and holds up Sheriff Coodle's shining star.

"Give me that." The sheriff glares and snatches the badge out of Casey's hand.

Chapter Eighteen

THE VINTAGE SURFBOARDS

The sheriff orders everyone to get off the beach. Rain is falling now, in heavy plops, making starfish splashes on the sand. Trustin accepts Casey's help carrying Francie; Grand Ella walks beside Charlene; Trippy and Glinda hurry on ahead to join Pippa and the other nervous Beachlings, knowing they might be needed if the rescue workers get impatient. Lorelei and Condi lag behind, carrying yoga mats and the Beachlings' sparse belongings, heading toward the beach stairs up to the low parking lot.

"Casey's so mad," Lorelei confides to Condi as they hurry along. "His mom is refusing to open up their hotel to the Beachlings." She grimaces. "Mrs. Arondale's the worst. But Casey says he's going to find a way to make her say yes, no matter what."

Worried, Condi looks at Lorelei. "I hope he does. The art shop is way too small for everyone."

"I know," Lorelei sighs. "Casey and his mom got in a big fight about it. Mr. Arondale says Casey is right to want to help, but his awful mother refuses to budge."

Condi hates what she's hearing. The art shop will be unbearable with everyone packed in like sardines in a too small can.

"Mr. Arondale had to tell Grand Ella that his wife wouldn't let the Beachlings stay at the B&B," Lorelei goes on. "Casey says Grand Ella was pretty upset."

Condi nods. She hasn't often seen Grand Ella mad, but she bets her grandmother is steaming about this.

At the beach stairs leading up to the parking lot, rescue workers are cajoling the Beachlings, lifting them into the dune buggies that will shuttle them up the winding hill of Upper Main and drop them off at the art shop. Grand Ella instructs Condi to ride with the Beachlings, while one of the rescue workers drives her back to the yellow cottage to pick up the packed van.

Trustin boosts Condi up into one of the crowded buggies, next to Casey and Lorelei. She smiles at him, then notices that Marissa is waving goodbye, dancing back down the beach stairs, her hair a bright flame in the silver mist.

"Where's Marissa off to?" she asks.

Trustin squeezes Condi's hand. "Other people on the beach need help. I'm going, too. Stay here. Take care of the Beachlings."

Condi nods, squeezing back. "Be careful. Wish I could come, but Grand Ella—"

"Would worry," he finishes for her, grinning.

"I worry, too," she tells him softly. "You and Marissa

need to be careful."

His turquoise eyes gaze at her. "You don't have to worry about us, Condi. Don't you know that by now?" Letting go of her hand, he races down the stairs to the beach.

As the dune buggy lurches and weaves its way up the hill, the wide fat wheels plow through sand drifting across the road. A throb of urgency surrounds the town, where a massive evacuation is underway. Shopkeepers are boarding up store fronts along Lower Main, frantic parents gathering children and pets. Everyone's in a hurry, preparing to drive inland to ride out the storm.

At last, the buggy reaches the summit of Upper Main, the highest point in the town. The wind is blowing ferociously now and the sky is dripping with moisture.

Somehow the rescue workers manage to get most of the Beachlings inside the art shop, with plenty of loud bossing from Glinda. Trippy is waiting outside in a dune buggy with Francie. Tucked into a nest of beach blankets, cushioned by Trippy's net of seaweed kelp, Francie moans softly, paper-thin eyelids fluttering, translucent as butterfly wings.

"Condi," Triponica says quietly. "Can you find a place inside the shop where Francie can lie down without getting jostled or stepped on?"

"I'll try," Condi mumbles, already thinking it's no use. Everything inside is going to be awful. The art shop is overcrowded, the thought of the smell of too many unwashed bodies and stuffy air is enough to make her scream with frustration. Across the street is the Arondale's' spacious B&B, with its luxurious rooms left empty—all because of one selfish woman with a closed mind.

When Grand Ella arrives with the van, Condi rushes to help her unpack, putting away supplies and stowing Aquamarine safely on the back porch of the shop. As she's finishing up, she glances out at the street, where Triponica is getting out of the dune buggy with Francie in her arms. Grand Ella and Condi hurry over to help. Triponica repeats the request she made to Condi to Grand Ella. Condi is horrified. How could she have forgotten? She was so busy being mad about Mrs. Arondale, she forgot to find room for Francie.

"Of course, Trippy. We'll make space," Grand Ella answers. "Condi, put Francie's blankets in the kitchen. Prepare a pallet." Quickly, she motions for Condi to go inside.

After they get Francie settled, Condi kneels beside Triponica, who is opening her nurse's pouch. Flakes of old leather sift from the crumbling red medical cross on the battered bag, remnants of another time.

"Triponica, I'm sorry," Condi says softly. "I don't have an excuse. I was mad at Mrs. Arondale, so I forgot to do what you asked."

Shaking her head, Triponica fingers through the contents of her bag until she locates a stoppered bottle. Pouring a bit of liquid into a fraying handkerchief, she gently wipes off Francie's dusty face. A scent of freshly laundered cotton, like sheets bleaching in the sun, wafts through the tiny kitchen.

Finished, Triponica slips the bottle back into the bag. Sitting back on her heels, she looks at Condi, eyes deep and black as a twilight sea. "The weak and sick come first. The rest of us must wait."

Condi lowers her head in shame.

"Child, look at me."

Slowly, Condi raises her eyes.

"A lesson learned, my dear." Trippy's dark eyes twinkle. Reaching into her bag, she draws out a small indigo vial with a dew drop stopper. "Tincture of Sapphire. A gift from the sea." Holding the bottle under Condi's nose, she says, "Let go of your anger—or it will blind you from finding solutions to things within your control, as it did this afternoon."

Soothed by the peculiar odor of salt and seaweed and something unknown, Condi nods, relief flooding through her.

"Thank you for not staying mad, Trippy," she says. "I'll remember."

"See that you do," Trippy answers.

With renewed energy and a lighter step, Condi leaves the kitchen. She goes into the big room to help Sheriff Coodle and Grand Ella push display cases against the walls, clearing space so the Beachling's yoga mats can be rolled out into a circle on the floor.

Outside, the storm is building, the wind rising in long, plaintive howls. Pippa falls to her knees, keening with the rhythm of the wind. The other Beachlings whimper nervously.

"Pippa!" Glinda yanks her sister down to a yoga mat.

"You're scaring the others. What would Father say?"

Abruptly, Pippa stops moaning. Pulling her knees up into her chest, she lies down on her side. Glinda strokes Pippa's hair. Then she, too, lies down on the mat, back-to-back with her sister.

Tiny, stalwart Charlene makes rounds with Grand Ella, covering the women with blankets, whispering soothing words. At last, the women settle, talking quietly or curling up to rest.

At last, Charlene folds herself into a restful position on her mat and Grand Ella collapses into her rocking chair next to Sheriff Coodle. Frantically tracking weather on his phone, the sheriff is checking on rescue personnel, helpless now against the impending storm.

Folding her hands in her lap, Grand Ella closes her eyes to meditate. Condi makes her way to the kitchen, hoping for a mug of tea. But Triponica is dozing against the wall, keeping watch over Francie, blocking the way to the kettle. Condi tiptoes past the kitchen, sneaking out the door to the porch.

Breathing in the cool fresh air, she goes over to the railing where Triponica's net of kelp, glistening blue and purple and glazed with sea salt, is draped to catch the rain. She raises her face to the mist. Despite the storm, it's a relief to be outside the crowded shop.

"Condi!" The front door of the B&B flies open and Lorelei hurries across the street to the shop. "Papa's almost here to pick me up. It's taken him forever to make it through town and up the hill." She frowns. "I hate to leave you and Casey."

"We're good," Condi tells her. "The B&B and the art

shop are way above the possible high-water line. We're fine no matter how high the incoming waves get."

Lorelei bites her lip. "Well, maybe. Casey says the hurricane bands are spinning in a way that should push most of the biggest waves to the far side of the cove—the north side—toward the Hollow."

Condi winces.

"Oh, Condi, I'm sorry!" Lorelei claps her hand over her mouth. "I'm so stupid—that's where the yellow cottage is."

Condi tries to smile. "Grand Ella says the cottage is in bigger hands than ours." She hugs her friend. "Be safe."

"We'll be fine. We live inland. For once I'm glad we don't live on the beach."

An old jeep chugs out of the mist. In front of the B&B, the jeep stops and Lorelei's father jumps out. The wind whistles through his hair, standing it on end. "Hurry up, Lorelei. We've got to go."

Blowing a kiss to Condi, Lorelei runs to jump in the back seat. The jeep disappears around the bend.

"Hey, Condi!"

A shout bursts out from the top of Upper Main. She squints into the mist. Silhouetted against the gathering dark, Trustin stands on the crest of the hill. "C'mon. Marissa and I need you. To the Billabong!"

Without hesitating, she leaps off the porch and runs to meet him. She knows she should tell Grand Ella, but there's not time. At the top of the hill, he grabs her hand and they start down the long flight of beach stairs. The rain is blinding, pelting her glasses. Reluctantly, she stops and takes them off, sliding them into her hoodie pocket.

"Can't see without them," she yells over the wind.

"I've got you," Trustin answers.

Holding her steady, Trustin helps her navigate the stairs and jog through wicked blasts of sand toward the Billabong. A blurry Mr. Marshall passes them, lurching into the wind, struggling with an armful of surfboards.

"Get the rest of the vintage boards!" he yells at Trustin. "Meet you at the beach stairs."

When they reach the surf shop, Trustin tugs Condi inside. The air is surprisingly silent and still. Sliding her glasses out of her pocket, Condi wipes them off. Trustin gently pushes them back up on her nose. Hand in hand, they hurry down the hall to the storeroom.

"Hey," Marissa calls out to Condi. "Glad you made it. Grab those two boards in the corner. Be careful—vintage boards are heavy."

"On it," Condi tells her. Striding across the room, she lifts a golden-green board down from its rack. The citrine surfboard is weighty yet light, like a boat skimming across water. A yearning rises in her chest. In the odd light, a green sail seems to float over the mirrored surface of the board.

With a catch in her throat, she props the board against the wall and moves toward a tangerine-colored board in a wooden floor mount. The sweet smell of citrus drifts over her. The scent is sad and familiar. She pauses, staring in confusion at the board.

Trustin comes to stand beside her.

"That smell..." she says.

"Do you remember, Condi?" he asks quietly.

"Remember what?" Puzzled, she searches his turquoise eyes.

"Stop it, Trustin. She doesn't get it," Marissa snaps.

"Get what?" Condi asks.

Marissa shakes her head. "See? She's forgotten everything." She shrugs, glaring at Trustin. "On you, bro. You're resisting Koan. She can't remember. Not until you solve the riddle."

"What are you talking about?" Condi exclaims, looking back and forth between the twins.

A powerful wind gust rocks the Billabong. The old walls shudder. The light in the storeroom snuffs out like a candle, casting the room in shadow.

"Never mind, " Trustin says. "C'mon."

"Get going," Marissa barks, hoisting a pair of jewel-colored boards to her shoulders. "Condi, can you handle two boards?"

Nodding, Condi picks up the tangerine board and heads for the door, where she grabs the citrine board. Trustin swings the remaining two carved wooden boards out of their mounts. Shouldering the surfboards, they hurry out of the shop.

Outside, the sky is the color of slate. Rain is whipping, lashing at the sand.

"Hurry," Marissa cries, jogging on ahead.

In Trustin's wake, Condi fights through wet and wind to the base of the beach stairs with the citrine and tangerine boards. There Mr. Marshall is waiting, ready to lift them from her shoulders.

As the boards slide through her hands, she catches a

glimpse of the shaper's marks.

On the golden-green board is an elegant sea lily.

On the tangerine board, a smooth white shell.

#

Tired but triumphant, they make their way up the winding road to the top of Upper Main, climbing the steep hill to Wafting Rafters. When they arrive at the art shop, they scramble to stack the rescued surfboards under the eaves of the porch, next to Aquamarine.

"You old fool!" The door to the shop flies open. Grand Ella bursts outside, angry as Condi's ever seen her. She glares at Mr. Marshall. "What were you thinking?"

Mr. Marshall looks stricken. Contrite, he hangs his head. "Now Ella..."

"Later, Andy." Holding the shop door open, Grand Ella shoos them inside. "Quickly, my dears. You're soaked."

"Thanks, but we can't," Trustin tells her. "Our dad's here." He points to the top of the hill where a lone car is idling, the headlights two orbs of white in the deepening mist.

Grand Ella sighs and pushes Mr. Marshall through the doorway. "Very well," she says, smiling at the twins. "Take care. Condi, say your good-byes, then come inside." She steps into the shop, shutting the door behind her.

"Where are you going?" Condi asks Trustin.

He takes her hand. His eyes telegraph regret—and something more. "Who knows?" he answers.

"Later, Condi," Marissa says. Tugging her brother's arm away, she pulls him down the porch steps until they're standing in the rain.

"Wish you could stay," Condi calls to them.

"Me, too," Trustin answers.

The twins dash to the two halos of light, through twirling sideways rain.

Chapter Nineteen

CANDLES AND SCARVES

Inside the art shop, the stench of stressed bodies is overwhelming. Leaning against the door to the porch, Condi is tempted to slip back outside, but she doesn't want to upset Grand Ella.

The shop is packed to the max. The Beachlings are crammed into the main room, while Mr. Marshall's long legs stretch out of the small bathroom. Trippy and Francie are two people too many for the cramped kitchen. Trippy is lying on her side under the cabinet above the counter, Francie below her, on the floor on blankets. One of Trippy's arms hangs down over the counter as she sings and softly strokes Francie's hair. Grand Ella and Charlene move among the circle of yoga mats comforting the old ladies, crying and wailing with every pitch of the wind. Even Sheriff Coodle is trying to calm them, awkwardly patting Pippa's back with a meaty hand while barking orders into his cell phone.

Grand Ella smiles reassuringly at Condi from the other side of the room. Relieved to know she's not in trouble, Condi stays put in the hall by the door, sliding down to the floor, resting her forehead on her knees. It promises to be a long night.

Rap, rap.

Startled, she sits up straight.

"It's me, Casey," a voice calls through the shop door.

Jumping to her feet, Condi opens the door, letting in a blast of wet wind. Outside, Casey is standing on the porch with his dad, jackets dripping with rain.

"We've come to take a few of the Beachlings over to the B&B," Casey says to Condi.

"We have two empty rooms," Mr. Arondale adds.

Casey winks at Condi behind his father's back. She smiles at him gratefully. He did it, just as Lorelei said he would.

Grand Ella makes her way over to the door, stepping nimbly over wall-to-wall bodies on yoga mats. "Bless you, David," she breathes in relief.

"Should've come sooner, Ella," Casey's dad answers gruffly. "Sorry about that—but Amber's on board now." He peers into the densely crowded main room. "Who should we take?"

"Francie and Triponica," Grand Ella tells him swiftly. "Andy Marshall and the sheriff."

"Absolutely not, Ella." The sheriff gets to his feet. "I'm staying. You need me."

Grand Ella shakes her head. "We're fine, Clive. The other Beachlings will insist on staying together, but

Francie needs the luxury of a bed. Besides," she points to Mr. Marshall's legs sticking out of the bathroom, "we need the bathroom." Eyeing the sheriff's phone, buzzing with messages, she adds, "And you need reliable Wi-Fi —like you'll have at the Arondale's. It's going to be a long night."

"But Ella," the sheriff protests weakly.

"Yes, Clive. Come to the B&B," Mr. Arondale says. "We won't lose power there. We have a backup generator."

"Fine." Grumbling, the sheriff steps out onto the porch while Grand Ella rouses Mr. Marshall and Condi helps Triponica gather Francie's things.

"Condi," Triponica says in her deep powerful voice. "I have a task for you." From her nurse's pouch she draws out the indigo vial with the dewdrop stopper and looks at Grand Ella. "Tincture of Sapphire, Ella. Do you know it?"

Grand Ella shakes her head.

"It's a calming essence. Culled from a rare kelp found in the depths of the sea. If you give your permission, I'll ask Condi to administer it to the Beachlings tonight—but only if it's needed. I've already shown her how it works."

Grand Ella nods. "Of course, Trippy. I'm sure your medicines are sound."

Triponica hands the vial to Condi. "Use it if it is necessary—but see that you bring only your healing energy to its use." She smiles. "No more anger."

Condi clutches the vial. "I understand," she whispers.

Gracefully, Triponica bends and gathers Francie into her arms, standing to her great height. Casey and his dad, both tall themselves, step back, gawking up at her. With her strong-jawed face, rippling muscles and majestic coiled gray hair, she is powerful, a fierce goddess.

"Your mother's going to have a fit about that one," Mr. Arondale whispers to Casey.

"She'll get over it," Casey answers.

As evening falls to night, Grand Ella and Condi make tea in the kitchen and hand out comforting mugs of steaming chamomile and honey to the Beachlings. Now that there's more room, the yoga mats are spread in a spacious circle on the old polished wooden planks of the shop. Each mat has two blankets, one for warmth and one for a pillow.

As the storm intensifies, Grand Ella and Charlene take turns reading from Grand Ella's poetry books, even making it though the entirety of Tolkien's "The Sea-Bell", the poem about the white shell and the simmering sea that Madelaine loves. Wrapping her fingers around the white shell in her pocket, Condi wonders, for the umpteenth time, how in the world the shell came to be in her pocket that day—and how Maddie knew it was there.

Around midnight, the hilltop shakes with the shrill relentless scream of the tsunami warning, signaling the return of the goliath tide to the cove. As the towering wall of water surges back to shore, the crash of the waves is deafening, shaking and rattling the windows of the shop. With a tremendous pop and flash of eerie light, the power goes out, thrusting the shop into total blackness.

Pippa jumps up and wails, almost drowning out the tsunami warning. Stumbling around in the dark, Grand Ella and Charlene rush to comfort her. Awake and agitated, the Beachlings moan and keen. Even Glinda freaks. Terrified, she rises from her mat, stepping on bodies, staggering toward the door of the shop. When Condi tries to stop her from flinging it open, Glinda trips and falls, bumping her head on Grand Ella's rocker.

Crawling over to the display cabinet in the corner, Condi fumbles for a scented beeswax candle and a safety lighter. Placing the candle in an empty tea mug, she lights it and then, shielding it with her hand, carefully brings it to the center of the circle of yoga mats. The small flame flickers bravely against the dark, the soothing scent of lavender and vanilla spilling into the room. On the ceiling rafters, the painted scarves ripple from eaves of indigo shadow, catching bits of light and color, like waves in a starlit sea.

In the steady gaze of the cozy candlelight, Condi takes out the vial of Tincture of Sapphire. Going around the yoga mat circle, she gently holds it under each Beachlings nose, whispering, "This is the breath of the sea. Breathe it in...all will be well."

Despite the siren and the howling winds, the old ladies smile gratefully, cuddle up in their blankets, and fall asleep.

The tsunami warning wails through the long night as the giant waves crash and pound at the cove, surging back home.

At last, in the deepest part of the night, the most ferocious of the winds fall away. The tide eases, banking down. The sun lifts weary fingers of light, pushing back the storm curtain, breaking to an uneasy dawn.

Chapter Twenty

HOME

The next few days are a blur. The hurricane and storm surge tore the beach and Lower Main apart, making a complete mess of the town. The Billabong and the Mirage are destroyed—leveled by the raging wall of water. Remarkably, the yellow cottage was unharmed, though the north side of the cove was altered in significant ways. Except for Triponica and Francie's caves, the Beachling's caves are underwater, well below the new tideline. The high peninsula of Windy Hollow was razed, wind and water shearing off the ruins of the Stinson mansion and the spa hotel, banishing them to the sea.

As hoped, Wafting Rafters and the Arondale's B&B were left untouched, though until today, there's been a barricade at the bottom of Upper Main. With downtown Dipitous nearly destroyed, it's not been safe to go up and down the hill.

Despite the isolation, Condi is content, though she worries about Trustin and Marissa. At least she knows they're safe with their dad. She and Grand Ella have been busy caring for the Beachlings, grateful to be among the few who haven't lost their shops or homes. In fact, things have been almost blissful at the top of the hill. The first morning after the storm, the Arondales opened their kitchen and veranda to the Beachlings. Every day at dawn the Beachlings roll up their yoga mats, leave the art shop and sit basking in the sun on the veranda with the exquisite sea view, close once again to their beloved ocean home.

"Amber Arondale adores Triponica now," Grand Ella tells Condi, as they lift their faces to the fresh ocean breeze, leaning over the porch railing of the art shop.

"I know," Condi says. "Casey told me yesterday that she let Triponica use the winepress at the B&B's vineyard to harvest Tincture of Sapphire."

"Ah, Triponica," Grand Ella muses. "She's a powerful one. That tincture made from deep sea kelp is special, almost like a magic potion."

"Yes," Condi nods. Though Trippy's tincture worked wonders the night of the storm, Condi's never used it again. At bedtime each night, after a cup of Grand Ella's lavender-honey tea and a bit of poetry read by Charlene, the Beachlings fall fast asleep.

Sheriff Coodle's patrol car appears at the top of the hill. Condi bites her lip in annoyance. The sheriff's been sleeping in his office since the night of the storm, directing the cleanup in the town, but he comes to see them each day, one of the few people allowed to pass through the barricade at the bottom of the hill.

He pulls his big frame out of the car. "Good morning, ladies," he says, tipping his hat. "Good news, the barricade's been lifted."

"Wonderful, Clive!" Grand Ella claps her hands.

The sheriff's face softens with pleasure. Condi turns away. She can't wait to get home to the yellow cottage. The sheriff is way too focused on Grand Ella.

"Well, would you look at that?" Grand Ella says. Smiling, she waves good morning to Mrs. Arondale, stepping out onto the sweeping front porch of the B&B, a billowing peach sundress showing off the strawberry gold of her hair. Behind her, a great shadow in the doorway, is Triponica, carrying Francie in her arms. Mrs. Arondale goes over to the porch swing, fluffs the floral cushions and makes a comforting nest. Then she helps Triponica gently place Francie on the swing.

"Funny how people are at their best after a catastrophe," Grand Ella muses.

"Or at their worst," Sheriff Coodle mutters darkly. "Gas gouging, looting—"

"Oh, Clive," Grand Ella says. "There's been mercifully little of that."

Grand Ella slips her arm around Condi. "Tomorrow we'll be going home," she says. "Won't it be wonderful?"

"That's right," the sheriff says proudly. "The beach road's been cleared. Today it's safe to go into town." He beams at Grand Ella.

A huge camera truck chugs up over the top of Upper Main. The sheriff groans. "Might have known. First truck up the hill belongs to the news crews."

Reporters leap from the truck and storm the steps of the B&B. The media is loving the story of the Beachlings, reporting on the sweet old women who cannot return to their beloved caves in the cliffs. Soon, Mrs. Arondale is posing on the front steps of the B&B, showing off her radical hospitality, while Triponica glowers at the crew snapping photos and refuses to have her picture taken. Francie happily smiles and waves from her pallet on the porch swing.

"I hate the media," the sheriff grumbles.

"There's good that will come of this," Grand Ella says. "Wait and see. Things have a way of working out." She turns to Condi. "Why don't you take a break, my dear? Go down to town. I can handle things here. Just be careful, please."

"Oh, I will!" Condi tells her, glad to be free again. School is cancelled for another few days. Maybe she'll hear news of Trustin and Marissa in town.

As Condi swings down the winding road of Upper Main, she stops at the top of the beach stairs leading down to the cove. Mr. Marshall and a bunch of his surfer dude friends are scavenging wood off the beach, most of it the remains of the old Billabong. The surf shop was ripped away by the surge. And there's nothing much left of the Mirage, only an eerie pile of splintered glass and chrome, gleaming on the sand.

Mr. Marshall looks up at her and grins, throwing up a triumphant fist. She waves back at him, proud that she and Trustin and Marissa helped to save his precious surfboard collection. Nothing will prevent the old surf master from rebuilding. He's got tons of friends to help him—everything he needs.

In town, the townspeople are cheerfully pulling together, getting on with the cleanup. Volunteers from nearby towns, even other states, have poured into Dipitous Beach, eager to help. There's no shortage of willing and able hands to clean up the debris left by winds and the giant wall of water

When she reaches Lower Main, a body in hot pink rounds the corner. "Condi!" Lorelei exclaims, sweeping Condi up into a giant hug. "Am I ever glad to see you. My parents said I could come to town today and check on you and Casey."

Condi hugs her back. "Casey's been talking about you every day. It's been wild with the Beachlings roaming around on the top of the hill. The only other kid we've seen up there is Anda. Her parents are allowed through the barricade, to bring us a hot breakfast each day."

"I didn't know any of that," Lorelei says. "Until this morning, our cell service was down. Casey and I couldn't text. I'm so out of touch."

"Did you hear about how he got his mom to take in the Beachlings the night of the storm?" Condi asks with a giggle. "His dad was intimidated by Triponica, but Casey stood fast. You would have been proud of him."

"Oh, I am!" Lorelei's eyes shine. "He says his mom loves Trippy and Francie now. Did you know the Arondales have offered them free room and board until the town figures out where the Beachlings can live?"

Condi whistles. "Wow, that's awesome. Grand Ella and I are bringing Charlene home with us to the yellow cottage tomorrow."

"How is the cottage?" Lorelei asks. "Any damage?"

"No," Condi's face lights up. "A miracle, really. The sheriff went to check it out. Everything's fine. Only the zigzag stairs down to the beach were torn away. We're lucky. What about you?"

"Our house didn't have a bit of damage, but..." Lorelei shakes her head.

"What is it, Lore?" Condi asks.

"Since the Mirage was destroyed, my dad is out of work." Lorelei sighs. "That's a bad thing for our family—almost as bad as losing our house would've been."

"Won't Mr. Holmes rebuild?" Condi asks.

"Not in Dipitous," Lorelei answers miserably. "He's rebuilding fifty miles up the coast." She sighs. "We might have to move, too. Oh, Condi, I don't want to leave you and Casey!"

"Don't worry yet." Condi gives her friend a hug. "Things have a way of working out," she says, echoing Grand Ella.

Lorelei puts on a brave smile. "That's what Mama keeps saying. She says it's too soon to know how things might turn out."

"At least school is starting soon," Condi says. "That's one good thing."

"True. I've been missing everyone. Are Trustin and Marissa back?"

"No one's heard," Condi answers carefully. "But I'm not worried."

"Liar, liar," Lorelei says kindly. "Of course you're worried."

Sadly, Condi nods. "The peninsula where the mansion

and the spa hotel used to be is gone. Where will Mr. Davis build now?"

Putting her arm around Condi's waist, Lorelei says, "Hey, remember what you just told me? Don't worry yet."

"Yeah, you're right." Condi looks around, taking in the damage in the town. "I still can't believe we've been through a hurricane—and the worst storm surge in years."

Dipitous Beach is hardly recognizable. All of the buildings on Lower Main are gutted. Carpeting and drywall litter the streets. Swarms of volunteers are hosing down the empty shells of stores, washing off layers of salt and mud.

"Place is scary looking," Lorelei observes, grimacing.

"At least the cleanup's going fast," Condi tells her. "Everyone's working together."

The two girls walk through the town, heading toward the Lindgren's food truck, parked across from what's left of Dipitous Beach Grocery, where volunteers are sweeping up a pile of glass.

Anda is at the window of the food truck, helping her parents pass out sandwiches and drinks to tired workers. When she sees Lorelei and Condi, she squeals, "Hey, you two, wait up." Jumping out of the truck, she rushes toward them.

"Here she comes," Lorelei says under her breath. "The girl I *didn't* miss."

Condi nods, steeling herself, determined not to forget how dismissive Anda was the night before the storm when she called to say Javed was okay and demanded to know where Trustin lived. Now the Mirage is gone—and so is Trustin.

Anda bounces up to them. "Hi guys. Hey, did you hear what happened to Mr. Poirot?"

Lorelei and Condi look at each other and shrug.

"He almost blew himself up!" Anda announces. "He was sanitizing the pharmacy, and he mixed the wrong cleaners together. Kaboom!" She giggles. "Singed his awful eyebrows right off."

"You've got to be kidding." Lorelei shakes her head. "He mixed an acid cleaner with a base? What a moron. Do you know what products he used?"

Anda looks helplessly at Condi. "No clue."

"Hard to believe a science teacher doesn't understand the pH scale." Lorelei groans. "Wait till Casey hears."

Anda looks perplexed. Condi laughs, giving Lorelei a playful shove. "You should go tell him. He's dying to see you."

Lorelei blushes. "Thanks. See you guys." Butterscotch hair flying, she jogs toward Upper Main.

Anda looks after her wistfully. "She and Casey have a good thing, don't they?"

"They do," Condi agrees. "But Lorelei's worried they might have to leave so her dad can find work. Did you know Mr. Holmes isn't planning to rebuild the Mirage?"

Anda nods. "Javed's dad hates this town because of the Beachlings. They're moving up the coast. Mr. Holmes thinks Dipitous is haunted."

Condi rolls her eyes. "Seriously?"

"No kidding." Anda's eyes are wide. "Before the storm, weird things were happening at the Mirage that couldn't be explained. Things falling off shelves. Food disappearing. And then that giant squid attack on Javed..."

Anda's dead serious. Sighing, Condi asks, "What about you? Sorry Javed's leaving?"

Anda shakes her head. "He was pressuring me to do stuff I'm not ready for." She points to bruise marks on her wrist. "Hurting me, too," she says softly. "You were right. He's not a nice guy." Her voice drops low. "Can you forgive me, Condi?"

Condi stands very still, gazing at Anda. Javed Holmes is cruel. He hurt Madelaine, Lorelei and Anda—and who knows who else?

"You sold out to a bully, all because he was hot," she says quietly.

"I know...and I was terrible to you and Lorelei," Anda goes on miserably.

Condi thinks for a long moment. "I'll forgive you," she finally answers, "but you have to make it up to Lorelei."

"I will. I just want to forget Javed," Anda says, tossing back her hair.

Condi sighs.

Some things remain to be seen.

The next morning, Condi, Grand Ella, and Charlene pile out of the van in front of the yellow cottage, eager to drink in their favorite view of the sea. Today the ocean is a magnificent rippling teal beneath a lemon and chalk-blue sky.

Things are working out for the Beachlings. The townspeople have opened up their homes so that every pair of old ladies has temporary shelter. Triponica and

Francie are tucked in at the B&B, along with Pippa and Glinda. Charlene will be staying at the yellow cottage for as long as she likes.

Except for the damage to the zigzag stairs, everything at the cottage is unchanged. Inside, they can't wait to throw the windows open wide and rush out to the terrace. Though the coral roses are battered and torn, the elegant white sea lily vine is unblemished, winding up the trellis to the spot outside Condi's loft window—nodding serenely as it always has.

"Odd that delicate flower survived the storm," Grand Ella observes, taking Condi's hand. "You'd think it would've been ripped away. Strange how the winds blow."

"Strange indeed," Charlene murmurs.

"If only Madelaine and Lucky were here," Grand Ella sighs.

"Madelaine is home," Charlene's words are gentle and clear. "Maddie and Lucky are where they're meant to be. We must let them go—and simply remember."

"Thank you, Charly," Grand Ella answers, hugging Condi close.

Leaning out over the terrace rails, they survey the changes wrought by the storm. The whole landscape of the coast is changed. The hurricane altered the shape of the cove; the beach is smaller, the waterline much higher.

"It's going to be hard to get up and down to the yoga cove," Condi observes. With the zigzag stairs destroyed, it's a steep climb up and down from the cottage to the curve of sand.

Grand Ella blushes. "We'll soon have a way," she says. "Clive is cutting wood for new zigzag stairs."

Condi sighs. The sheriff's thing for Grand Ella isn't changing...and her grandmother doesn't seem to mind.

"Going to unpack," she says. Heading back inside, she climbs the ladder up to the loft, eager to think about something else.

#

"I can't believe how well things are turning out for the Beachlings," Grand Ella says to Condi that evening on the terrace.

Nestled in blankets, they savor being home again, admiring the crimson and lilac-gold sunset fading over the sea. In the cottage kitchen, Charlene's rattling around happily, the delicious smell of steamed clams and roast potatoes drifting from the window.

Grand Ella's prediction is coming true. The reports on the evening news were amazing. The town is overwhelmed with good press about the Beachlings. The Arondale's B&B is being called "the friendliest hotel around". Photos of the Beachlings are inspirational: the old ladies eating breakfast at the Lindgren's food truck, sleeping in the sun at the B&B, Francie on the porch swing, Triponica keeping watch.

"Who would have believed it?" Grand Ella is saying. "Because of the storm, the Beachlings made national news." She chuckles. "The media is calling us 'The Town That Came Together When It Mattered.' "

"I'm surprised you're glad about all the fuss," Condi says.

"I have to be," Grand Ella answers. "Donations are

227

pouring in. There's a plan to create new, safe homes for the Beachlings. The town is building open-air decks with bunk rooms near Craggy Point. Isn't that wonderful? Those awful caves in the cliffs were dangerous." She stretches her legs, wiggling her toes. "And Ava Ragsdale just called. The donors heard about our sunrise yoga class with the Beachlings. A yoga pavilion is going up next to the open-air decks. It's wonderful to see the town united. Like it used to be, with everyone pulling together."

Condi huddles into her blanket, pulling it tight around her neck. She doesn't want to be a killjoy, but not everything is fine. School will start soon. Still no news of Trustin and Marissa, though other evacuated families are returning to Dipitous.

Grand Ella looks over at her. "Oh, Condi, I'm sorry. I haven't let you say a single word. What is it?"

"My friend Marissa Davis hasn't come back," Condi blurts out. "You know, the red-haired girl you met at the Billabong?"

"The pretty surfer girl who's teaching you to surf?""

"Yes. She and her brother haven't come back since the storm."

"I see," Grand Ella says thoughtfully. "And Marissa's brother is Trustin Davis—the brave boy who rescued Javed Holmes."

Condi shifts around in her chair. "Yeah." She didn't know Grand Ella knew so much about the Davis twins. "Never mind about that," she says stiffly. "The thing is, I want Marissa and Trustin to be here when I surf for the first time." Taking off her glasses, she wipes a tear away. "It won't be fun without them."

"Are you sure you're ready, Condi?"

Condi flinches at the hesitation in Grand Ella's voice.

"Yes. I can go in the water with my board now—Mr. Marshall says so."

Taking a long breath, Grand Ella gazes out to sea. "I'm not planning to disappoint you, you know."

Condi flushes. "I'm sorry."

"In fact, I have a surprise for you," Grand Ella says brightly. "I was going to wait until your birthday next month, but, well, I think maybe you need some good news right now." She turns to Condi. "I've saved enough money for your contact lenses," she goes on proudly. "You won't have to wear glasses under your goggles—though goggles are still a good idea, so you won't lose your new lenses."

"Oh, Grand Ella, thank you! If only Marissa and Trustin would come back, everything would be perfect."

Grand Ella shakes her head. "Things aren't often perfect, my dear. I'm not sure what to think about your friends. Some folks aren't coming back. Many things have changed. The peninsula is washed away. Maddie is gone..."

"I know. It's awful," Condi says miserably.

"I never thought I'd say it, but I'm glad Madelaine isn't here to see the mansion swept away. She never got over losing her old home," Grand Ella says. "It's hard to imagine Maddie living in such grandeur, but she and her husband, Errol, ran the Double Palm successfully for more than twenty years." Grand Ella hesitates. "Then something terrible happened."

"What?" Condi asks.

"Never mind." Grand Ella's voice trails off. "I'm sure Charly has dinner ready. Let's go inside."

"Please tell me what happened that was so terrible. It's not fair not to—"

"You're right." Grand Ella's brown eyes soften. "It was a surfing accident—a young girl was killed off the Hollow."

"Oh." Thoughtful, Condi stays quiet. If it's about surfing, better not press.

"I'd rather not talk about it right now." Grand Ella sighs. "I promise to tell you, but could you wait till I'm ready? It's our first night home. I want it to be a happy one."

Smiling, Condi pulls Grand Ella to her feet. "Let's go inside. Dinner smells great. We haven't had clams for ages."

Chapter Twenty-One

THE MOLTEN-BLACK SURFBOARD

During the next week, Condi gets fitted for contacts. Except for that, the rest of the week is dismal. She's pretty sure Marissa and Trustin aren't coming back.

No one's heard a word from Mr. Davis. In fact, it turns out that the Davis family wasn't actually staying at the Mirage. At least, that's what Duke Holmes claims. He says they were never registered there, though his security team found Trustin's molten-black surfboard in an empty room the morning they cleared the beach. No one can explain it.

Things are returning to normal. School is starting, Mr. Marshall's Billabong is nearly complete, and the open-air decks and bunk rooms for the Beachlings are going up fast—along with Grand Ella's yoga pavilion. Thanks to Sheriff Coodle, the zig zag stairs are back in place at the yellow cottage. Mrs. Arondale is once again attending the sunrise yoga class in the yoga cove.

As for Condi—all she wants is for Trustin and Marissa to come home.

#

In Mr. Poirot's science class the following week, Condi looks wistfully out the window. Tomorrow she'll get to surf for the first time, though Trustin and Marissa won't be there to cheer her on.

"Miss Bloom, may I draw your attention to the screen, please? No daydreaming." Mr. Poirot raps his ruler on the lab table in front of Condi.

She looks up and blinks, trying to focus on the science lesson. Today Mr. Poirot looks extra crazy. His face is blotted with blisters and band aids, and he's made a pitiful attempt to cover his missing eyebrows.

"Pathetic," Casey mutters to Lorelei. "Can't believe dude was dumb enough to cause an explosion with cleaning products."

"I know," Lorelei whispers. "I was going to ask him what he thought about Trustin and Javed and that squid, but I'll never listen to him again." She turns to Casey. "Something odd happened that day."

"Yeah," Casey agrees. "I wish Trustin were here. Even Javed. Since those two left town, we'll never know what really went down that day."

"And Marissa," Lorelei moans. "I really miss Marissa."

Condi turns her head away from them. She wishes they'd stop talking about the twins. Her heart hasn't felt this bruised and battered since Mama and Papa died.

Today the subject of the science class is the hurricane

and storm surge. Droning on and on, Mr. Poirot pontificates about how lucky the town of Dipitous was. He explains that, due to the increasing volcanic activity in the Ring of Fire, the storm could have easily produced a full-blown tsunami.

Waggling his non-existent eyebrows, the teacher direly predicts, "A deadly tsunami is likely to occur in the near future, class. Remain aware."

"He's full of it," Casey whispers to Lorelei. "No one who blows themselves up with drain cleaner is capable of predicting a tsunami."

But Condi's not so sure. She recalls the day they saw the underwater volcano erupt on the live feed from the oceanographer's sub. She wonders if Mr. Poirot might be right. That steaming volcano looked angry, almost like it was shouting.

In fact, Condi is starting to feel nothing but uncertainty about pretty much everything. Since Trustin and Marissa left town, she feels like she's living in the wrong space and time. Everything that's happened lately feels vaguely familiar—the volcano, the giant red squid—Condi's certain there's something important she's missing.

After Science, she refuses Casey and Lorelei's invitation to hang out with them at lunch and wanders down to the library. Maybe a book will help.

As always, the library smells like a thousand stories. She stops and breathes it in. The air reminds her of Trustin—but then everything does these days. He understood her, even from that very first day, when they went for the walk on the beach.

Avoiding Mrs. Lowry's inquisitive eyes, she goes to the

alcove behind the curved bank of books and sits down in the seaweed-green chair. The chair, the porthole window, the salt mountains on the glass...

Fighting away a sob, she looks for a book to distract her. The World War II book with the black-and-white cover is on the shelf next to the saggy-bottomed brown chair, where Trustin left it in the days before the storm. Though she dreads reading about sea accidents, she slides the book onto her lap, and opens it. Then, taking a deep breath, she looks out the porthole window, drawing courage from the sea. Reading Trustin's book just so she can feel close to him is silly; it won't bring him back to her. But then, people do silly things when they miss someone.

The book falls open to the story about a submarine lost off the California coast, near Dipitous Beach, in the closing days of World War II. Strangely, the sub wasn't lost to enemy fire. It was a worse tragedy than that. A deranged cook on the sub started a fire; everyone on the sub died—except for one of the galley boys.

She stares at the page in shock.

The galley boy who survived the fire on the submarine was named Errol Stinson—Madelaine's husband.

After school, Condi cuts away from the other kids and heads across the beach, rushing past the yellow cottage, toward the remains of Windy Hollow.

Near the domino rocks, on what's left of the scree shore, she hesitates. It is mid-tide. The domino rocks are glazed with water and will soon be covered by the rising sea. The ledge that once connected the tower of the Hollow to shore is gone, thanks to the hurricane, though the ocean still spins circles around the tips of spear-shaped rocks below. Today a mean riptide is gnashing at the sandbar leading out to the island and the tower.

Wrapping her fingers around the seashell in her pocket, she slips out of her sandals, slowly sidestepping across the shifting sandbar until her toes touch the island. Looking back at the water she just crossed, she shivers. Sandbars are fickle things. The shoal is fast blending into the current. She glances up at the sun. As long as she crosses back before high tide, everything will be fine.

Quickly, she climbs the stairs up to the Hollow. At the top, the breeze tickles her hair. Climbing up onto the orange-red rescue kayak wedged between the two half-moon rocks, she sits cross-legged, staring out to sea. What is going on? Why is there no record of the Davis family living at the Mirage? Why was Trustin reading about that submarine?

She sighs, trying to accept it. She'll never know the answers. Trustin and Marissa are not coming back.

De capo, Condoleeza.

Begin again.

Dal segno.

Pay attention to the signs.

The breeze spins and lifts her hair. A faint scent of citrus drifts in from sea, a lingering tang carried to shore from somewhere she cannot see. Turning, she looks over to the barren shore where the Stinson mansion once stood beside the old spa hotel. The once majestic shore is stripped bare.

A thought floats in, like scent on the wind, forming an idea. Below her, the tide is turning, spinning, like the questions in her mind.

Perhaps...

There is one person who might be able to help.

But she'll have to wait.

Quickly, she descends the stairs, crosses lightly over the sandbar, and returns to shore.

Chapter Twenty-Two

GHOST STORIES

Oh, no. Not again.

On the beach below the yellow cottage, a deep male voice is booming out from the terrace. Sheriff Coodle is upstairs with Grand Ella.

Condi flushes. The sheriff is coming by the yellow cottage way too often—and he's probably sitting way too close to her grandmother right now. Backing away from the new zigzag stairs, she glares out to sea. Grand Ella is hers....

C'mon, Condi. Nobody belongs to anybody, you know that.

Sliding down to the sand, she covers her face with her hands. How she misses Trustin. He pointed out the truth of things.

"Condi!"

Condi looks up. Charlene is uncurling from the spot

where she was kneeling on the shore, the ivory and pink scarf given to her by Grand Ella fluttering around her bent shoulders. With remarkable swiftness, she moves toward Condi.

"My dear, what's wrong?"

Condi shrugs. "I'm just tired of losing people, I guess," she says.

Crouching beside Condi, Charlene draws the familiar floppy orange sock out from among the folds of the scarf and spills shells onto the sand.

"Life is like the tides," she says. "Ebbing and flowing. An in-breath and an out-breath to everything. Don't hold on too tight—let things move and change." Fingers flying, Charlene arranges the shells into circular patterns, shaping them into a majestic swirling sea. Every shell fits somewhere—but in unexpected ways.

"Oh, Charly. It's beautiful."

"Yes," Charlene smiles. "But also fleeting." Quickly, she picks up the shells and drops them back in the floppy sock. "Do you see, Condi? Nothing gold can stay. It's impossible to hold on to things you love." Patting Condi's hand, she asks, "Remember the day of the storm? You told me to leave my art—so I could create something new."

"I remember." Condi smiles.

Together, they climb the zigzag stairs up to the yellow cottage.

Grand Ella's invited Sheriff Coodle to dinner. After her conversation with Charlene, Condi vows to make the best of things. Pushing food around on her plate, she listens to the adults discuss the renovations in Dipitous.

"Your new homes on the open-air decks above Craggy Point are wonderful, don't you think?" Grand Ella says, looking at Charlene.

Charlene nods, sipping her tea. "Even Glinda is pleased, Ella." She chuckles. "Pippa and Glinda squabble, though neither likes to be alone. A bunkroom with twin beds is perfect for them."

Grand Ella smiles. "It's all coming together. The storm was a blessing in many ways."

"It's wonderful, Ella." Charlene agrees. "Francie and I are going to live together. Trippy will have her own room, right next door." She claps her hands with delight. "I can't believe the town has given Francie a wheelchair! She'll no longer be shut up, like she was in the cliffs." She looks at Grand Ella and Condi. "I'll be leaving tomorrow. Thank you for opening up your home, my dears."

"Oh, Charly," Condi exclaims, "I'll miss you a lot."

Grand Ella sighs. "Yes, we'll miss you, Charly. Please let this be your second home. You're always welcome here."

Folding her small hand over Grand Ella's, Charlene pats it lovingly. "I'll come to visit often, and I'll be at sunrise yoga every morning." Wincing, she straightens her spine. "But I must return to my own. We are a community of beach souls—we belong together."

"You've earned my respect, Charlene," Sheriff Coodle says gruffly. "All of you. You're amazing women."

"Thank you, Sheriff," Charlene says, neatly wiping the corner of her mouth with her napkin, trying not to smile.

The Beachlings are earning their keep. Now that most of the volunteers are gone, they work tirelessly in the cove, clearing the storm debris still washing up on the beach, no job too lowly or nasty for them.

Longingly, Condi looks over at the pie stand on the sideboard, catching Grand Ella's eye. Charlene's made a scrumptious blueberry cinnamon pie. She's going to miss her cooking, too.

After dessert, Sheriff Coodle wipes his whiskered chin with his napkin and clears his throat. "An odd thing happened today, ladies. An EMT named Garfield Lewis came to see me. He was the young man who went to check the Stinson mansion the day of the storm."

Grand Ella puts her hand on the sheriff's. "Oh, Clive. I thought you didn't send anyone?"

The sheriff looks embarrassed. "I couldn't take a chance on letting anyone spend the storm on the top of the Hollow. Especially a helpless old woman like Madelaine." He avoids Condi's reproachful eyes. "Besides, Garfield Lewis is an experienced climber."

"What did he say?" Condi presses.

The sheriff shakes his head. "It's peculiar. He asked a strange question—wanted to know if there were any reports of missing girls after the storm."

"What?" Grand Ella exclaims.

"Of course, there've been no such reports." The sheriff pushes back his chair. "Garfield says he saw a red-haired girl and a black puppy up on the top of the Hollow that day. It's been bothering him. He chased her through the mist—but she disappeared."

Grand Ella turns pale. "Oh, Clive! Not a red-haired

girl?" She moves her hand to her heart.

The sheriff gets a funny look. "I know what you're thinking, Ella. That's why I don't want this getting out. It'll lead to more ghost stories about the Hollow."

"Ghost stories?" Condi blurts out. "That makes no sense. So what if Garfield Lewis saw a girl up there on the Hollow. My friend, Marissa Davis, has red hair."

The sheriff throws down his napkin. "Your surfing friend, Marissa? That blasted girl."

"She's cool," Condi says hotly. "But she's a daredevil. She probably climbed up to the Hollow. After all, her dad was going to rebuild the mansion and the old spa hotel. The Hollow is their property, after all."

The sheriff sits back in his chair, looking helplessly at Grand Ella.

Quietly, Grand Ella says to Condi, "I don't know what Marissa Davis told you, but the property on the Hollow's been condemned for years now. No one's allowed to build up there."

Condi stares at Grand Ella "I don't understand." She pushes away her plate. "Oh, everything's awful! Nothing makes sense." She looks accusingly at the sheriff. "And what's all this got to do with ghost stories anyway?"

"Tell her, Ella," Charlene's voice is firm.

Grand Ella sighs. "I guess it's time for you to know, Condi." She settles back in her chair and takes a deep breath. "A long time ago Maddie was married to a wonderful man named Errol Stinson. He was a World War II vet, the sole survivor of a terrible submarine accident off the Hollow. After Errol and Maddie made their fortune, they built the Double Palm Hotel. But it wasn't a hotel for tourists, you see. Maddie and Errol never opened their doors to vacationers. The Double Palm was a safe haven for the grieving families of World War II veterans, a retreat hotel for widows and orphans, many of them poor and homeless. The families who stayed at the Double Palm had lost husbands, fathers, and brothers during the war." She looks at Charlene.

"I lost my father in the war," Charlene sighs. "And shortly after that my mother died. I came to work for Maddie and Errol as a housekeeper when I was a young teen." Charlene's eyes float far away. "How I loved working there. The Stinsons made sure we were all well fed and comfortable. Maddie made sure we spent long hours on the beach, being healed by the sea."

"I remember seeing beautiful lights on the top of the Hollow when I was a little girl living here at the cottage," Grand Ella says. "Every evening, lovely music came floating across the sea."

"Maddie and Errol always had music at the hotel," Charlene says. "Every evening they taught dancing out on the deck, then Maddie read poems and stories to the children. Every day at the Double Palm was happy and comforting in some small way, Errol and Maddie made sure of that."

"Oh, it was a wonderful thing the Stinsons did, wasn't it?" Grand Ella exclaims.

Charlene nods. "Families who lost so much during the war had a common bond—they endured terrible losses. But the Stinsons helped us help one another." She smiles wistfully. "It was a privilege to work for them."

The sheriff shakes his head. "Shame it all fell apart

when their daughter died in that surfing accident."

Condi turns her eyes to Grand Ella. So this was the surfing accident she didn't want to talk about.

"Yes, Condi," Grand Ella says. "It was Madelaine and Errol's young daughter who was killed surfing off the Hollow." She pauses, her voice catching.

"May I, Ella?" Charlene asks quietly.

Grand Ella nods gratefully.

"Condi, your grandmother was only four when the accident happened. But it was a terrible blow to everyone in town. Madelaine and Errol's daughter was a beautiful red-haired girl—fifteen years old, and a gifted surfer." Charlene's eyes meet Condi's. "Your friend Marissa Davis looks a lot like Maddie's daughter, Mari. It's a striking resemblance really."

"That's why Marissa looked so familiar," Grand Ella says. "My mother showed me pictures. Mother and Maddie were friends."

"Poor lovely Mari," Charlene says softly. "After she died, Madelaine lost her will to live for a long time."

"And Errol couldn't cope," the sheriff says gruffly, "not with his PTSD and all. He went through hell during the war. That submarine catastrophe was a freakish thing. Losing Mari was the last straw."

"How did the surfing accident happen?" Condi asks softly.

Grand Ella twists her fingers nervously. "Do we have to re-live the details?"

The sheriff looks at Grand Ella fondly. "Condi deserves to hear the whole story."

Grand Ella sighs. "True, Clive. Go ahead, Charlene."

"Mari was an amazing girl," Charlene says. "A girl with a reckless spirit and a grand heart. She fought as well as any boy, always standing up for the kids in Dipitous who were down and out." Charlene bursts out laughing. "Trust me—all the bullies steered clear of her."

The sheriff guffaws. "That's the truth. She beat up Dabney Mincher pretty good one day, because he pushed me down the beach stairs." Sheriff Coodle's eyes dew over. "I remember a little about Mari, too, though I was only six. She was always laughing, always shaking back that shiny red hair." The sheriff stops and clears his throat. "I was only a little fella, but I think I may have had a crush on her."

"The crush is obvious, Clive." Grand Ella smiles, patting the back of the sheriff's hand.

"So what happened?" Condi presses.

Charlene sighs. "Mari was a risk-taker. Never afraid of anything. Maddie constantly worried about her." She sighs again. "It was a wickedly beautiful day—blustery, you know, with the wind shifting like it is now, signaling the change of seasons. The surf that day was magnificent, whitecaps like mountains, sky pulling blue from the sea." Charlene pauses, knitting her knotted fingers. "Of course, the dear girl couldn't resist going out to surf, though Madelaine had strictly forbidden it."

Charlene takes a deep breath. Grand Ella's anxious eyes flicker over to Condi's.

"I want to hear it all," Condi tells her fiercely. "Keep going. What happened?"

"Mari surfed too close to the spear-tipped rocks off the Hollow. Her puppy was caught by the tide—stranded on the domino rocks. She wanted to save him." Charlene bows her head.

Silence.

"You can guess what happened next." Charlene raises her eyes and looks grave. "Condi, if you want to be a surfer, you must learn from Mari's terrible mistake. The day we lost her was an unpredictable wind day. Wise surfers use good judgment, *always*."

"I promise to be careful," Condi says, hating the stricken way Grand Ella is looking at her. "May I be excused now?"

"You may," Grand Ella says.

Hurrying up the ladder to the loft, Condi throws herself into the softness of her bed, staring up at the protector stars catching the first bits of starlight twinkling through the window. The elegant white sea lily nods in the rising breeze. Nothing makes sense. The mysteries surrounding the Davis twins are a swirling vortex in her mind, no landing place in sight.

Tomorrow is her first surfing day.

She's not as eager to go out as she thought she'd be.

What she wants is answers.

Chapter Twenty-Three

THE FLAME

When Condi wakes up the next morning, she slumps against the pillows. Instead of an even relaxed tide outside the loft window, there's a wild booming surf. Another ugly weather change. Slipping on her glasses, she looks up at the painted stars on the ceiling.

Fretta, Condoleeza.

Hurry.

Premere.

Press on.

The elegant sea lily at the window flutters, rushing her out the door. Jumping out of bed, she dresses quickly for the beach, piling on extra layers.

In the kitchen, Grand Ella looks at her with concern, a furrow etched between her brows. Cupping her fingers around a mug of tea, she hands Condi a basket with steaming black cherry chocolate muffins. "Still going, I see.

You know you can't surf today. It's brutal out there. Cold and choppy seas."

"I'll help Lorelei," Condi says. "I'm teaching her yoga poses to use on her board." Nibbling on a muffin, she adds, "We won't go near the water."

Grand Ella nods. "Excellent plan, my dear."

When Condi reaches Mr. Marshall's newly constructed Billabong, she's amazed how the surf shop resembles the original, except this time it's wisely built higher on the beach.

"I can't believe you're back in business already," Condi says as she enters the shop, inhaling the smell of fresh wood and paint.

The old surf master smiles. "My surfing buddies showed up to help." He scratches his chin grizzle. "Rebuilding the shop was a piece of cake. I used reclaimed wood—ghost wood—left on the beach by the storm."

"Hey, guys, we're here!" From the front porch of the Billabong, Lorelei pokes her head in the door and grins.

Condi and Mr. Marshall join Lorelei and Casey outside on the sand. Casey sets up the sawhorses and docks Amethyst in the grooves. Lorelei eyes the sawhorses with wariness. "You're kidding, right? Yoga moves on a surfboard...balanced on that?"

"You can do it," Condi answers.

"I doubt it," Lorelei says dismally.

Condi drapes her arm around her friend's shoulders. "You're just nervous, Lore. No one's watching. Today's cold and rough. No one's even on the beach."

"I know you're trying to help, but I wish Trustin and Marissa were here. It's not your job to teach me to surf." Lorelei shrugs off Condi's arm.

Stung, Condi steps back. "I know. Marissa and Trustin were great teachers."

"Sorry," Lorelei mumbles. "Don't take it personally."

"I get how you feel," Condi answers, lifting her chin. "Marissa and Trustin helped me—I was thinking it's my turn to help you." She sighs. "But I totally get it. I really wish they were here."

"Now, now," Mr. Marshall interrupts. "Time to get on with the lesson. Nasty beach weather, but a prime day for practicing balancing in the wind." He winks at Lorelei. "Let Condi show you yoga poses. It will help your surfing."

"Hope you're right, Mr. Marshall," Lorelei answers glumly. "So far nothing's helped."

The old surf master steps toward Lorelei's surfboard. "I think you need a bit of inspiration. Look here. See this shaper's mark?" He points to a small sparkling octopus on the nose of the board, each winding arm a different color.

"That's the coolest shaper's mark ever, Lore," Casey blurts out. "I mean—the way you love sea creatures, and all."

Lorelei smiles at him. "Marissa loved sea creatures, too."

"The octopus is one of the smartest creatures in the sea," Mr. Marshall proclaims, nodding his head. "Anyone surfing on a board marked with an octopus is bound to do well."

Lorelei giggles. "Oh, Mr. Marshall. You're a funny

one." She smiles at Condi. "The octopus mark feels like a special message from Marissa. Maybe I *can* learn to surf, after all."

The next hour flies by. With Condi teaching and Casey spotting, Lorelei easily learns yoga moves, balancing on the board, moving gracefully through the wind.

"I can do it!" she exclaims at the end of class. Taking Casey's hand, Lorelei leaps down to the sand. "Thanks guys."

Condi beams. "Don't thank us—thank the octopus. They're beyond flexible—as well as smart."

Lorelei laughs.

"You girls are ready to go in the water," Mr. Marshall declares. "Next week, if the weather's good, you and Condi can both surf."

"Yay!" Lorelei cries.

Condi smiles. Without Trustin and Marissa it won't be the same, but having her first surfing day with Lorelei is definitely the next best thing.

After Casey and Lorelei head for home, Condi hangs around the surf shop.

"Mr. Marshall," she ventures slowly, "I have a question for you. Grand Ella says the security team at the Mirage found Trustin's surfboard at the hotel before it was destroyed. Do you know what happened to it?"

He smiles. "Funny you should ask. One of the guards at the Mirage took it home. Yesterday he sent it to me for safekeeping."

"Can I see it?" she asks.

"Come with me, my girl." Leading her down the hall, he shows her the way to the new surfboard storeroom and proudly flings open the door.

"Oh, I love it," Condi says softly, stepping inside, inhaling the heady smell of sea salt and well-polished wood. Despite the cloudy day, the room is infused with light, a garage-style window sweeping in breezes off the beach.

"I'm mighty happy with this room," Mr. Marshall says. "Thanks to you and the Davis twins, my vintage collection survived the storm." He pats one of the carved wooden boards of the Pacific Islanders. Around them the jewel-toned boards gleam, sparkling like polished stones. In the corner, leaning against the wall next to the window, are the citrine and tangerine boards. Parked next to them is Trustin's molten-black board.

"Delivered without a scratch yesterday." Mr. Marshall's eyes twinkle at her. "Who knows, those amazing Davis twins might be back yet. Don't give up hope."

"Do you think so?" Condi asks carefully. "It's been awhile."

"True," he agrees, scratching his chin.

"Mr. Marshall, did you ever actually ever meet Mr. Davis?" She asks, watching the old man's eyes.

The surf master winces. "Oh, you've caught me there, my girl." He shakes his head. "I got an email from Jay Davis, with an article about Trustin and Marissa winning Surfing Pacifica. Asked if they could train with me to be Junior Surfing Instructors. Of course I jumped at the chance. Signed all the permission forms and emailed them—but I never actually met the man."

"That's what I thought," she says sadly.

He puts his hand on her shoulder. "I'm sorry, Condi. Now that the twins have disappeared and there's no record of them at the Mirage...well, I'm wondering what was going on."

She turns away from him. "This board is the only proof that Trustin existed, isn't it?" Touching the molten-black board, she stares out to sea.

The old surf master nods. "Perhaps. But his surfboard may explain more than you know." He points to the tallest of the vintage boards. "There are countless stories hidden in all these boards, Condi," he says quietly. "Sacred stories. Revealed to only a chosen few."

He runs a craggy finger over the nose of the richly grained board. The shaper's mark is a bird feather. "A Tongan board," he explains. "Swept up on the beach when I was a boy. No one knows how it came to drift this far. My first board—crafted by a powerful chieftain." He straightens his back and stands to his full height, losing all the years. "Turns on a dime, carves pipes like butter." He caresses the board. "Won a surfing contest with this board back in the day. Took on high rollers with skills I could never access again. Swear I could fly. The power of the chieftain who shaped this board was with me that day—I rode waves I never again was able to surf on my own."

He stops, looking intently into her eyes. "Do you understand, Condi?"

She holds onto his gaze. "I think so."

"You must be sure, my girl."

Squaring her chin, she answers. "I am."

The surf master studies her face for a long time. "If a story is revealed to you today, you must trust it. No matter what—you must believe."

"I will," she answers.

The old surf master nods. "Then I'll leave you to it. Good luck."

Slowly, she lifts Trustin's molten-black board away from the wall and turns it around. The shaper's mark on the nose of the board glows, a bright orange-red flame.

Reaching out a finger, she touches the shaper's mark.

Instantly, the light in the storage room shifts, swirling thick and opaque—like smoke. Condi steps back and coughs, eyes burning. Through an acrid gray cloud, she squints at the surfboard as a scene on appears on the blurred surface, floating up through the ebony depths. A small, cramped room with a curved roof comes into view, a metal ladder hanging on one wall, a tiny stove attached to the other. Next to the stove, a muscular man in a uniform holds a frying pan with a sputtering flame. Two young boys, not quite men, push and shove their way down the ladder, horsing around, almost falling into the cramped room. Their eyes widen when they see the man, chuckling cruelly, holding the smoking pan.

Condi cannot breathe. Flames are flaring and leaping from the pan. The man's body jerks taut as a bow, then snaps with rage. Maniacal laughter—horrible, crazy laughter—rings in her ears. Lunging forward, the man flings the fire in the pan toward the boys.

A flash, an awful scream.

One of the boys catches fire. Frantically, he clutches at the burning collar of his shirt. The other boy scrambles back up the ladder. The burning boy lunges toward the man, grabs the pan and tries to fight him. Falling to the floor, they scream, rolling in the flames.

A fire bell sounds.

Condi recoils, stepping back away from the surfboard. Her throat is burning. Gasping for air, she climbs out the garage-style window, dazed, and heads down to the beach. Eyes fixed on the north shore, she runs down the new shoreline to the yellow cottage and flies up the zig zag stairs. Grand Ella is at the art shop. Charlene moved to the bunk rooms on the open-air decks today.

All she wants is to be alone.

Chapter Twenty-Four

THE DOUBLE PALM HOTEL

Somehow, she gets through dinner. She can't talk to Grand Ella, not until she understands things—and maybe never at all. What she saw in Trustin's surfboard doesn't make sense—and yet somehow it does. Though the scene on the surfboard was terrible, it means something important. She's certain now that there's something she's supposed to be remembering. Something that explains everything....

After dinner, Grand Ella goes into the living room and shakes out a yellowed newspaper. "Clive brought this by the art shop today, Condi. He was pleased about your interest in the history of the Stinsons and Windy Hollow. He thought you might like to read this article about Errol and Maddie and the Double Palm Hotel."

Kneeling on the floor in front of the rose-splotched sofa, Condi smooths the wrinkled paper out on the floor. The article is dated May 1950.

"Strange," Grand Ella says, curling up on the sofa and taking a sip of tea. "Clive says the article was shoved under some old papers in the Dipitous Beach Sheriff's Office. He found it when he was straightening up after the storm. He swears he looked in that same drawer before, and never noticed it was there."

Condi glances at her grandmother. Not for the first time, she wonders if Grand Ella knows more than she's saying.

"I'll make you some cocoa," Grand Ella says, slipping into the kitchen.

Condi's heart aches as she reads the article about the Stinsons. So many families came to stay at the Double Palm in the years after the war. Grieving women and children.

With the establishment of the Double Palm Spa Hotel, Errol and Madelaine Stinson have created a place of rest and healing for the wives and families of the veterans of the war who never came home. Errol—a survivor of a tragic submarine fire—and his wife, Madelaine, are honoring families of those who were not so lucky.

A grainy photo in the paper tears at Condi's heart. Maddie, young and raven-haired, is dancing with a young boy in a wheelchair. The boy is laughing as she spins and twirls him across the deck of the Double Palm. The article concludes with a list of veterans lost in the war. Their families were invited to stay at the spa hotel to seek solace with others who shared their grief.

Slowly, Condi gets up from her place on the floor. Grand Ella returns from the kitchen with cocoa. She sits on the sofa; Condi slides in quietly beside her.

"Tell the sheriff thanks for the article," Condi says softly.

"Sad and inspiring, isn't it?" Grand Ella asks, handing Condi a mug of cocoa laced with cinnamon. "There's more news, my dear. Prepare yourself for a shock. Charlene says your aquamarine surfboard belonged to Mari Stinson."

"What?" Condi exclaims. "I found it on the beach."

"The board wasn't recovered the day of Mari's surfing accident," Grand Ella goes on. "Maddie recognized your board when she stayed on the terrace. She told Charly."

"Oh, Grand Ella," Condi says, remembering how Maddie reacted when she saw the board. "She kept crying *Mar! Mar*! It was heartbreaking."

"Don't feel badly," Grand Ella assures her. "I'm sure Maddie was comforted that the sea returned the board to you." She brushes the curls off Condi's forehead and gives her a light kiss. "Now that you know Mari's tragic story, I'm certain you won't take the surfing risks she did."

Condi looks at Grand Ella, amazed. "You're not scared?"

Grand Ella laughs. "I'll always be a little bit scared, Condi. It's the nature of mothers and grandmothers to want to protect their children."

Condi hugs Grand Ella. "I won't let you down."

In the next week, Condi gets contact lenses. Not wearing glasses is wonderful, especially at the beach. Nothing to push up when she sweats, nothing to slide off in the wind, nothing to get blurry—everything new and clear and fresh.

Today is a beautiful beach day. After school, she heads down to the cove to walk the shoreline to the cottage. Looking up at the top of the Hollow, she remembers the day she met Trustin—the best day of her life.

Suddenly, a great wind gust lifts foam off the sea, showering her with water droplets.

A tempo, Condoleeza.

It is time.

In a great wave, a memory rises and breaks over her. Clutching the shell in her pocket, she draws in her breath.

Why, I was up there that day—on the top of the Hollow, in my summer-blue dress, holding it down against a wild wind—waiting to watch Trustin surf. The memory clarifies and deepens, rushing back. Trustin *did* show up that day to surf.

The time under the sea floods back in crystal clear waves, Lily, the Locker, the Distiller, the Siphoners and Infusers—and, of course, Koan, the Master of the Sea. As the memory of the Locker clicks in place, it confirms what she guessed. The story revealed to her in Trustin's surfboard is Errol Stinson's story—the story of a terrible fire, a very bad man, and a sea tragedy that killed a lot of brave men.

Sucking in gulps of air, she runs down the shore, heading for the new open-air decks where the Beachlings now live. There is only one person alive who knew the Stinsons back then.

On the open-air decks, Francie is outside, sunning in her new wheelchair, eyes closed, face to the light. Triponica stands beside her, hair a glorious pewter fan in the morning sun. She is massaging Francie's frail shoulders with Tincture of Sapphire, the small indigo vial unstoppered on the deck. Charlene, wrapped in an ivory beach blanket, is huddled on the warm wood outside her bunkroom. Beside her, the floppy orange sock spills out shiny sea glass and shells.

The Beachlings smile a greeting to Condi. Kneeling beside Charlene and her latest shell mosaic, Condi's heart hammers, beating out questions.

"Beautiful and mysterious, Charly. Like the Hollow," she says.

Charlene nods. The shell mosaic is a dreamy rendering of the Hollow before the storm; the ruins of the Stinson mansion etched with wisps of seaweed, barely, barely there. Condi swallows, searching to find the words.

Charlene studies Condi's face. "You are here for answers, aren't you, my child?" She sits back on her heels. "Maddie and I knew when you found Mari's surfboard— you are meant to know the truth of things."

"I've figured out some things already," Condi answers, "though there's still a lot I don't understand. Please—tell me the rest."

"If I tell you what I know, it will change your understanding of the whole world," Charlene answers. "Are you sure you're ready for that?"

"I think so," Condi answers slowly.

Charlene reaches for her hand. "Very well." Wrapping the blanket tighter, she sits up straight. "Maddie and Errol were heartbroken over Mari's death, Condi. I stayed on to care for them. They were too grief-stricken to keep the Double Palm open. It closed, and Errol gambled the rest of their fortune away." Charlene sighs. "Errol's nickname in the billiard room was Lucky, because he survived the submarine fire—but he was lucky no more." Charlene pauses. "One night, as a storm approached, I stood on the front porch of the mansion and watched Maddie and Errol run into the sea."

Condi's eyes widen. "They killed themselves?" Everything comes rushing back. Madelaine, at the Hollow the night before the storm, cobalt-black hair streaming, running with Lucky into the waves, shouting poetry into the wind.

"Yes. Terrible and beautiful at the same time," Charlene murmurs. "They had suffered greatly. But Maddie and Errol were finally free." She smiles sadly. "So now you know the truth. Maddie Stinson died many years ago."

"Maddie and Lucky haunt the Hollow?" Condi stammers out. "They're ghosts?"

Charlene giggles. "Maddie and Errol, you mean. Errol came back as Lucky, Mari's dog." She winks at Condi. "People don't tolerate homeless men, you know." She grows serious. "Please understand, my dear. Maddie and Errol aren't ghosts like you think. They don't scare and *haunt*. Not at all. They're sea spirits—taken by the sea and called to bring healing to the world. When things got tough for the Beachlings in Dipitous, Maddie and Errol returned to protect us. A good thing, too. Duke Holmes was set on hurting us or sending us away. Maddie and Errol wouldn't let that happen."

"Maddie fought with Javed Holmes," Condi tells her, smiling.

"Yes," Charlene laughs. "And Errol gave him a nasty

bite on the arm. Maddie and Lucky saved that foolish little girlfriend of yours, too—that boy was up to no good."

Condi sighs. "I hope Anda's learned her lesson."

Charlene shakes her head. "If she hasn't, that same lesson will come around again—you can be certain of that." She pats Condi's hand. "For now, the Beachlings are safe. Maddie and Errol's work is done. We have you and Grand Ella—both of you changed the town's heart."

"I don't know what I did," Condi mumbles. "It was mostly Grand Ella."

"Your grandmother is an extraordinary woman," Charlene agrees. "But you also changed the town—by taking chances, by being brave."

"I wasn't always brave," Condi says quietly. Taking a deep breath, she asks, "Charlene, does Grand Ella know?"

Charlene shakes her head. "No, Condi. But be assured that your grandmother knows many other things that you do not. Her purpose in this life is different, and so is her path to knowing."

Condi swallows hard. "And what about Marissa Davis—is she Mari Stinson? Nothing makes sense about the Davis twins, you know. Garfield Lewis saw a red-haired girl playing with a puppy on the Hollow during the storm."

Charlene nods. "Mari returned to Dipitous Beach to help you learn to surf, Condi—all because her own surfing dreams were left unfinished. But, of course, once you'd learned, she couldn't stay."

"Nothing gold can stay," Condi whispers sadly.

Charlene hugs her. "How Maddie loved poetry. Remember her in that way. And the sea gave you Mari's surfboard—Aquamarine—the color of the sea on a perfect surfing day."

Triponica comes to stand beside them, pushing Francie's wheelchair. "People you love stay with you, Condi. You know that now, don't you?"

"I've learned," Condi says quietly. She studies Trippy, backlit by a halo of sun. "Trippy—are you...?"

"Hush." Triponica places a great hand on Condi's shoulder. The mysterious scent of Tincture of Sapphire surrounds her. "Some things are to be discovered in time."

"Well, it is hard to know some things and not others," Condi says sadly.

"Not as hard as you think," Triponica says. "Now that you understand the connections, you'll find more ways of knowing."

"And *show* what you know by sharing love and hope and joy," Francie whispers. "Always show, never tell."

"Telling never works anyway." Trippy says with a snort. "People must find their own way."

"Don't ever interfere with another's journey," Charlene cautions.

"I understand," Condi promises.

Patiently, she waits, breathing with the tide. But the Beachlings have said all they're going to say. Triponica pushes Francie back to her bunk room. Charlene picks up her shells and fills the orange sock.

At last Condi gathers her courage. "Charly, there's one another thing you can tell me, surely? What about Trustin? You haven't mentioned a single word about him."

"Oh, my dear, I'm sorry." Charlene shakes her head. "I can't explain Trustin Davis. Mari Stinson didn't have a twin—she was an only child."

Chapter Twenty-Five

TOP OF THE HOLLOW

Later that night, after Grand Ella goes into bed, Condi takes the cell phone off the charger and creeps out into the dark of the terrace. The stars are a brilliant silver, the moon hanging over the sea in a golden curve of light. The waves are whispering softly—Papa's lullaby tide.

Though it's difficult to take in, Condi knows now that the time under the sea with Trustin was real. Mari Stinson died surfing off the rocks of the Hollow on Aquamarine back in the sixties, then came back as Marissa Davis to help her learn to surf. Maddie and Errol Stinson, Mari's loving parents, came back to help the Beachlings. And how thankful Condi is to know that Papa and Mama are with her always, in ways she never expected.

The breeze stirs, the cool night tasting crisp on her lips. For an instant, tears glaze her eyes. She looks to the top of the Hollow, where the light of the moon flickers on and off the shell of the orange-red kayak.

If only she knew the answers to the questions about Trustin. Can she dare to hope? Is it possible that since he left the molten-black surfboard at the Mirage that he might return to Dipitous?

Sighing long, she opens Grand Ella's phone, and flips to the photo library, ready to look at old pictures of Mama and Papa. After all, tonight is a night to remember.

Starlight catches on the phone as she taps a finger on the family album. A blinding flash lights up her palm, and a video emerges—one she's never seen before.

Startled, she leans in to watch it. The scene is eerily familiar, a dark, dark night on the top of the Hollow beneath the light of a cloudy half-moon. She makes the video larger. Moonlight smudges the black water of the excavation pit, the site of the old spa hotel. The video glows brighter in her hand, playing a slow-motion movie across the tile walls of the old steam room. She recalls the sudden flash when she tossed the phone and it clattered across the tiles—it must have recorded this scene, on the night when her dream was not a dream.

She watches the video carefully. Shadowy figures in old-timey clothes, dancing shadows, twirling, whirling across the old, cracked walls of the steam room—figures identical to the black-and-white photo she saw in the newspaper article about Errol Stinson, but the video is colorful and alive. Young Madelaine Stinson: cobalt-black hair, an emerald-green dress, dancing with a boy in a wheelchair; violin music playing like a breaking heart, wafting over the sea...

Spinning, spinning...

Laughing, laughing...
The young boy turns his face to the camera...
Joy in his turquoise eyes.

#

She stares up at the Hollow. A burst of stardust clouds the night. As it fades away, a familiar silhouette appears, framed in the light of the moon.

No time to lose.

Slipping back into the yellow cottage, Condi retrieves the newspaper article, and folds it into her pocket with the phone. Flying down the zigzag stairs, she hurries to the cove, and takes off across the sand, racing to the scree shore, where the domino rocks are underwater. It is high tide—the ocean spinning inky circles around the spears of rocks—water too dark and deep to know where the shifting sand shoal lies.

Her breath catches.

The hand of the moon slips in and out of a cloud, a magician's sleight of hand. When it emerges, it blooms bright, disappearing in a scatter of moonlight. A trail of water diamonds spreads like breadcrumbs across the dark water, marking a safe passage through the sea.

Thanking the moon, she steps into the water, toes searching for the plush firm sand of the bar. Guided by trembling sparkles of starlight, she wades to the island's shore and climbs up the rock stairs to the top of the tower.

#

He is there, waiting—just as she knew he would be.

"You came," Trustin says simply, holding out his hand.

She slips her arm through his. "I remembered."

Together, they sit side by side on the orange-red kayak, looking out at a canopy of stars twinkling over the sea.

"I know about Marissa," she tells him. "She was killed surfing off the Hollow years ago. But she didn't have a twin—so who are you?"

He looks at her with sweet sadness. "Condi..."

"I have questions, Trustin," she tells him. "Things only you can explain. That day I tried to rescue you in the kayak and got sucked under, I didn't drown." Intently, she searches his eyes. "Why didn't I drown? Plenty of other people do."

'Yes," he answers bitterly. "Or get burned to death in a fire..."

She stops. His hand is real and firm in hers, but he is trembling. Moonbeams catch in his onyx hair, drawing out the pain in his turquoise eyes.

Her hand goes to her throat. "*You* died in the fire on the sub?"

He squares his shoulders and nods. "I was fifteen when I died on a US submarine off the coast of Dipitous Beach a few weeks before the end World War II. Only Errol Stinson survived that fire." He stares out to sea. "We were both galley boys. I called him Erry, he called me Trus. I never knew his name was Errol Stinson, Condi—not until I found that book in the library. We gave the Navy fake last names because we were underage. Both of us were big for our years, and they didn't do much real checking back then. It was all going to be fine until the cook on the sub turned out to be a psychopath named Bernardo."

"The Voice in the Locker," Condi whispers.

"Meanest, most soulless man I've ever met." Trustin's jaw tightens. "The worst kind of madness. Bernardo cared about killing—but not whether he lived or died doing it. Errol and I were terrified of him. We were his galley boys. He constantly threatened to start a fire in the kitchen—so we would burn in hell."

"Oh, Trustin," Condi clutches his hand. She shudders, remembering Bernardo's Voice raging out of the Locker filled with the lust of killing.

"Erry and I made a pact," Trustin goes on. "We kept a stash of wet rags in slop water, hidden under our bunk. If Bernardo ever made a move, it was Erry's job to run up top and sound the alarm, mine to douse the fire." His shoulders slump. "We were foolish, kids playing at war. Rough housing one boring afternoon, he caught us off guard." His voice breaks. "You know the rest."

They sit quietly for a long moment. Condi hopes he can feel her trying to share the pain. Grand Ella's taught her that you can't take away hurt—but you can be in it with someone.

"Remember the day we watched the Beachlings from the top of the Hollow?" she says slowly. "The old lady with the black dog, Madelaine Stinson? Did you get to know her?"

He shakes his head. "I never saw her again, even when Marissa and I went to the cliffs to make friends with the Beachlings. I wanted to meet Madelaine, especially after I found out that Erry was Errol Stinson and she was his wife."

Condi's eyes widen. "Wait. I'm confused. Didn't you know that Marissa is Mari Stinson—Errol and Maddie's daughter?"

"Marissa is Errol's daughter?" His eyes search hers, flashing with questions. "That's nuts." He shakes his head. "Marissa and I are from two different time periods. I'm from the forties and she's a sixties girl. I guess I shouldn't be surprised. Koan never explains a thing when he sends us on a mission. And we're not allowed to discuss our pasts." Pushing the lock of onyx hair out of his eyes, he sighs. "The only thing I knew was that Marissa's purpose was different from yours and mine." He grins. "She's a Dare-Dreamer. Her purpose is to dare people to live out their dreams. She came back to help you learn to surf. And, for the record, you better end up being a darn good surfer, Condi. You know how fierce she is—she'll haunt you forever if you let her down."

Condi laughs. No doubt Marissa would love every minute of a good haunting.

"Trustin," she says softly, "I still don't understand why you and Marissa died—and Koan allowed me to come back to my life."

"Koan's unpredictable," Trustin answers. "The ultimate Riddle." He lets out a long breath. "It drives all of us sea spirits crazy, the way he loves to play games. Like having Marissa and me be twins... when we're from completely different time periods in the past. I didn't understand half the stuff she was saying. Talking surfing slang—stuff I'd never heard before—calling junior surfing class kids *grommets* and every big wave *gnarly*."

Condi laughs, then she gets serious. "Marissa said you

can't find the answer to Koan's riddle because you're resisting Koan." She watches his face. "Is that true?"

He sighs. "She's right. But I can't seem to change how I am, Condi. The riddles Koan asks us to solve are for our own good—but we can decide if we don't want to solve them." He gets to his feet and goes to the lip of the ledge, shaking his fist at the sea. "I can't do what he asks." He turns back to face her, broken and lost, a beautiful shadow backlit by stars. "I can't stop hating Bernardo. That's why I can't solve the riddle. I'm failing as a Knower. Koan says what I need is not knowledge, but 'knowing'—believing that even the darkest souls can let in a little light." He reaches for her hand. "But I can't do it. I don't understand how evil can work for good."

Holding tight to his hand, she believes more in Trustin than he believes in himself. But she's learned enough about Koan to know that things won't make sense—until they do.

"Let's go for a walk on the beach," she says.

Hand in hand, they go down the stone stairs, Condi holding Trustin tight, rather than the other way around. Gentle tidewater splashes across their feet as they cross the shallows over the sand shoal. It is now the deep of night, the tide is receding, the ocean sounds a hush.

"Why did you run away to war?" she asks him, as they follow the winding tideline to the domino rocks. "Were you unhappy at home?"

"Not at all," he answers. "But we were poor; my

parents had too many mouths to feed. One of my brothers had a wasting disease. It was breaking my mother's heart. My dad couldn't enlist. He'd lost an eye in a machinist's accident. Not being able to serve killed his pride—so I got the foolish idea I could serve for him." He stops and hangs his head. "I loved my family—I truly did—but I wanted adventure, Condi. I thought joining the Navy was a way to see the world." He shakes his head. "The captain of the sub was a harsh man, but a kind one. Erry and I knew if we talked to him about Bernardo's threats, he'd guess our ages and put us off the sub at the next port. Besides, we were kids, and we wanted to be war heroes."

Silent, they walk the star-studded beach. Condi holds on tightly to Trustin's hand like it's the last real thing she will ever do.

"World War II diesel subs surfaced often and mostly floated on the top of the ocean," Trustin says, breaking the quiet. "Not much time was spent under water. The conning tower of a diesel submarine is a lookout, sticking out of the water when the sub isn't submerged."

"Like those old-time movies with periscopes," she says.

"Yeah, I guess," he answers, winking at her. "But those movies were after my time, remember?"

"Sorry," she says, feeling bad about forgetting.

"It's okay. Being from different time periods is confusing. Now you understand how confused I was when Marissa said *hang ten* and *kook* all the time. And I jumped sky-high every time she called a big wave a *bomb*. He laughs, then grows serious. "I saw enough of bombs and torpedoes during the war." A shadow crosses his face.

"Then I died in a stupid grease fire at sea."

"How did Errol survive? she asks quietly.

"Erry stuck to our plan and rang the alarm, but I didn't have a chance. Wet rags don't put out grease. I tried to fight, but flames were everywhere. The last thing I remember I passed out. When I woke up, I was in a life raft, covered in screaming burns." Trustin's voice chokes. "I don't know how Erry did it, but he got us out of there. The rest of the crew went down with the sub."

Condi stares at him. "You lived?"

"Naw," he answers. "It was too late for me. Erry only had time to ask me my real name. Trustin O'Kenny. Those were my last words...before I died in his arms."

"That's the bravest story I've ever heard," Condi whispers.

The puckered ridge of scars at the base of Trustin's neck gleams in the moonlight. "Strange how things end up. Until that day in the library, I didn't even know Erry was Errol Stinson." He wipes a tear away. "What I hate the most is that my family never knew what happened to me, Condi. There was no way to notify them since I'd lied about my name and run away." he sighs. "When I read that Errol Stinson survived, I didn't want to find out anything more about him. Marissa tried to tell me I was making a big mistake—overlooking something important."

"You are," Condi tells him quietly. "Koan told us to help one another, remember? It's time for me to tell you what I know."

She leads him over to the highest of the domino rocks and they perch on the edge, dangling their toes in the sea. Without a word, he pulls her close and she leans her head on his shoulder.

"I missed you so much after the storm that I kept going to the library and sitting in the seaweed-green chair, reading about World War II," she tells him. "That book you were reading—well, it helped me feel close to you somehow. I learned that Errol Stinson survived the sub accident and returned to Dipitous Beach, where he made a fortune, fell in love with Maddie, and they had Mari. Then, like we saw in the surfboard story, the Stinson's built the Double Palm, the finest spa hotel for miles around." She pulls the newspaper article from her pocket and holds it out to him.

Puzzled, he takes it and opens it, a ray of moonlight illuminating the wrinkled page.

"It's the story of the Double Palm Hotel, and why Errol and Maddie built it," she explains. "Trustin, the spa hotel wasn't a place for rich people. Errol and Madelaine built it as a retreat hotel to comfort the grieving families of World War II vets. Errol never forgot you, or how lucky he was to have survived. He built the Double Palm to honor vets like you. Look."

She hands him the phone and opens it to the mysterious video. "This was taken the other night on the Hollow when I went there looking for Maddie and Lucky before the storm. I can't explain it, but this video was taken when you saved me from Bernardo in the excavation pit. I tossed my phone into the old steam room. Look."

She taps the screen and the video plays.

He gazes at the video for a long time, playing it over and over, the phone in his palm lit with moonlight, trembling with color—Maddie's cobalt-black hair, her emerald-green dress, the boy's turquoise eyes.

"Do you know that boy?" she asks softly. "He looks a lot like you."

He turns to her. "The boy in the wheelchair is my little brother Jack." His voice breaks. "Erry found them...my family." Tears slide down his cheeks.

"Yes, look here," Condi points to the names listed in the newspaper article. "Here's your family, Trustin—Patrick and Nellie O'Kenny, sons Ben and Jack, daughter Stella May. They stayed at the Double Palm."

In wonder, Trustin looks up at the remains of Windy Hollow—the barren shore—the Stinson mansion—the miracle of the Double Palm Hotel now washed into the sea.

"My mom and dad found out what happened to me, after all." He chokes back a sob. "They didn't live their whole lives believing I didn't want to come home again. Erry found them. He and Maddie took care of my family and others hurt by that awful war." He gazes at Condi, hope blazing. "Maybe Jack lived. Maybe they found a cure."

"Yes," Condi cries. "It might have happened that way. And all because Errol never forgot that he was the lucky one who got to live."

"The answer to the riddle," Trustin says slowly. "This is it. Some good came from Bernardo's evil life. The submarine fire was terrible and awful, but in the end, Errol built the spa hotel and helped lots of grieving families."

The ocean shoots up a magnificent fountain of glittering spray.

"May I kiss you, Condi?"

She lifts her face to his.

He kisses her gently.

It is her first kiss—and it is everything.

Slowly, they make their way back toward the beach below the yellow cottage. The deepest part of night is slipping away, the moon fading to ether, making room for the sun.

Below the zigzag stairs, he lets go of her hand. "I've found the answer to the riddle," he tells her, "I must return to the sea."

"Oh, no," she says softly, though she's known it all along. "I wish we could be together."

"We will be, Condi. But not in the usual way," he promises, whispering into her hair. "Think of it: You and Marissa and I are from three different times—yet somehow we became good friends."

"Yes." She breaks into a smile. "Three friends from three different times came together..."

He kisses her once more. "...in Koan's time...where there is no time."

Chapter Twenty-Six

SURFING DREAMS

Later that night, Condi sighs in her dreams for Trustin, lost in the world where first kisses live. In the morning, the high tide sings. The elegant white sea lily on the trellis peeks in through the loft window, sunlight dapples the floor, the painted stars shimmer like playful tickles.

Giocoso, Condoleeza.

Time to have fun!

We lived our dream.

Go live yours.

Thankful, she lets herself remember. Mama and Papa, sailing the coast, making beautiful music—loving Grand Ella and Condi well.

#

When she leaves the yellow cottage, Grand Ella kisses Condi on the top of the head. "Have fun, darling girl. Be safe. I'll be there to watch."

Today the sky is cream and pink and ginger yellow, the wind fresh and clear. Condi makes her way to the Billabong, Aquamarine on her shoulder, wearing the sweet yellow swim suit under her hoodie, pink goggles slung around her neck.

Tucked safely in her pocket is the smooth white shell that breathed for her under the sea. Nothing in her life will ever be the way she expects. She knows this now. With Koan's magic—in Koan's time—it is all surprises.

Reaching the cove, she waves to the Beachlings. Trippy, Pippa, and Francie are out sunning on the open-air decks, basking in the cleansing ocean breeze. In the new yoga pavilion, Charlene and Glinda are stretching, arms lifting to the sky.

It's a stellar surfing day. The water in the cove is a wrinkled blue, soft cotton-tipped waves gracing the shore. Off Craggy Point, the waves are high, rolling with a steady rhythm, the kind that surfers love.

At the base of the beach stairs, Lorelei waits in her ruffled pink swim suit.

"I can't believe it—it's happening!"

"Let's do this!"

Parking Amethyst and Aquamarine in the sand, the girls race up to the Billabong to put on wet suits. Outside the surf shop, they pass Mr. Poirot, aimlessly poking around in the sand. Dressed in old-school swim trunks, he probes a pile of rocks with a long stick that looks like a wand.

Lorelei nudges Condi. "What's he doing? Scouting uranium?"

"Bet it has something to do with predicting tsunamis," Condi says. "You know how he is—that's all he talks about." She pauses, then asks softly, "Do you really think Dipitous could get wiped out by a tsunami, Lore?"

Lorelei stares out at the cove. "It's possible—probably more than possible, in fact."

Condi nods. Of course Lorelei's right. Under the sea, there's a volcano named Nami who belches steam and rages to Koan about sending a tsunami to Dipitous. A last resort—if the town doesn't keep building community. She shivers. Things haven't changed that much. A threat still hangs over Dipitous.

Lorelei smiles reassuringly. "No one can predict these things, Condi. They call them acts of God, you know."

Condi laughs. "Well, I know one thing. I'm going to start being nicer to Mr. Poirot. He's keeping us aware. Everybody has a purpose in this world, you know."

As she says it, she considers her purpose as a Connector. She's only taken baby steps. Her work is far from done. The people of the town came together after the storm and kids are getting along better, but who knows how long the good times will last now that the crisis is over?

"You're right," Lorelei says. "I'll be nicer to Mr. Poirot, too. It felt awful when Javed made fun of me. I guess it doesn't feel any better when you're grown-up."

#

When they reach the Billabong, Casey is there waiting for them.

"Isn't he just the cutest boy you've ever seen?" Lorelei whispers.

"I'm going to change," Condi says, dodging the question. Leaving Lorelei with Casey, she goes inside the Billabong.

Mr. Marshall winks. "Ready, my girl?"

"You bet." She shoots him the hang loose sign and heads toward the small dressing room in the back of the shop, stopping along the way to peek into the surfboard storeroom. Trustin's molten-black board is leaning against the wall, turned to display the shaper's mark—the orange-red flame—a symbol of courage.

When she hurries out of the Billabong, Lorelei is squealing with delight. "Guess what, Condi? Mr. Marshall's starting a free surfing class for any kid who wants to learn."

Mr. Marshall grins, trying to look chill. "My vintage boards aren't doing what they're intended to do, stuck in a back room. It's a waste. If you kids will help, we'll offer free lessons. I'll loan out my boards. Plenty of wet suits to go around."

Condi smiles. Free surfing classes are bound to bring the kids in town closer together. "Awesome! I'm in."

Mr. Marshall blows the whistle around his neck. "It's time, girls. Get out there and surf."

Condi picks up Aquamarine.

Thank you, Trustin and Marissa.

My dream is coming true.

At the tideline she pauses, icy blue water rinsing over her toes. Then, flopping on her tummy, she paddles out, spray misting her goggles, splashing into her mouth. Beyond the Point, at the slope of a roller, she hovers in the trough. Taking a deep breath, she grasps the sides of the board, pulls up into a surfer's crouch, and smoothly swivels the board toward shore.

The water skims beneath her. Surfer kids cheer. On the shore, Grand Ella stands beside Mr. Marshall and Sheriff Coodle, beaming, hand over her heart.

Lorelei tries her turn on Amethyst. Standing for a moment, she wobbles, then falls sideways into the surf. Bobbing up out of the waves, she laughs, Casey there to retrieve her board.

Condi paddles out again, eyes scanning the far horizon, searching for a bigger wave. The first ride felt too easy, every turn smooth as cream, every move as sure as when she practiced on the beach.

At the base of a big one, she hops up onto the board. Her back foot slips. Windmilling her arms, she falls to her knees, preparing to roll safely into the water. The board stabilizes and rights itself. Regaining her footing, she slides into a low lunge. The powerful wave shoves her forward.

Standing tall, she rises up, singing over the waves, the sea beneath Aquamarine a brilliant azure blue. Glancing down, she smiles. No wonder she's surfing so well. Under the bright glaze of water, Marissa is gliding beside the board, laughing up at her. Bold and beautiful—the best the sea can conjure.

With an open heart, Condi slides into the curve of a shining wave, lifting her eyes to the top of the Hollow, certain she can see him.

An onyx-haired boy with turquoise eyes...

...on an orange-red kayak between two half-moon rocks...

...in the place where sea meets sky.

REFERENCES AND CREDITS

"Renascence" by Edna St. Vincent Millay
https://poets.org/poem/renascence

"Nothing Gold Can Stay" by Robert Frost
https://poets.org/poem/nothing-gold-can-stay

Vance, Paul and Pockriss, Lee. "Itsy Bitsy Teeny Weeny
    Yellow Polka Dot Bikini"
http://www.songfacts.com

"The Sea-Bell, or Frodo's Dreme" by J.R.R. Tolkien
http://www.councilofelrond.com/poem/the-sea-bell-or-
    frodos-dreme/

ACKNOWLEDGMENTS

This book was inspired by a magical trip to Laguna Beach to spend time with my dad remembering my wonderful mother. Thank you, Mom and Dad—for encouraging your shy, bookish daughter to be brave and independent. (I'm discovering that bringing a book into the world, especially a story written from the heart, takes a great deal of courage indeed.)

To my inspiring writing critique group friends, Amy Kelly and Emily Roberson—thank you for speaking hard truths with grace, reading countless drafts and always making this book better.

To the friends and family who have long wondered about this whole crazy writing thing I do. Thank you for supporting and encouraging me because you know I love it.

To the incredible team at Atmosphere Press, the expansive and inspiring DFW writing community, librarians, booksellers, book club members, fellow readers and writers everywhere. Where would we be without our books?

ABOUT THE AUTHOR

Kellye Abernathy is a former business executive, happily transformed into a yoga teacher and practical life skills advocate for trauma survivors.  She believes in creatively building unique and supportive communities, one relationship at a time. A graduate of the University of Kansas, she holds a Bachelor of Science degree in Secondary English Education. She lives in landlocked Plano, Texas, dreaming of her next trip to the sea. *The Aquamarine Surfboard* is her first novel.

Find her at **kellyeabernathy.com**